CLOUD DUST

R-D SERIES, BOOK ONE

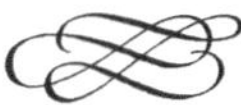

CONNIE SUTTLE

Print Second Edition (2018)
Print ISBN: 1-63478-059-0
Print ISBN-13: 978-1-63478-059-9
eBook ISBN: 1-93975-929-3
eBook ISBN-13: 978-1-93975-929-0

Published by:
SubtleDemon Publishing, LLC
PO Box 95696
Oklahoma City, OK 73143

Cover art by Renée Barratt @ The Cover Counts

To Walter, Joe, Larry, Lee, Dianne, Sarah and Mark.
Thank you.

And for Clare and Dave B. for invaluable assistance and information.

ACKNOWLEDGMENTS

As always, this book is the result of collaboration. If it weren't for the support of my editor, my cover artist and my beta readers, it would be less than it is. All mistakes, as usual, are mine and no other's.

About the Author:
Connie Suttle lives in Oklahoma with her husband and a conglomerate of cats. They have finally banded together to make their demands, which has proven disconcerting to all humans involved.

You may find Connie in the following ways:
Facebook: Connie Suttle Author
Twitter: @subtledemon
Website and Blog: subtledemon.com

ALSO BY CONNIE SUTTLE

Blood Destiny Series:

Blood Wager

Blood Passage

Blood Sense

Blood Domination

Blood Royal

Blood Queen

Blood Rebellion

Blood War

Blood Redemption

Blood Reunion

Blood Destiny Series Boxed Set (Books 1-10)

Blood Recall

Blood Alliance*

Legend of the Ir'Indicti Series:

Bumble

Shadowed

Target

Vendetta

Destroyer

Legend of the Ir'Inditi Boxed Set

High Demon Series:
Demon Lost
Demon Revealed
Demon's King
Demon's Quest
Demon's Revenge
Demon's Dream

God Wars Series:
Blood Double
Blood Trouble
Blood Revolution
Blood Love
Blood Finale

Saa Thalarr Series:
Hope and Vengeance
Wyvern and Company
Observe and Protect*

First Ordinance Series:
Finder
Keeper
BlackWing
SpellBreaker
WhiteWing

R-D Series:

Cloud Dust

Cloud Invasion

Cloud Rebel

Latter Day Demons Series:

Hot Demon in the City

A Demon's Work is Never Done

A Demon's Due

Seattle Elementals Series:

Your Money's Worth

Worth Your While*

~

BlackWing Pirates Series

MindSighted

MindMage

MindRogue

MindMaster*

~

Black Rose Sorceress Series

The Rose Mark

Rose and Thorn

Black Rose Queen

Queen of Thorns and Roses

Future Wars Series

Buffer Zone

Black Zone*

Other Titles from SubtleDemon Publishing:

Malefactor

Transgressor

Underhanded*

by Joe Scholes

*Forthcoming

CONTENTS

CHAPTER 1

I got out five years ago.

Untalented, they said.

In other words, they didn't know what to do with me, and murder usually leaves a mess.

I understood messes. Saw too many of them in my dreams. That's why I live where I do, still in their shadow but outside their walls. The conditions, of course, are that I have to move every five years, check in now and then, and never, ever, talk about *them* to anyone.

It was time to move.

"I don't want you to go." Eric, my next-door neighbor looked like a sad puppy as the movers loaded my caramel-colored sofa onto their truck and wrapped it in heavy plastic.

"Honey, I'll send postcards, I promise." He peered over our shared side fence, watching as five years of my life were loaded into a moving van.

I didn't want to go, either. Eric and his partner, Max, were the only friends I had, and even they knew little about me. I knew all about them, though, and fed their cat when they went on vacation or out of town for weekends with Eric's family.

"You'll send me the next book?"

"Yes. It's such a burden and all, but I'll send it," I teased.

That's what I do—I write books. Mysteries. Under a pen name. There wasn't any way I wanted to give up an entire catalog of work again, just because I used my current name.

To Eric, Max and the rest of the world, I'm twenty-seven. It says so, right on my driver's license—Corinne Watson, born May 29, twenty-seven years ago. I look younger than my listed age—by at least four years. People would be shocked to learn that I'm actually seventy-three, but that would be giving away secrets. Unless I wanted *them* on my doorstep the next day, that secret would remain a secret.

"Will you call us?"

"Absolutely." *Lie.*

"How long will you live in France?"

"Until I finish the book. I'll be back after that." *Another lie.*

Eric and Max thought I was renting a house in a small village in France, so I could soak up local culture and write a mystery. They thought my furniture was going into storage until my return, and that I was renting my house out in the interim. *Big lie.*

The house was never mine—they'd purchased it for me. They couldn't help themselves—control was their thing. Who knows what would happen to the house—perhaps someone else they were content to watch from a distance might have it for five years.

"What if the cookie recipe doesn't turn out right?" Eric frowned. He'd been eating my oatmeal cookies for five years. I'd sent him the recipe the night before in an e-mail.

"It will, if you follow the directions. Stop worrying, all right?"

"That's the last of it, ma'am," one of the movers came to me with a clipboard in his hand. "Sign here." He tapped the bottom of a paper filled with legal garbage that nobody in their right mind would ever want to read.

I signed and handed the clipboard back, my hand shaking. That's another thing that Eric and Max don't know.

I have PTSD. And GAD. I take medication for it, and hide it quite well on most days. Why do I have those things?

That's the stuff nightmares are made of.

❧

"Corinne, you're welcome to redecorate. Major changes have to be approved."

"So a sunroom to grow marijuana is out of the question?" I blinked at Colonel August Hunter as he led me through my new home. He was my contact. Handler. Whatever.

Can a seventy-three-year-old say whatever and get away with it?

If you look twenty-three, with long, black hair, fair skin and gray eyes, you can get away with a lot. August grimaced at my joke. Of all the people belonging to the hive-mind-collective of *them*, he was one of the least offensive.

August was tall, straight-spined, black, late-forties and a former Marine. Handsome, too, but I didn't want to point that out. He'd officially given up his job with the armed forces to join the collective of *them*. Shortly after that, he'd been assigned to me.

I was a problem for him, but he accepted the job with long-suffering patience if not good humor. The best course of action for me, therefore, is to fly under the radar and make his job as easy as possible. My warped sense of humor gets the best of me at times, but that's all.

Everything else ends up in my books.

"You can stay at a hotel tonight; your belongings won't arrive until tomorrow," August pointed out.

I didn't make any observations on how I was only moving from Arlington, Virginia to Silver Spring, Maryland, roughly a distance of fifteen miles. It took me barely half an hour to drive to my new address.

I also didn't add that taking that long to replace the bugs they'd installed on my furniture and appliances was amateurish.

August probably knew that I knew about the bugs. I knew that he knew that I knew. We never discussed it; that would place implication and blame. Paperwork would ensue. Probably another move.

I—and the bugs—would stay in Silver Spring. "Do you know the neighbors?" I asked.

"A file will be delivered tomorrow, with your things."

"Those poor people." I lifted a slat in wood blinds to stare at the house next door. It, like mine, was a narrow townhouse with three floors. I hate stairs. Yes, I look and feel young, but carrying laundry from the top to the bottom floor and then back again is still a chore, and getting from the top floor to the bottom floor to answer the door and explain to the salesperson there what *No Soliciting* actually means is downright annoying.

"Corinne, it's standard procedure. We wouldn't have chosen this location if your neighbors weren't safe."

In *them* speak, safe meant oblivious.

"Have you considered the self-defense course I suggested?"

"Yes." My shoulders sagged. I'm five-four and weigh one-hundred-three pounds. I might be able to wrestle a nine-year-old to the ground. Maybe.

"Corinne, Krav Maga is good exercise. I saw that pathetic treadmill you own."

"Hey, I can run three miles on that thing," I huffed.

"But that doesn't improve your arm strength."

"I can type five thousand words in one sitting."

"Cori."

When August calls me Cori, he's flabbergasted. Disgusted. Probably several other words that end in –ed, too.

"When are the classes?" My shoulders sagged another notch.

"Tuesday and Thursday evenings," he said, a smile touching the corner of his mouth. "I set it up already. The gym is five minutes away, and I know the instructor."

"Right. Mincemeat, here I come."

"Cori."

"Auggie."

He frowned deeply at the corruption of his name. "I've disciplined soldiers for less than that," he said.

"You know, I get that about you." I let the slat in my fingers fall—I was done staring at my unfortunate neighbor's house. I'd have to go to a window on the opposite side to see my other neighbor's home, but that could wait.

"Any nearby hotels on the list of approved vendors?" I asked. "I'll pay my own way, unless you can't restrain yourself."

"I'll allow it."

"Wow. Thanks. Can we go for ice cream, now?"

"You know I can't."

"I know. Your wife and your department won't approve. I'm not trying to steal you or embarrass you, you know. I realize I can't cut it compared to the others. That's embarrassing enough."

"Corinne, the others had a choice in the matter. You didn't."

"But it messes with your tough-guy mojo."

"I have a tough-guy mojo? I'll add that to my job description."

"Holy cow, is that sarcasm? There's hope for you, yet," I said.

"Cori."

"Yeah."

Maybe it would have made a difference if I'd bothered to watch the news in my hotel room.

I didn't.

Instead, I unpacked my laptop and brushed aside the events of the day to lose myself in writing. That's what writing is for me—an escape. I didn't bother to turn on the news until three days later, after my cable was hooked up and turned on in the new house.

There he was, standing behind Vice President Al Flint, looking as smugly innocent as a cat that had just swallowed the pet goldfish.

CHAPTER 2

"I promise that General Edwards' killer will be brought to justice," the VP announced at the White House press conference. After a while, I tuned him out and focused on the man standing behind him.

Hugh Lawrence. *Secretary of Defense* Hugh Lawrence. I shuddered as I studied him. Of all people—well, too bad, I guess. "So sorry you're going to die unexpectedly, dude," I whispered, before turning off the television and tossing the remote onto the coffee table with a sigh.

"It has just been announced that Hugh Lawrence, Secretary of Defense and trusted adviser to President Sanders, was found dead this morning of an apparent heart attack," the newscaster announced while I peeled a banana for breakfast. "An autopsy will be performed to confirm the cause of death, but doctors are unanimous in their preliminary findings. Mr. Lawrence appeared in good health, and leaves behind two sons and his ex-wife, Stacia. Hugh Lawrence, dead at fifty-six."

"Hugh Lawrence, dead at fifty-six," I mimicked before tossing my

6

banana peel into the wastebasket. *Murdering, filthy bastard,* I added mentally.

～

Notes—Colonel Hunter

There are six of them in the Program. Actually five, since one of them isn't talented. Everybody else who got the drug is dead—all ninety-five of them. Nobody has figured out why some live and most die. Time and resources have been allocated to that problem, with the best scientists working on it. Nothing has been determined as yet.

Of the six living, I was assigned to the untalented one, because Hugh Lawrence and the Joint Chiefs disliked me.

It takes a very high clearance to know about the Program. Cloud Dust, they call it. Who knows where the name came from? There are many things about it that even I don't know.

I like Corinne. Funny, beautiful, can write mysteries that show up regularly on the bestseller lists. She's also the best judge of character I've ever met, and can read situations accurately in seconds. I figure she's been studying people all her life and has developed the talent over time. That talent consistently comes through in her books.

She self-publishes—it's the only way the bigwigs will allow her to do it, and she has to write under a pen name. People who read Sarah Fox's books have no idea who Corinne Watson is. The bigwigs—and the big publishing houses—despise her.

It's better that way.

"Colonel?" Maye stepped gracefully into my office. She is deadly at several martial arts. I'd hesitate to take her on, and I'm seldom taken down, even by the best.

Maye is one of the talented ones. She hears thoughts. That talent has saved many lives.

"Maye?" I blinked at her in surprise. Her handler, Jeff Chambers, wasn't with her.

"I got a transfer," she began, her green eyes filled with concern while unruly red hair clouded about her face. Maye was an alias. Her old name no longer fits her appearance, but that's how Cloud Dust works. She'd been Asian, before. Still spoke fluent Japanese. Strange? *Yes.*

Transfer meant she'd picked something up. If she knew the person, she'd recognized the mental voice as well. "What's that? Has Captain Chambers been notified?"

"I wanted to talk to you first," Maye said. "The transfer came from Corinne."

"We have to be sure before we take this to anybody else," I snapped.

"Of course, Colonel," Corporal James Draper replied. James is my assistant. He knows about the Program. Enough, actually, that he has quarters at the Mansion, where the Five are housed.

The recordings from the past two days had to be played back—nobody bothered to listen to Corinne's recordings unless requested. I hadn't asked; Corinne deserved some privacy. Three hours later, James handed a flash drive to me. "Images and sound, Colonel," he said. "She said, *so sorry you're going to die unexpectedly, dude,* before she turned off the television."

"And the next morning, Hugh is discovered dead of a heart attack." I shook my head. "James, this is what I want you to do—call the Oval Office. See if you can get an appointment for me to meet with the President. I think we found what Corinne can do—looks like she may be able to see a death coming. I'm not sure what to make of the transfer Maye captured, so we'll table that for now."

"Seeing a death ahead of time—that would be pretty handy to know," James breathed. "I'll call the Oval Office right away."

Corinne

Wednesdays, I have a standing appointment with my department-assigned shrink. I've been seeing him for six years. He gets pissy every time I refuse to tell him what happened.

He knows I was held hostage for six days.

He knows all the others are dead. He's not sure how I survived. I'm not going to tell him.

He also wants to know what happened—and how and when all the other hostages died. He knows I almost died, too.

Well, that's not exactly true. I *did* die. August Hunter was correct when he said I hadn't had a choice. I was flat-lining when they gave me the drug, and couldn't make an informed choice. Now, they wanted names and answers.

So far, I hadn't given them anything they could use.

I had my reasons.

"How did your first Krav Maga lesson go?" Doctor Shaw asked. The hive-mind-collective at work again—what one knows, they all know.

"I spent most of the night on the floor, begging for mercy," I sighed. "I have bruises."

"Corinne, Colonel Hunter would prefer that you were able to protect yourself. This isn't retribution for imagined wrongdoing."

"I didn't suggest otherwise."

"I'd like to see you try to make this work. Build up your strength."

Like everybody else in the Program, Doctor Shaw was military. Army, actually. A Lieutenant Colonel. I leaned my head against the soft leather of the chair I sat on and closed my eyes.

I wasn't military. Everybody in the Program thought I was weak and ineffective. In some ways, I was. "Corinne, there's no need to feel inferior," Doctor Shaw said.

True. There's no need to feel inferior, when everyone, overtly or not, reminds you of the truth of it almost daily. What did they care that I'd sold a few million books and had a truckload of money in the bank?

I couldn't spend much of it, or travel, or do anything others with money might do—that would draw attention.

No attention. Dr. Shaw would be furious if I drew attention. Colonel August Hunter would be furious if I drew attention. I sighed.

"What?" Dr. Shaw lifted a hopeful eyebrow.

"Nothing." I waved off his question.

"Do you like your new house?"

"It's okay."

"What's wrong with it?"

"Three stories."

"Ah."

~

Notes—Colonel Hunter

"Shaw?" I said.

Dr. Shaw called me as expected after a session with Corinne; we spoke once a week, at least.

"Corinne is withdrawn."

"Are you surprised? She has PTSD. And panic attacks," I pointed out. Shaw and I had the same conversation every two months or so.

"She says she has bruises from Krav Maga lessons."

"Everybody gets bruises in Krav Maga. If she learns how to put an elbow in somebody's ribs, it'll be worth it."

"Need I remind you that she's not military?"

"Nobody needs to remind me of that." I couldn't keep the bitterness from my voice.

"I hope you don't belittle her like that when you see her."

"I have better sense than that. I like Corinne—as a civilian."

"But she'd never make it in the military. Is that what you're saying?"

"It doesn't take a genius to know that. A lot of people aren't suited for it. Corinne is one of them. Do you think I'll mistreat her because of it?"

"I know how the others feel about her. I treat them, too, remember?"

"Yeah. I remember. Are you telling me that the Five are schoolyard bullies?"

"I wouldn't classify three of them as bullies—just indifferent or superior in their attitudes. The other two are definite bullies."

"How the hell do you pull that shit out of them? Seems to me it would be wiser to keep their mouths shut." I was getting angry, and that wouldn't do. I had more research to go through and Shaw was interrupting.

"They don't consider that sensitive information. These were elite soldiers before they volunteered. Inevitably, they'd see Corinne as the weakest one in the pecking order."

"Do they have hearts, or are they just machines, now?" I snapped. Yeah, Corinne has been a sore spot for me for more than six years. I'm teased regularly by the other handlers. It pisses me off. They have Dobermans, while I have a toy poodle.

"This isn't a competition, August. I try to tell the others that—that Corinne didn't choose to compete, as they did. It never sinks in."

"You got that right," I muttered.

"Colonel?" James was back.

"Hold on a minute," I said, putting a hand over the receiver. "What is it, James?" He'd never interrupt unless it was important.

"Word just came in. NCIS found evidence that Hugh Lawrence murdered General Edwards. They found the gun in his belongings. He obviously didn't have time to get rid of it."

"What the fuck?" I exploded. It wasn't any secret that Lawrence and Edwards didn't like each other, but what the hell was Lawrence thinking? I went cold for a moment. "Let me call you back," I said to Shaw before dropping the receiver in its cradle and staring at my assistant. "This is what Corinne saw. What she meant in the transfer Maye picked up. Maye says she heard Corinne thinking *murdering, filthy bastard.* Get me everything you can on Hugh's death," I demanded. "Start a file."

"Right away, sir." James left my office in a rush to collect the required information.

There's a small restaurant on the Mansion's first floor. It's open until eight every day and serves breakfast, lunch and dinner to those who get tired of cafeteria food. That's where I'd asked Jeff to meet with me. The cafeteria is on the third floor, and their fries are always soggy.

"Rumor has it that Lawrence wanted Edwards out of the way so he could control the Program." Jeff Chambers, Maye Canton's handler, stuffed a French fry in his mouth.

"When did that rumor start?" I asked. James hears everything, then reports it to me. He hadn't reported this.

"It started when they found the gun that killed Edwards in Lawrence's sock drawer. Standard investigation—the President wasn't satisfied with the preliminary cause of death. Lawrence was a health nut."

"I know that," I said. I'd ordered coffee while Jeff got a burger and fries. The burger disappeared in roughly four bites. The fries looked to last only slightly longer.

I couldn't begin to say how thankful I was that Edwards had been a hands-off Director. Well, lazy might be a better term, but I didn't want to emphasize that. I preferred to make my own decisions, and Edwards didn't care as long as no laws were broken.

"How's your poodle?" Jeff grinned. Maye was considered a pit-bull. I had the pampered show dog, in his opinion.

"Corinne is fine. Just went through the move."

"Has it been that long? Damn," Jeff chewed another French fry. "Any ideas on Edwards' replacement?"

"None. The President will weigh in, and it'll likely be her replacement for Secretary of Defense."

"You think so?"

"Yeah. I think so."

"We could get a pool started. My money's on Cutter."

"Cutter's an asshole," I said. "Wouldn't want to see that happen. Can you imagine what he'll say when he's briefed on the Program?"

"The work of the devil?" Jeff grinned.

"That's mild to what I was thinking," I said.

Corinne

While they scrutinize everything else I buy, examining it for equipment, plans or information on an attempt to overthrow the government, they barely glance at my purchases for office supplies.

I wandered down the aisles in the local office-supply warehouse, dumping pens, binder clips, folders, staples and anything else I wanted into a basket.

Some women buy shoes.

I buy office supplies.

Just in case a pair of boots might be considered contraband or a cover-up.

The taxpayers foot the bills for the Five. I pay my own way whenever possible. I wanted to hire an assistant. August put the kibosh on that.

I had an editor and two attorneys already, with all business handled by e-mail or phone. That was hard enough to push through, and they don't do my filing. I do that, along with the housework, cooking and laundry. Sometimes, I dream about a big house or condo on the beach. I don't live in one because they don't want me to get that far away from them, and not because I can't afford it.

When I'd lived next to Max and Eric, I had somebody to talk to about books. Eric was a huge fan. Max didn't like to read that much but he always read mine after Eric was finished with them.

Eric frequently asked questions and requested spoilers. I seldom gave anything that might ruin an upcoming novel if the information got out. Poor Eric—I'd never see him again, and that was sad.

Notes—Colonel Hunter

"This was the worst possible time for Edwards to be killed," Brigadier General Safer said. "We have a situation."

The meeting was called in minutes, and came as a surprise to the

Five and their handlers. Safer was Edwards' Second-in-Command and knew all about the Program. He didn't want the top spot, however; he was ready to retire in six months.

We knew what situation meant—it meant somebody important was dying, and the drug was being considered.

"Who?" Jeff asked.

"Recognize the name Ilya Kuznetsov?"

"The Blacksmith?" I almost couldn't breathe. That's what Kuznetsov meant, and it was easier to use Blacksmith as his code name. "He has to be nearly eighty," I sputtered. In his day, he'd been the best spy Russia had. Nobody had heard of him for twenty years. Most of us suspected he was already dead.

"Eighty-one," Safer acknowledged. "He came to us a week ago, dying of cancer. Offered us sensitive information in exchange for medical treatment. He's been in a Russian prison for the past six years. Had to call in a favor from an old friend to get out—they wanted him dead."

"Why?" Becker asked. Becker was talented, just not the sharpest tool in the shed. After all, he'd chosen his new first name from a tennis player's last. All Five had aliases. Corinne, too, but I'd never been given her old name. That was a buried secret.

"Because he knows too much," Maye snapped at Becker.

"So they're considering him," Jeff shook his head. "How's that supposed to work?"

"If he survives, he'll be watched. If he doesn't cooperate, he's gone."

"Sounds dangerous," Kevin observed.

"Think you can't take down an old Russian?" Ken teased.

Those two—Kevin and Ken, used to be identical twins. They look nothing alike, now. It was a test—to see if twins could survive. Kevin was given the drug, first. When he survived it, Ken was brought in.

Three other sets of twins didn't make it—all in the name of science.

"Stop worrying about the Russian. I hear he's angry enough with his country to do whatever it takes to make them pay. Regardless, we'll watch him carefully. This, of course, is assuming he makes it in the first place. You know the odds. We want information. Never forget that," Safer said.

"When?" I asked. The drug took two weeks to work—if it were going to work. If the Blacksmith survived, we'd get a new resident—and a new handler—in a few weeks. I had things to do in between. One of those things involved a trip to the Oval Office.

"Tonight," Safer replied. "His health is failing, even with the best treatment."

"Have they chosen a handler?" Jeff asked. His was a good question, and one that would prove important to all of us.

"Three are under consideration. I'll let you know how things proceed. Dismissed," Safer gruffed.

"Did you see how quick he left? He didn't want any of us to know who's under consideration," Jeff growled. This time, we'd met in the cafeteria with the other three handlers.

"I think we're jumping the gun," Vance pointed out. "He'll die. Face it—six out of one-hundred-and-one? Not good odds. Stop worrying. Our little kingdom is safe."

"If he makes it, he'd better not step out of line," Gene muttered. Gene was Becker's handler, and as close to being a thug as any of us might get. I figured Becker was one of Dr. Shaw's schoolyard bullies, and Gene did nothing to discourage him.

"All conjecture at this point," Preston leaned back in his chair with a sigh. "If the drug is given tonight, we'll know in two days whether we have something to worry about."

Preston, Nick's handler, was something of a fatalist. Probably for the best, since Nick was called *the Hound* for a reason. He was right, though. If the body started showing signs of change, we'd have to open a new suite of rooms.

Corinne

Yes, they read everything, including the Sarah Fox books as I write them. Nothing I do is private. It's the price I pay for living outside the Mansion. Sometimes I get messages from James, August's assistant. He's a big fan and usually acts as a beta reader of sorts. It makes me laugh at the irony of it all.

Hey, Cori, his message began. *I'm a little upset with you. Why did you kill off Hector? I know he was a bad guy, but he had a great sense of humor.*

Bigger, funnier bad guy coming, I typed. *Nastier, too. Hector was a minor baddie—admit it, lol.*

You mean Hector's boss is gonna go, too?

No. Hector's boss is getting a boss. Does that make sense?

I guess. When are you writing that?

Near the end. A lot of things have to happen between now and then, I replied. *Keep your shirt on; I still don't have all my stuff unpacked.*

Shirt still on but getting itchy, James informed me.

Right. TMI. Don't they make a cream for that?

There's only one thing that'll cure this itch, and it's the rest of this book, he said.

Uh-huh. Maybe I'll take a year off from writing.

Nooooo! At least give me a name.

Okay. West (short for Weston) Alvarez.

That's gonna keep me up tonight. Is he related to?

Yep. Back to work. It's not five, yet.

Are you still writing?

If I can stop answering nosy messages, lmao.

All right, already. Bye, Cori.

Bye, James.

I didn't fool myself—James might be considered a friend, but I had no doubt where his loyalties lay. If asked, he'd shoot me without a second thought and cry over my novels later.

∼

Notes, Colonel Hunter

"The President will see you, now, Colonel."

It had taken exactly four hours to get an appointment with the President when I called a second time. She was taking an interest in every part of the Program, looked like. Since General Edwards' death, it had likely been on her mind often. Hugh Lawrence likely wanted Edwards' job, so the Program was responsible for jealousy and murder.

"Madam President," I nodded respectfully to her. She extended her hand and we shook. "Colonel, have a seat," she gestured toward a guest chair in the Oval Office. I waited for her to sit behind the desk, first.

"I understand you have some concerns?" she asked immediately. I noticed she was toying with a gold pen on her desk instead of looking at me. Not a good sign.

"Not concerns exactly," I said. "Just curiosity, mostly, and I wanted to bring my findings to you, first." I wasn't about to point out that I didn't trust the Joint Chiefs at all, and they wouldn't listen, anyway.

"What do you have?" She looked at me then, her curiosity getting the better of her.

"I have this file," I laid it on her desk.

"That's a file on Hugh Lawrence." She'd lowered her eyes just long enough to catch the name on the folder before coming back to me.

"That's true, ma'am. His death coincides with this." I pulled the flash drive from my pocket and laid it on the President's desk.

"I don't want to alarm her or raise suspicion," the President said as she walked me toward the door. "Just tell her that I want all of them together, in case there's an emergency. It's my decision, after all, and nobody else's. Make sure she knows nothing of this," she handed the file back to me. "If this theory has any merit, I want to know about it."

"Yes, Madam President. How quickly do you want her at the Mansion?"

"Tonight."

"I'll make arrangements immediately."

～

Corinne

"Is this because I wrote *lmao* in a message?" I asked when August Hunter and the movers stalked into my new house. "What will the neighbors think?"

"Corinne, the President asked me to bring you in. She's still spooked about Edwards' death, and she guards this secret better than they guard Fort Knox."

"Great," I hunched my shoulders.

"Don't worry—just pack your laptop. These guys will take care of everything else."

"That's what worries me," I pointed out. "I just had my desktop hooked up," I added petulantly.

"Cori, we already have everything on it. Your book is safe."

"That's what worries me," I repeated. "What about the Five? Won't they take umbrage?"

"I only use my umbrage when it rains."

"Very funny. It's too late for that, Colonel. I don't know where you got that joke, but you really ought to give it back."

"Corinne, see reason," he turned dark eyes on me. "The President ordered this, and I can't refuse that order. I'll do my best to see that the Five leave you alone. I have a suite waiting on the third floor—they're on the fourth. You have a kitchen—they don't. I'll have somebody run errands for you, and I'll even request an assistant. I can't guarantee that the expense will be approved, but I promise I'll ask."

"But I'll still be just as trapped."

"I'll ask James to make himself available if you really need to go out. You'll have another guard with you, but that ought to be enough. Don't have a panic attack," he held up a hand. Yes, my breathing had gone rough and labored.

"Too late," I wheezed.

～

Notes—Colonel Hunter

"What did you think would happen?" Dr. Shaw snapped. I'd called him first thing after the medics arrived. Corinne ended up riding to the Mansion in the back of a military ambulance.

"She was held hostage by terrorists. Couldn't escape. Remember, I suggested that she be allowed outside the walls in the first place," Shaw continued. "This isn't good for her; you know that. At least keep the bullies away from her."

"I'll do what I can." If Shaw meant to hand me a verbal beating, he was doing a good job of it. The bullies, as he put it, could find a way to get to her, no matter how closely she was watched.

"How goes it with the new one?" Shaw had heard about the Blacksmith.

"No change, yet," I reported. "But it's only been twenty-four hours. After forty-eight, we'll have a better idea."

"Not sure how I feel about it," he said.

"I know."

～

Corinne

Everybody at the Mansion knew of my arrival.

They also knew of my method of arrival.

It was the wimpiest way anybody could get there—by ambulance.

I imagined the Five staring through fourth-floor windows as I was unloaded on a stretcher, protesting the whole time that I could walk.

I would have—if they'd let me.

They didn't. I was wheeled straight to the elevator on the first floor, and then driven into my suite on the third floor. The only thing I was thankful for was that the cafeteria lay on the opposite end of the Mansion, next to the gym and workout facility.

Two suites near mine were unoccupied, and I was grateful. I needed quiet to write, not the sounds of constant foot traffic outside my door. As it was, I figured I'd have enough people knocking on my door for official reasons, and that made me nervous.

The first knock came ten minutes after I was deposited in my new suite—one of the nurses from the Mansion's med-unit stood outside my door, a syringe in her hand and orders to give me a sedative.

"I don't want that," I said, backing away as she strode purposely into my room.

"I have orders from Dr. Shaw to give it to you."

"Then I owe Dr. Shaw a kick in the ass."

"You can give me a hip voluntarily, or I can call someone to hold you down."

"You enjoy this, don't you?" I wanted to take another step back but didn't. A second panic attack threatened, and that would be disastrous.

"It's my job. Turn around." She waved a packet containing an alcohol wipe in her free hand—the one not holding the syringe—indicating that I ought to turn and drop trou. I turned and dropped trou.

"Now, the bedroom's this way," she took my elbow after jabbing me with the needle. "You'll have your furniture and personal things tomorrow. Tonight, you get military bedding."

It didn't matter what kind of bedding I got; she shoved me onto the bed and in five minutes, I was asleep. I barely had time to kick off my shoes before passing out. The Nasty Nurse of the North didn't even bother to cover me up.

CHAPTER 3

ear Dr. Shaw, I question your choice of sedative, the strength of same and those instructed to deliver it.

Sincerely, Corinne.

Corinne, what happened?

Shaw.

Dear Dr. Shaw, I slept for sixteen hours, nobody checked on me (that I know of) during that time and I almost peed my pants trying to make it to the bathroom when I woke up. The state of my dress, the frigidity of my skin and the dandelion-look to my hair attest to the unprofessional manner I was left on the military bedding supplied in my suite.*

**Their term, not mine.*

Sincerely, Corinne.

I'll have a word with the nurse.

Shaw.

Dear Dr. Shaw, I don't think one word will suffice.

Sincerely, Corinne.

"Are we incensed?" August stood outside my door, copies of my e-mail correspondence with Dr. Shaw held ominously aloft in his left hand.

"Incensed is insufficient. I refer you to any thesaurus. I pray the military has seen fit to purchase at least one for the use of its several divisions?"

Yeah, I was pissed. I'd just gotten out of the shower, there were no towels in the bathroom, I'd been forced to use kitchen towels to dry off and then I had to dress in the same clothes I'd worn the night before because my things still hadn't arrived.

I figured they'd gotten lost in New Jersey, somewhere. My hair was wet, it was sixty-nine degrees inside my suite and I couldn't find a thermostat anywhere to make it warmer.

"My skin is blue," I held out an arm for Colonel Hunter to see. It was covered in goose pimples, too, but he could see that for himself. "My hair practically has icicles on it," I complained.

"You're on the same centrally-controlled thermostat as the gym," August frowned. "They keep it cooler in there."

"Well, it's sure as hell cooler in here," I sputtered. "Are you coming in or getting out?" I flung up a hand. "We wouldn't want all the frigid, polar temperatures to slip away, now would we?"

"Cori, I get that you're upset. Shaw already called and chewed me a new one." He stepped inside my suite and studied the stark emptiness I'd been assigned with a less than critical eye. "I'd appreciate it if you'd come to me first, from now on. Dragging Shaw into this just complicates matters."

"You weren't the one who ordered the sedative—he did."

"Then demand to see me the next time somebody shows up from the med-unit. I'm in charge of your wellbeing, remember?"

"Sure. I'll let you wrestle the nurse next time. I was as respectful as I could be; she was waving a syringe and making threats."

"What kind of threats?"

"She said if I didn't drop my pants, she'd call somebody to hold me down."

"That's not," August sounded angry for a moment. "I'll go, now." He left without explaining where he was going or what he intended to do when he got there. I hoped he was prepared to tell somebody off for threatening to hold me down. I ought to have a choice whether I accepted a sedative or not; the one I'd gotten was extremely unwelcome.

～

Notes—Colonel Hunter

"Dr. Shaw prescribed a sedative," he snapped.

I stared down the doctor on duty in the med-unit. "Shaw says he prescribed half what you gave her," I snarled back. "The patient was threatened, also something Shaw would have discouraged, and the treatment was completely unprofessional."

"Look, she's on duty at night for a reason—we're not usually needed then," he raked fingers through his hair. "I saw the report. I'm just grateful she didn't bother to lie about it. Her report matches what is on the security video. She isn't a psychiatric nurse, by any stretch."

"I'm not sure she should be a nurse at all," I fumed. "Don't let her near Corinne again. If you can't find somebody better than that, call me. I'll get Shaw over here to handle it."

"Yes, sir."

He'd better damn well call me sir. I outranked him and had access to the security videos, just as he did. I'd already seen them—with James. James was pissed about the way Corinne was shoved onto the bed and left there for sixteen fucking hours. "Unless it's an emergency, I expect to be notified of any medical treatment for Corinne in the future. You got that?"

"Yes, sir."

"Good." I stalked away from the med-unit, still fuming.

～

"Colonel, we've had word," James placed a folder on my desk. "The Blacksmith is changing. He didn't die."

"I have mixed feelings about this," I said, shaking my head before opening the folder. I'd gotten a dossier on the Blacksmith, just as the other handlers would receive the information. All of us had intelligence on the Five, plus Corinne, to make sure safeguards were in place. The Program was too important to allow a single death to debilitate it. If information on the Program was leaked, the Five, the handlers and Corinne were in jeopardy.

"What do you think the odds are that he'll fit in?"

"Almost as poor as Corinne's odds. I put him ahead of Corinne because this guy, young and strong, could probably handle two or three of the Five at once. He has a reputation for a reason."

"I read his stuff last night. Scary," James agreed. "He may draw a handler just as tough."

"What you read probably wasn't the half of it."

"Yes, sir."

Corinne

My stuff showed up after five. Nobody came up to help. I wasn't surprised. I'd walked downstairs to the restaurant at three to get a late lunch. I was watched the whole time. Somebody, somewhere, was watching while I unpacked my stuff for the second time in a week.

I pretended that wasn't true as I filled drawers in my small kitchen with kitchen gadgets. If I thought about it too much, I'd lose the beef stew I'd had for lunch. With crackers.

"What are you doing in there?" I pulled my mp-3 player out of a box of ladles and spatulas. Sticking earphones in my ears, I listened to music the rest of the evening while I put things away.

James showed up with two lattes the following morning. "I'm here to hook up your desktop," he grinned.

"Hi, James. How long will this take?" I asked.

"Maybe an hour, why?"

James has blue eyes, brown, curly hair and probably got into everything when he was a child. He has an air of curiosity about him that hasn't been taken away as yet.

"I have time to bake cookies for you," I nodded and let him in. I took my vanilla latte, too—I wasn't about to turn that down.

"Oatmeal cookies?"

"Yep."

"Nobody bakes cookies around here," he sighed and followed me to the kitchen. I didn't point out that the hour he took watching me bake cookies was under surveillance; he had warm cookies to eat in forty-five minutes and ate almost a dozen. I packed another dozen for him to take with him after he hooked up my computer.

"I wish I could tell my family that I just hooked up Sarah Fox's computer," he said as he walked out my door. "Thanks for the cookies."

"Oh, you could tell them," I shrugged. "I just can't say what might happen to you afterward."

"True." He grinned and waved before heading toward the elevator.

"Look, it's Corinne. Itty, bitty, helpless Corinne," he mimed a fainting fit. Becker, my least favorite of the Five walked up, tossing an insult in my direction. He'd been to the gym to work out and just happened to walk all the way to the other end of the Mansion's third floor to ride down the west end elevators.

Nosy bastard.

"Look, it's Becker," I said, waving an arm. "I'm surprised you can say my name without pointing. Or drooling." I didn't wait for him to think up a comeback—that could take a while. I shut the door and locked it instead. He didn't walk away for several minutes. Yeah, I listened shamelessly for his footsteps.

"Corinne, you shouldn't bait him like that," August speared chunks of salad with a fork. He'd forced me to have dinner with him in the cafeteria later, before he went home to his wife.

"So, you want me to just listen to the insults and say nothing?"

"What did he say to you?"

"Come on, you know what he said." I figured everybody in the Mansion knew what he said.

"Yeah." August shook his head and kept eating.

"When the President waved her hand and ordered me here, didn't you step up and argue with her? Why didn't you tell her what happens when the Five and I get together?"

"I think she's seen the reports."

"Everybody sees the reports," I muttered, hugging myself. I had chicken and noodles in front of me and hadn't touched them. My stomach would rebel, and the cafeteria floor was mostly clean. The staff would probably prefer that it stay that way. "Nobody does anything about them," I added.

"The Five are special," August said, refusing to look at me.

"Yeah."

"Maye and Becker are with the President, tonight," August said.

"Of course they are. I understand things are a bit strained with the Russian Ambassador. Is the Prez trying to soothe ruffled ushankas?"

"Cori, most people don't even know what those things are called."

"Yeah."

"Corinne, I wish, well, fuck." He dropped his fork and pinched the bridge of his nose.

I blinked at August—he seldom used profanity around me. I didn't mind when he did—I knew what all those words meant. I'd used them, too, in my seventy-plus years.

"Auggie, I have a long list of I wishes, and none of them are on anybody's list to be granted. I'm stuck here. You're stuck with me. We're both miserable. Admit it."

"I guess that's what makes you such a good writer," he finally looked me in the eye. "You read situations better than anybody I ever met, and you were never trained to do it. I don't know how you knew about the Russians, but there it is. Again."

"Something's going on, isn't it?" I lifted an eyebrow. "Somebody's gotten the drug, haven't they? That's why Russian panties are in a knot."

"That's why Russian panties are in a knot," he agreed with a grim smile. "We have an old spy with a ton of information he wants to hand over. They suspect we have him. What they think is that he's dying and we won't get much. If he survives, we could get everything."

"A double-edged sword," I said, allowing my shoulders to droop. "You don't know if he can be trusted. You don't know what he might be able to do when he wakes. You don't even know what he'll look like when he does," I ticked things off on fingers.

"You don't know that he'll live," August began.

"Count on it," I grumbled.

"How do you know this shit?" he frowned.

"August, stop asking questions if you don't really want answers."

"What do you see when you look at me?"

That question surprised me and definitely took an unusual turn. I blinked at him for a moment before answering. "I see a confused man," I said.

"Fuck," he said again. "Eat your dinner, Corinne." He rose and stalked out of the cafeteria.

"Two hours after having dinner with the President, the Russian Ambassador was murdered outside a bar in Arlington," the reporter announced.

I'd been rousted out of bed at two-thirty in the morning and herded toward the cafeteria by a decidedly grumpy Colonel Hunter. The Five were already there, with handlers in tow. I had no idea why I was included in this meet and greet, but I didn't want to have an argument with August about it; I just wanted to go back to bed.

Nevertheless, I sat at a table with August, watching the large television in a corner of the dimly-lit dining section as the news was announced.

"They think the President had something to do with this?" Maye turned to her handler, Jeff Chambers.

"You'd know better than I would," Jeff muttered.

"I didn't pick anything up from her," Maye huffed before turning back to the news program.

"What about the Ambassador's guards? Where were they?" Kevin asked.

"They were asleep at the Russian Embassy. Where the Ambassador was supposed to be," Preston Childers said. Preston was Nick's handler, who decided to answer Kevin's question before Carol, Kevin's handler, had a chance to do so.

Carol White was the only female handler in the bunch, and I could see she didn't like Preston's interruption. The corner of her mouth tightened and she turned her back on him.

"Do we have proof they were there and asleep?" Vance Johnson asked.

"None yet—all we have is their word," Brigadier General George Safer said as he strode into the cafeteria. "There's no evidence at the crime scene that says otherwise, though." He held up a flash drive and nodded to Ken Harvey, Kevin's brother.

Ken rose, took the drive from Safer and plugged it into the computer system connected to the television.

The crime scene was bloody and the images had been recorded before the body was covered. I closed my eyes against the violence of the scene and fought down nausea. Once the initial ill feeling passed, I opened my eyes and watched the scene while Safer described it in detail.

"No prints at the scene. Killed with a nine millimeter," Safer said. "No records of any meetings set up on his calendar, and nobody knew he was outside the Embassy."

"Somebody had to know. You just don't sneak out of there—all the doors are guarded," Nick huffed.

Becker was my least favorite of the Five. Nick was my second least favorite. Nick was smarter than Becker, though. By a lot.

"The Russian President is demanding answers, of course, and we have nothing to give him. Nick, we'd like you to come with us while the crime scene is still fresh, to see if there's anything you might tell us."

"I'll get dressed." Nick rose from his seat. All of us were in robes and pajamas—we hadn't had time to get dressed before we'd been pulled into the cafeteria.

"Maye, you should come, too; we're questioning anybody who was in the area around midnight."

"I'll be ready in fifteen," she rose and followed Nick from the room. Both handlers nodded to Safer and followed their charges.

"Corinne, I know it will be hard for you to see this up close, but will you come?" Safer stood in front of our table.

"But," I stuttered.

"We know you're a damn fine mystery writer. Maybe you'll see something we miss. It never hurts to have fresh eyes on something like this."

"August?" I turned to him in shock.

"Cori, get your clothes on and let's go."

We walked through the bar, where several people were either in the process of being questioned or waiting their turn. I watched them closely as we headed toward the back door of the upscale bar—the crime scene wasn't far from there, according to Safer.

"August," I tugged on his sleeve.

"What?" he stopped abruptly and I almost plowed into him.

"That man sitting at the table against the wall? Who is he?" I asked after regaining my balance.

"I don't know. General, do you know?" Safer had stopped shortly after we did and turned toward us.

"Let's find out." Safer led us toward the man, who lounged against the back wall, watching as police questioned bar patrons on what they'd seen and heard shortly before the bar closed.

"Don't come any closer." He'd stood so fast I almost didn't see it. He held a gun in his hand and pointed it right at General Safer.

"Gun," somebody shouted. I stared as things slowed. The man, in his fifties and blond but going gray, shot at the officer who'd shouted.

At least six officers fired back, killing the man instantly.

~

"I can't tell you, because I don't know," I said for the fortieth time. "I just had a feeling, that's all. Trying to explain this is like asking an earthworm to describe why the sky is blue. He lives in the dark and doesn't know."

The blond man's gun was a nine millimeter and the same one used to kill the Russian Ambassador. The ID on the man was a forgery, and his fingerprints weren't in any database. August was just as tired as I was, but he wanted an answer he could take to the Chief of Staff and the President. They'd utilize their time better if they concentrated on identifying the shooter.

"Who do you think he was, since you can't explain why he stood out?"

"I think they knew each other," I said. "This guy and the Ambassador. I think the Ambassador had a reason to meet him, and the guy had a reason to shoot the Ambassador. Ask your Russian spy when he wakes up. I'll bet you ten bucks he knows something."

"Not a bad idea," August sighed. "If you get any more of these feelings, will you let me know? He might have killed somebody, or gotten away last night and we'd be nowhere with this. We have one police officer with a shoulder wound and that's it. Could have been a lot worse."

"Right. Can I go to bed, now?"

"Yeah. Want James to walk you back to your suite?"

"If he has time."

"He has time. One last thing, Corinne."

"What's that?"

"General Safer wants to keep this between us and the President—that you pointed this guy out. The others think he just went crazy. They were already outside at the crime scene and didn't see anything."

"Fine with me."

"A sausage and mushroom pizza, please, to Miss Watson's suite," James said before ending the call to the restaurant downstairs. I was exhausted and hadn't eaten since the night before. It was a difficult decision to make—sleep or food, first. James said it would be easier to sleep on a full stomach, so I asked him to order something for me.

I ate with my eyes closed at least half the time, drank a glass of milk and went to bed after brushing my teeth.

Notes—Colonel Hunter

"Colonel, that's outstanding. The Russian President says he's never seen the shooter and is giving us the usual bluster about our defective security, but the Secretary of State pointed out that his security let the Ambassador get away from the Embassy in the first place. We're having a small, cold war at the moment, but we'll find out who that bastard was and we'll have the Russians by the balls. Your theory is looking pretty sound from where I'm sitting. You say she stopped you and asked about the shooter right away?"

"She sure did, Madam President. General Safer can't get over it, either."

"Keep me informed. This could turn out better than we thought."

"Yes, Madam President. It sure could."

"You know she won't say anything. She never talks about it." Shaw met me for dinner, as requested. "You're telling me she went right to the guy, without even sizing anybody else up?"

"The minute she saw him, she stopped me. Safer knew something was up, so he stopped, too. The guy knew he was made, so he stood and pulled his weapon."

"If he were involved with something deeper, he knew he had to die before we arrested him," Shaw agreed around a mouthful of steak.

"Nobody has anything on this guy. He's a spook."

"No money trail?"

"None to follow. Not yet, anyway. Picture's sent everywhere. Nobody knows him."

"Did Maye walk right past him and not pick anything up?"

"That's what I hear."

"It may be a good thing he's dead, then."

"We all worry about that—that somebody knows. So far, we've been safe."

"I worry about what will happen if ninety-five families find out their relatives didn't die in combat."

"We had nothing to do with that, and you know it. Those were volunteers. The life insurance payouts given to the families weren't refused, either."

"No comment."

~

Corinne

Waking up in the afternoon after sleeping all day after staying up most of the night before always leaves me groggy and nauseated. I wouldn't have awakened when I did if there hadn't been a knock on my door.

Shuffling toward my front door and silently cursing whoever stood on the other side, I peered through my peephole to see who it was.

Colonel August Hunter. He didn't look happy.

"Who pissed in your Post Toasties?" I asked when I opened the door.

"I don't eat Post Toasties."

"Shredded Wheat?" I asked innocently.

"This isn't about breakfast cereal."

"Then come in and tell me what it is about," I waved him in. Yes, I was dressed in pajamas and a robe, which wasn't exactly military issue. Colonel Hunter ignored my dress and walked inside my suite.

"I just got word," he began, "While I was downstairs having a late lunch with Doctor Shaw."

"What word is that?" I asked.

"That we'll be getting a new resident soon," August muttered.

"Great. Didn't I tell you that? I thought I told you that," I said trying to comb fingers through my hair. It likely looked as if birds had nested in it. Condors, maybe. I didn't have a mirror to check.

"Corinne, will you stop and listen for a minute?"

"I'm listening."

"They want to put him in the suite next to yours, because he likes to cook. You'll be sharing your kitchen with him, looks like, since it's the only one available to a resident. They'll install a connecting door in the next few days, and they'll put up something sturdier between your living space and the kitchen, so you can lock yourself in. The kitchen is the only thing you're expected to share."

"No. That's not acceptable," I snapped, immediately angry. "It's one thing to be hauled here without being given a choice in the matter. It's something else to share any space with one of the others. You know how they all feel about me." I tossed up a hand, as if that might make a difference.

"Corinne, the decision wasn't mine to make. I objected when I heard, but that didn't sway the ones in charge."

"So they don't even know how things will turn out with him and already he's getting perks? Typical," I huffed. "When have they ever given me perks? Want to answer that?" I rounded on August, as if he could wave a hand and make things different for me.

"I know," I held up a hand. "Neither of us has a choice in this. Thank you for voicing your concerns. When will the wrecking crew arrive?"

"Thursday."

"Fine. Will he be sharing my groceries and kitchen gadgets, in addition to insulting me every chance he gets?"

"They didn't say. I assume that's true."

"Will the smell of borsht be permeating my office?"

"I don't know."

"You know," I pointed a finger at August, "Every time I think things can't get any worse, they always do."

"There's more," August winced.

"Oh, joy. Please—do tell."

"He's an expert in Krav Maga."

"Great."

"Corinne, they'll ask him to take over your lessons."

"Just to keep him busy, huh?" I shook my head in disbelief. "If he's occupied with obliterating the least important person in the building, maybe he can't get into too much trouble?"

"I think they want you to help keep an eye on him."

"No. There are enough people in this building watching what everybody else does. You don't need my help for that."

"Corinne, I'm asking you to do that. With that special insight you seem to have, maybe you can let us know if he's on the level or not."

"Wow. There go my plans of avoiding him altogether."

"There's something else."

"Lemmings have invaded the White House?"

"Cori."

"Okay."

"You're expected to go to meetings with the Five from now on."

"Auggie, say it ain't so."

CHAPTER 4

*I*lya

"We'll allow leeway on your new name—within reason. Nothing Russian—that should be obvious."

"I'm from Ukraine." That should have explained everything to the dolt sitting behind the desk, but it didn't.

"Nothing Ukrainian, either."

Fucker. "Rafe," I said. "Rafe Black. That will do."

"You sure? You won't be able to change it, once it's entered in your dossier."

"I don't intend to change it."

He lifted an eyebrow but tapped the name on his computer anyway. "We'll have legal documents sent to you at the Mansion. Is there anything else?"

"You say I'll have a kitchen available?"

"Yes, but you'll share it with another resident."

"I prefer not to share."

"It's that or no kitchen at all. Those are your options."

"I hope he stays out of my way."

"*She* will likely stay as far away from you as possible, if the rumors are true."

"Is she part of the Program?"

"Yes, although she seldom participates."

"By her choice?"

"By her talent. She has little, according to my records."

"Her name?"

"Corinne."

Corinne

I eyed the new connecting door distrustfully, as if something might pop through it at any moment. Realistically, I knew I'd probably be introduced first, but that didn't keep my fear at bay while I checked on pot roast and vegetables.

Pot roast would last me two or three days, if I made sandwiches. That left more writing time, and with the impending Russian invasion, I could avoid seeing him as much as possible if I didn't cook so often.

Until he started beating me into a floor mat at the gym while pretending to teach Krav Maga.

August let me see the heavily redacted dossier on him, since we'd share space. I learned his original first name, too—Ilya. Common enough, and safe enough, since I didn't officially have a last name to go with it.

I heard he spoke English better than most Americans, with no trace of a Russian accent, and that he spoke many more languages—fluently. No surprise, since he was a spy. No wonder the Russians were experiencing palpitations.

Rafe Black was his new name. I'd see how well it fit him. No photographs were included in any of the information I'd been given, so I had no idea what he'd look like. It didn't matter; I intended to stay out of his way behind the new, steel door that divided my office and sleeping quarters from the kitchen.

Ilya

I didn't need the bulletproof vest I wore. My talent appeared to be shielding—good enough to stop bullets. They'd been afraid to test anything stronger against what I had. I could protect anyone standing near me, too—up to four feet. Past that, they died. Obviously, I'd only protected mannequins during the testing. That was a shame; I wouldn't have minded seeing a few doctors and scientists riddled with bullets.

"Here's the entrance to the tunnel," my companion, Dalton Parrish, announced. They'd named him my handler. We'd see who did the handling.

The tunnel was perhaps a quarter mile long, and the entrance lay beyond a guarded gate. Once we'd driven past the tunnel, I saw the Mansion.

It was impressive, but I'd stayed in better.

"Your quarters are on the third floor," Dalton informed me as I lifted my duffel from the trunk of the vehicle. "My suite is next to yours, but not connected."

"Good," I said.

"Uh, when do you want to meet the others?" He didn't know whether my last response meant that I was glad he was next door or glad his suite wasn't connected to mine. I let him worry about it.

"Tomorrow," I said. "That will be soon enough." Hefting the bag over a shoulder, I walked toward the nearest entrance.

Corinne

"He's here, so you may hear something next door if you're in the kitchen," August said. "He said he didn't want to meet anyone until tomorrow, so we're delivering a meal to his suite for tonight," he added.

"Thank God." I slouched onto a barstool and let my forehead drop to the island. "I can eat in peace tonight, at least."

I didn't add that I wished they'd put a sign on the connecting door, or some other way to let us know the other's preferred cooking schedules. I shoved that thought away and lifted my head to blink at August. He was frowning at me. No surprise.

"Corinne, I expect you to keep me informed," he said.

"August, if there's anything worthy of informing you about, you'll hear it from me, first. Okay?" I figured the new guy's brand of toothpaste wasn't important to national security.

"Okay."

Notes—Colonel Hunter

"Corinne's scared to death," Shaw informed me.

"Did she tell you that?"

I'd met Shaw in the coffee shop at his request; he'd seen Corinne the day before. "No, she didn't say it. I asked a few questions—how she felt about sharing space with a stranger, that sort of thing. It wasn't difficult to draw the logical conclusion."

"I don't blame her for being frightened. He's taller now than he was before, and looks even tougher, if that's possible."

"You've seen photographs?"

"Yes. I kept those away from Corinne."

"That was probably a mistake. The first time she walks into her kitchen for coffee and finds him there, she'll have a panic attack."

"We're making arrangements to introduce him to her and the others in a controlled setting," I argued. "So she won't have panic attacks. I'm hoping for a kitchen schedule, too, to keep the peace."

"Best laid plans, Colonel?" Shaw lifted a skeptical eyebrow.

"Probably. I don't know what will happen when he starts training her in Krav Maga."

"Don't let him hurt her. This isn't fun and games, you know, and beating on her for the pleasure of it will garner a complaint from me to the President."

"When are you scheduled to meet with her?" I asked, ignoring the threat. I figured the President wouldn't be happy if somebody broke Corinne—she was her new toy.

"Next Wednesday, right after Corinne's appointment."

"Convenient. You can yell at Rafe if he hurts her," I said.

"You know that's not the way things work. Those sessions are private and shouldn't bleed into the others."

"Yet you and I discuss," I began.

"I discuss with all the handlers. That's their job—to see that their assets don't get out of hand, or receive what they need to thrive. If they'd asked, and they didn't, I'd have suggested leaving Rafe and Corinne separate, and building a second kitchen."

"We were given enough money for a few doors, nothing else," I huffed.

"Corinne would have paid for a private kitchen," Shaw shot back. "You know that. Are you asking her to help keep an eye on him?"

"That's not common knowledge," I hissed. "Keep it to yourself."

"Not a problem," Shaw shrugged. "Just keep her safe, got it? I hear things, Colonel Hunter. I hear Corinne may be a lot more useful than you ever thought she'd be."

"The President doesn't want that spread around, and she doesn't want to alarm Corinne," I snapped.

"If she didn't want to alarm Corinne, she should have left her alone and found someone else to teach her Krav Maga."

"Point taken."

Corinne

"There's a formal breakfast meet and greet scheduled in the morning," James handed a note to me. "You and the Five will be there to meet the new guy."

"I'm not looking forward to it." I stood on one side of my doorway while James stood on the other, delivering the formal invitation to breakfast Friday morning.

"I know. I noticed you haven't written anything the last two days."

"It's difficult to write while you're mopey and depressed," I pointed out.

"Cori, you can't leave the book hanging like that."

"Wanna bet?"

"Please?" he wheedled. "I'd ask for cookies, too, but that would be too much. I'll settle for the end of the chapter."

"I can't make any promises, James," I said, leaning my head against the doorframe. "Not only does he get my kitchen, he gets to beat on me, too."

"If he's any good at all, that won't happen."

"Look, if he wants to impress the others, all he has to do is join in and bully the weakest member, or don't you remember that from high school?"

"Cori, what are you really worried about?"

"That the others will come to watch, and he'll hit harder because of it."

"It's only three days a week."

"Yeah."

Ilya

The best way to size anybody up, as they say in America, is to catch them off-guard. I intended to size up Corinne Watson before we were introduced. That's why I was in the kitchen quite early, sipping strong, black coffee and waiting for her to arrive.

Big mistake.

"Not the best way to make your presence known," Dalton shook his head.

"If you'd given me sufficient information, this could have been avoided."

"I didn't have Colonel Hunter's permission."

"Where is he, then? I'll talk to him myself."

"Stay put." Dalton held out a hand. "We're in enough trouble as it is, and this is just our first day."

"Hmmph," I snorted. "How was I to know she'd have a panic attack? You told me she wasn't very talented. I expected her to be military, at the very least, and prepared for things like this."

"Look, a big part of her file is redacted, so even I don't have access. If you get information, you may have to get it from her. Colonel Hunter is so mad he could breathe fire over this."

Corinne

"Why, Dr. Shaw," I muttered. I opened my eyes to find him leaning over me. "Whatever are you doing here?" I added.

"I believe you know why." He grimaced and straightened beside my bed. "You really need to handle surprises better than this."

"Did you see him?" I pulled myself up and leaned against my headboard. "He looks like a mountain."

"He's six-four. That's not a mountain."

"Says you."

"It appears you're feeling better," Shaw said, his voice dry.

"Look, just, well, never mind." I rubbed my forehead.

"I think he's willing to work out a schedule, or at least knock," Shaw said.

"Great."

"The meeting with the others went well."

"I imagine Becker is in his pocket already—Becker's never made me have a panic attack."

"Let's not add wild speculation to this debacle," Shaw said. "I have enough paperwork as it is."

Ilya

Becker and Nick are pigs masquerading as humans. Maye is an ice queen with telepathic talents. Kevin and Ken are tech geeks with acquired physical abilities.

All of them are sent out regularly on assignment; sometimes outside the country. I wasn't surprised that their handlers were with them; Dalton insisted on being with me when I met with the Five at breakfast.

I wasn't stupid enough to ask why they were called the Five and not the Six. To them, Corinne didn't count. I understood that—up to a point.

It wasn't difficult to determine that something was happening with Corinne—latent talents or such—because she'd only been brought to the Mansion recently, after being on the outside for more than five years.

That spelled one thing to me—she'd suddenly become more valuable. Whatever the talent was, it wasn't common knowledge. The Five thought her just as ineffective as they'd always imagined.

I'd gotten an earful, too, from Corinne's handler about PTSD, which Corinne has. I didn't interrupt the rant, although I knew more about the illness than he did. I'd seen too many—soldiers and spies— formerly strong and resilient, suddenly fall because of the affliction. Where I came from, a spy with PTSD didn't live long. They were too much of a liability.

It intrigued me, too, why they'd given Corinne—a civilian—the drug. Perhaps we were more alike than I wanted to think. Information can be quite valuable, and I figured Corinne held something they wanted.

Just as I did.

"I hear you're gonna teach Corinne Krav Maga," Becker snickered as I studied the remains of my breakfast. The eggs, toast and ham I'd consumed. I've never liked hash browns. Those stayed on my plate, untouched.

"Are you an expert?" I refused to blink as I turned to him, lifting an eyebrow in speculation.

"I'm good enough," he growled. *Easy to anger, that one.*

"Maye's the expert," Ken intervened. *Peacemaker.*

"I'd like to see you take her on," Nick said. *Instigator.*

"I just arrived," I said. "I'd like to settle in before anyone attempts to bloody me up."

"I believe it's my choice whether I bloody anyone or not," Maye lifted her cup of tea gracefully. *Deadly—no doubt about that.* Curly red hair? *The best disguise I'd ever seen.*

"I have news," General Safer walked up to our table. We'd met in a private corner of the cafeteria, but still visible to anyone who came inside. I recognized him, even before I'd been informed that he was currently in charge of the Program.

When the President replaced General Edwards, Safer would go back to his former position of second-in-command. Meanwhile, he had news. All of us at the table quieted, waiting to hear what it was.

"The President just named a new Secretary of Defense, who will be placed in charge of the Program."

"Who?" Carol White, Kevin Harvey's handler, asked.

"General Paul Cutter," Safer deadpanned.

Corinne

"One last thing," Dr. Shaw said before draining his coffee cup. I'd gotten up and made coffee for both of us in my kitchen, while we talked. I liked having our session there, instead of going to Dr. Shaw's office downstairs.

"There's a last thing?" I asked.

"The President named a new Secretary of State."

"It's Cutter, isn't it?" I mumbled, staring at my fuzzy slippers.

"It's Cutter. I'm surprised you know about him."

"You can't turn on the television and not know," I muttered. "He's a nightmare. Please tell me he won't be in charge of the Program."

"I can't tell you that."

"Dr. Shaw, the virus has been introduced. Be ready for the consequences," I said.

"What do you mean? He's charged with preserving national security."

"In his mind, that has nothing whatsoever to do with what we are," I snapped.

∼

"Corinne?" August walked in after barely tapping on the door outside the kitchen. He and Ilya/Rafe found Shaw and me at the kitchen island, having our debate about General Cutter, asshole extraordinaire. Cutter was army, so Shaw was doing his best to defend him.

I wasn't buying the load of excrement the good doctor thought to sell.

"Corinne, I wanted to introduce—properly—Rafe Black, the newest addition to the Program," August announced.

"Any more coffee?" Rafe asked immediately.

"Look, I figure you got enough in the cafeteria, but if you think it's necessary to break the ice, then sure, we have coffee. Caf? Decaf? I don't have anything that went through an animal first, so if that's what you want, you're on your own."

"There's something you should know," August nodded toward a barstool, silently telling Rafe to sit. "Corinne, here, writes the Sarah Fox mysteries. If you don't behave, she'll kill you at least twice in her next book."

"How did you escape your handler?" I ignored August and pointed my question directly at Rafe.

"Why do you want to know?" he asked, his voice cool, his face expressionless. That probably came in handy in the spy business when dealing with difficult people. I figured all the women in the Mansion were already signing up for nights with Rafe. He was attractive in a rough sort of way—tall, with dark hair, darker eyes and an air of command about him.

"Looking for pointers," I replied, setting a cup of full-caf in front of the former Soviet spy. "Want cream and/or sugar?"

"Neither. I don't intend to drink much," he shrugged.

"I thought so."

"Tell me," he said, "what do you think of the Five? Does it irritate you that they call themselves the Five instead of the Six?"

"Really?" I huffed. "Why would I want to be associated with that bunch of prejudiced jerks? Why do you want to know? Have they excluded you already, too?"

"Corinne," August warned. "Shaw and I are here, remember, and others may be listening."

"Really?" I said again. "Like I don't know already that every moment of every day is under microscopic scrutiny?"

"I," Rafe cleared his throat, "just wanted to drop by and apologize, for earlier and for later."

"Later what?" I narrowed my eyes at him.

"For when I knock you to the floor on multiple occasions during your lessons."

"Oh, for cripes' sake," I tossed up a hand and slid off my barstool. "Auggie, did you hear that? He's going to kill me. Look, why can't we not do this, and just say we did?"

"Auggie?" Shaw seemed interested, suddenly.

"We're not buying monogrammed towels," I snapped at Shaw. "If I call him Auggie, it's because he deserves to be irritated."

"You really write the Sarah Fox mysteries?" Rafe asked.

"What? That was five minutes ago. Are you slow or something?" I asked, shaking my head at him.

Ilya

Truthfully, I expected someone who'd hide in a corner the moment I reappeared. I certainly didn't expect what I found. After speaking with her for only a few minutes, I learned she was just as adept at assessing others as I was. I found it disconcerting, too, that she could read me just as easily.

"Is this talent you have for reading people part of your writing ability?" I asked. Yes, I'd read Sarah Fox's novels. *All of them*. I wasn't going to divulge that information. Let her think I disapproved of her talent. That would keep her unbalanced and easier to unsettle. Vulnerable people could be manipulated.

"You're not a spy, here," she pointed out. For the first time, I blinked first. "Auggie, did you show him any pictures of the guy who killed the Russian Ambassador?"

I turned quickly in Colonel Hunter's direction. I hadn't gotten that news. "He's dead?" I asked.

"Here." Colonel Hunter drew out his cell and scrolled through photographs before settling on one. "This one killed the Ambassador. Know who he is?"

Corinne

He knew. I know he knew. He shook his head anyway. August pocketed his cell with a sigh. "Just wanted to check," he said. "Thanks."

"No trouble," Rafe replied. Yes, he could lie with the best of them. I wasn't fooled for a minute. "Is he dead, too? The one in the photograph?"

"Yeah."

"Too bad you didn't get information from him, first."

"What makes you think we didn't?" August asked.

"He's fishing," I said. "Now he knows for sure."

"Cori," August warned.

"Yeah." I slumped in my chair.

Ilya

I was beginning to see already what it had taken them more than five years to find—Corinne Watson was dangerous. I'd perfected the craft of reading people and situations after years of practice. She had it naturally. To me, that meant it could be the least of her talents. That concerned me. Did they not see that she was concealing what she was?

While I considered keeping my mystery to myself, I began to worry that I might not unravel hers and I really wanted to solve that riddle.

"When do you have breakfast—or coffee?" I asked her.

"Usually around seven-thirty," she replied. I cut her off before she could ask what my schedule was. "I'll see you then," I said. "We'll avoid future surprises that way."

"Wait," she said as I waved and walked toward the door. Colonel Hunter watched me go, a deep frown on his face.

Corinne

The asshole didn't even wait for me to tell him that I wanted quiet time for myself in the mornings, to consider what I wanted to write during the day. He intended to interrupt. Likely, he knew it would unsettle me—that was his game plan, after all.

Ilya Kuznetsov, I thought at him, *you're a real jerk.*

Ilya

I heard her—as plainly as if I'd been standing next to her, and began my mental list of what it was, exactly, that Corinne Watson was capable of doing.

Notes—Colonel Hunter

I'd only known Rafe for a few hours and disliked him already. His handler, too, was an unknown to me. It made me wonder if General Cutter was making his presence known already.

"James, get me everything you can find on Dalton Parrish," I said the moment I walked into my office.

"Right away, sir."

Fifteen minutes later, James was back and setting a flash drive on my desk.

"Tell me," I said, fingering the tiny file.

"Worked as General Cutter's assistant in the past," James reported.

"Corinne was right," I muttered. "The virus has been introduced."

"Corinne is starting to scare me," James said.

"That makes two of us."

"We can't barge into the President's office and tell her she made a mistake," Shaw said.

We'd chosen a familiar haunt away from the Mansion to have our discussion—a small, nearby park devoid of bugs and listening devices. Thankfully, the Hound was still at the Mansion, or he might have heard what we said.

"Look, we both know Cutter was one of her picks for the Vice President's position when he ran for the presidency—as a conciliatory move after she won the nod at the primaries. The polls showed Flint was a better fit, so Cutter backed out. He's been kissing presidential ass for a while," I shook my head. "He's been retired from the military for eight years, in case he got the nod for Secretary of Defense. He was just waiting for this to come along so he could continue to rub us the wrong way."

"How long did Parrish act as his assistant?"

"Four years. The information I have says he's in Cutter's pocket, all the way, although he's been working in other departments for the military."

"Captain Dalton Parrish, here to spy on everything," Shaw sighed. "Everything will go right back to Cutter."

"What has the President told him already?" I snorted. "We'll be lucky if we're not shipped to Alaska."

"Or shoved onto a submarine," Shaw agreed. "I hate those things."

"What about the President's upcoming conference at Camp David?" I said. "She'll want Maye and Nick there, for sure."

"I hear she may take all of them," Shaw said.

"If that's the case, she'll ask for Corinne, too. And the Russian."

"I hate Camp David," Shaw muttered.

❧

"We have information."

"What information?" Dmitri lifted an eyebrow. He was acting as the Soviet Ambassador until someone else was appointed.

"Just a conversation," the informant shrugged. "But *the Russian* was mentioned. I believe you know what that could mean."

"I'll make contact immediately," Dmitri said and nodded his dismissal.

❧

Corinne

"You won't be smiling if I lose my coffee all over you," I said.

Rafe/Ilya was still grinning (*the bastard*) as he stared down at me. I was flat on my back, with his arm pressed against my throat. At least I wasn't gasping for breath, and I would have been if he'd pushed harder.

"You think I haven't gotten worse than that?" he said before leaning back and letting me up.

"I hope it was unpleasant every time," I said, struggling to rise. He didn't offer a hand.

Just as I'd feared, all five of the Five had shown up to watch my beating. I had no physical defense against this man. *He* knew it. *They* knew it. *I* knew it. "I'll bet you beat up kittens in your spare time," I rubbed my left hip—I'd landed on it after the last attack.

"I like cats," he responded, stepping back.

"That doesn't mean I'll like you any better," I snapped, "just because we both like cats."

"I expect you to go through those exercises we did earlier every morning. I don't care how sore you are," he said. "We're done today."

"Thank God," I muttered and walked stiffly toward the door.

"God had nothing to do with it. You should thank me," he said. I heard the Five laughing as I left the gym.

"I can't walk. That's how my lessons went," I said. Dr. Shaw arrived shortly after I got out of the shower, just to see how my beating had gone.

"We need to discuss the list," he said, taking a seat at my kitchen island and nodding when I offered coffee.

"You know how I feel about that," I said. Moving my arms felt like moving lead weights as I dropped a coffee pod into the brewer and hit the button. I figured I wouldn't be able to move anything later in the day, but didn't point that out to Dr. Shaw. I'd take ibuprofen and hope to get through it.

"Corinne, we know sex can relieve stress, as well as offering other benefits. You've ignored this as long as you've been in the Program. I think it's time you did something about it."

"Who's asking now?" I huffed, handing the fresh cup of coffee to him. I noticed my hand wasn't particularly steady as I did so.

"Dalton Parrish has added his name to the list. You know just about any male with breath in his body here at the Mansion is on that list."

"I don't want Dalton Parrish. That should be clear enough. If I don't take any of them, then none of them can be offended. Right?" I stuffed another pod into the brewer and shoved a thumb against the button.

"Corinne, if somebody you do want isn't on that list, you can add your name to their list," he said.

"Nope. Not going there, either." I figured part of Becker's

animosity toward me had to do with the fact that I'd ignored his name, just like all the others. The sad truth? We were only allowed to get close to somebody associated with the Program. If we wanted somebody from outside, that was considered a security breach. Dr. Shaw saw the need for intimate contact among the survivors of Cloud Dust, and had no trouble hooking the others up.

I was the one who balked.

I had my reasons.

"Dr. Shaw," I said, "I want to go to bed with somebody who cares about me, and not some warm-blooded dildo. We've had this discussion before. I hope we don't have it again."

CHAPTER 5

*C*orinne

The first meeting with all seven of us present came three days later. General Safer arrived to deliver the news.

"The President's meeting at Camp David is next week. All of you will go. Your handlers will advise you of your assignments before then."

"I hope my assignment is writing in my bungalow," I sighed.

"Cori," August warned.

"Yeah."

"You will run with the rest of them, instead of on that pathetic treadmill," August informed me as we walked toward my suite after the meeting.

"That's outside," I said.

"Along the perimeter of the wall. They run at least five. I'm willing to let you do the usual three," he said.

"There are insects out there," I complained.

"And fresh air."

"In this town? Seriously?"

"You don't get enough sunlight. Dr. Shaw commented on it recently."

"I'm sure he did." At that moment, I was hoping he hadn't discussed my sex life—or lack of same—with August. "I can build a sunroom onto my suite," I suggested.

"It's spring," August pointed out, ignoring me. "The air is warmer. Get new running clothes if you need them; you've only ordered groceries since you got here."

"You know I'll need them," I grumped. I ran in old sweats. Totally unattractive ones, too.

"Get them ordered today. And ask Ginny to order a suitable wardrobe for next week."

"I'm not wearing dresses."

"You will if you have dinners with the President."

"Please say I won't have dinners with the President."

"Dr. Shaw says you refused Dalton Parrish. You know we could use information," August began.

I slapped a hand over my eyes. Shaw did discuss my sex life with Auggie. "I'm not prostituting myself for anyone," I hissed. "Get the hell away from me." I ran toward my door, leaving Colonel August Hunter stewing behind me.

Notes—Colonel Hunter

"I told you not to say anything," Shaw said, slapping the saltshaker onto the cafeteria table.

"We have an opportunity to find out what that asshole knows, and she balks," I stuttered.

"He put his name on Maye's list, too. Maybe Cutter wants the same thing."

"Good luck on getting anything from either one of them," I said. "What did Maye say?"

"That she'd break his neck before she'd have sex with him."

"I tend to believe her when she says that," I agreed. "Anything new on the Russian?"

"Nothing unusual. We talked about his time in prison. He had an easier time of it than some of the others—privileges and such. Still wasn't getting medical care, though. They wanted him dead."

"Tough bastard."

"No doubt. The Five showed up for the first three Krav Maga lessons with Corinne. That's been whittled down to two."

"The bullies?"

"Of course."

"You think they'll lose interest? Corinne has bruises everywhere. She won't even look at Rafe when they're not sparring."

"Is he still showing up for breakfast?"

"As far as I know. Dalton said she wasn't talking then, either."

~

Corinne

I sat at the kitchen island, preparing to eat a quick bowl of chicken noodle soup for lunch while I considered the prospect of having my future breakfasts in the cafeteria. He walked in. I hadn't spoken to him in days.

"I wanted lunch," he said, taking the seat next to mine and pulling my bowl of soup toward him.

"Oh, dear God," I sighed and dropped my head on the island. I listened, my eyes shut, while I heard sounds of a spoon clinking against the bowl and slurping noises. I waited until he was finished before rising from my seat and elbowing him in the ribs.

He'd taught me the move—I just hadn't used it until then.

While he got his breath back, I made myself another bowl of soup.

"You're still here?" I asked as I set the bowl on the island and took my seat.

"Thinking about taking that bowl, too."

"You think so?"

"I could."

"I know." I allowed my shoulders to sag.

"I won't take your lunch. Eat," he nodded toward my bowl. "I'll find crackers for you." He rose and shuffled toward the cabinets. In a few seconds, I had a sleeve of crackers and a glass of orange juice in front of me.

"You're going to run with the rest of us tomorrow morning. At six."

"Six is too early," I moaned, leaning my head back and closing my eyes.

"If you didn't stay up until two working on that goddamn computer, you'd get up earlier."

"It's easier to write then," I said, opening my eyes and staring into his. They were quite dark. *I'll bet you're responsible for quite a lot of panty moisture throughout the Mansion,* I thought at him. He chose that moment to turn his head away.

"Your health is suffering for it," he said. "Staying up so late."

"Really? Got a medical degree, too?" I sniped.

"I've done some reading."

"I'm sure you have."

"Natural remedies are available to help you sleep. You don't need those drugs that Shaw offers."

"I don't take those drugs that Shaw offers."

"Colonel Hunter said you didn't."

"You've increased my intake of ibuprofen."

"I know. You could go to the whirlpool. That would help."

"The whole Mansion shows up there."

"And that is a problem because?"

"I'm an introvert."

He laughed. It wasn't a horrible sound. "Do you own a swimsuit?" he asked when he stopped chuckling.

"It's five years old and I've never worn it. Moths may have eaten it; I haven't checked."

"You could go in naked."

"While everybody in the Mansion has probably seen me naked, I don't want it to be voluntary," I said.

"You make me laugh," he said.

"Sure. Every time you toss me to the floor, you're grinning."

"Get your swimsuit, lightweight. We'll go to the spa."

"Where's your suit?" I demanded.

"I'm wearing it under my jeans."

"Of course you are."

"You should call me Rafe," he added.

"Of course I should."

Complete proof that everybody listened to everything going on in the Mansion waited for us when we arrived at the huge hot tub connected to the gym. Even James was there, grinning like a fool and scooting over so I could sit next to him.

Rafe the rat sat between us.

"You stopped in the middle of a paragraph," James said, forcing me to lean around the mountain sitting next to me so I could reply.

"I stopped for lunch. Which he ate," I poked Rafe in the ribs.

"You had more. I wouldn't have eaten all your tinned soup." He took my fingers from his ribs and set them in my lap.

"Really?" I made a face at Rafe. At least six women lined the other side of the spa, and all of them ogled him. James, who was fit enough, looked like a ninety-pound-weakling next to Rafe. *All six of those women will serve you soup—at the same time*, I thought in his direction.

At least hot, bubbling water hid my hand as I poked him in the ribs a second time. He covered it by turning to James and asking how he might get access to my books as I wrote them. James offered to send him what he had. I slapped a wet hand against my forehead. Rafe laughed.

Running three miles at six in the morning was bad enough. What made it worse was that a light rain fell as I ran. Becker lapped me twice, just to prove he could. The last time he passed me, one of his hands snaked out and shoved me. Waving my arms helplessly when he knocked me off balance, I fell in rain-soaked grass and mud with a splash and a grunted *oof*. Muttering obscenities, I struggled to rise while Rafe ran right past, his steady stride slurping up mud and flinging wet droplets about him. I watched him run for a moment before pulling myself from the slop I'd landed in.

Ilya

I ran at a steady pace behind Becker, content to let him have the lead. He was happiest thinking he was in charge of every situation. I allowed him his fantasies—until he shoved Corinne into the mud.

That's when I caught up with him.

Waiting for an opportunity, I held back until he was prepared to pass one of the brothers, then burst between them, making sure Becker went down. I smiled as he shouted names in my direction.

Corinne

"Are you packed?" Rafe drank coffee as I walked into the kitchen. I was still sore, but the whirlpool sessions helped. Today was the day we were heading to Camp David. I didn't want to go. At least I wasn't expected to run or have a Krav Maga lesson.

"Yes," I grumbled.

"You're not dressed to go."

"It's a Freudian slip."

"Looks like a bathrobe to me."

"You're so funny," I mocked. "I want coffee first, so I can be wide awake and miserable, instead of half-asleep and miserable."

"Corinne?"

August had arrived.

"Auggie, please sit, have coffee and tell me everything that I'm doing wrong today," I waved toward a barstool at the island.

"You, Rafe and the others will attend the meetings with the President. Rafe will be within four feet always, while you will be nearby, watching the others and taking notes."

"Physically taking notes?"

"That's what Cutter said."

"Cutter. Joy."

"Cori."

"Yeah."

"Rafe?" Dalton Parrish walked through the door connecting Rafe's quarters with my kitchen.

"Dalton." Rafe sipped coffee and didn't look up. Dalton repeated August's words to Rafe, and then to me. His eyes wandered over me, too, as if he'd never seen a rumpled woman in her bathrobe before.

"Coffee?" Dalton asked. I made coffee for August, Dalton and me. I drank in silence while the others talked—we'd be flying in helicopters to Camp David. The choppers would arrive shortly, so I didn't have a lot of time to get ready.

"Corinne, get in the shower," August said when I'd finished half my coffee.

"Fine." Taking my cup with me, I wandered toward the door leading into my suite. I took my time, too. That's why the chopper blew up before we left the Mansion, instead of after we were inside it.

Notes—Colonel Hunter

Burning debris was strewn across the yard and guards were everywhere, with more on the way. It took a while to determine that the pilot was involved—he'd taken off running seconds before the chopper exploded.

He sat in an interrogation room inside the Mansion while another chopper was ordered for us—the President was waiting, although she'd been briefed. James stood with us as we watched a fire crew put the last of the fires out—singed and blackened grass littered the lawn in front of us and the unpleasant scent of burned fuel, rubber and metal hung about the Mansion.

"Colonel?" James said, nodding toward the back entrance, near the helipad. He wanted to talk.

"Let's go," I said and followed him toward the Mansion.

"Do you think Corinne," he began before I held up a hand. He and I both knew—Corinne was never late. She'd dragged her feet today.

"We'll have this conversation later," I said. "What's the ETA on the second chopper? Do we have an inspection crew ready?"

"Yes, sir. And we have experts coming to examine the wreckage."

"Good. I want to be informed if they find anything."

"I'll keep you in the loop. Who would do this?" he added.

"That's what I want to know."

∼

"Our first attempt failed. We will try again."

"See that you do," the voice crackled over the secure line. "This problem must be eliminated."

"Agreed."

∼

Ilya

This looked familiar—I'd seen others die the same way. Dmitri could be behind this. How had he found the information? Had someone discussed me while Dmitri's watchdogs were listening?

It angered me that they'd killed Ambassador Bespalov; he'd secretly arranged to get me out of prison. I wouldn't reveal that information—his wife still lived in Novosibirsk. I was likely involved in her husband's death; I didn't want trouble to visit her, too.

More than anything, I wanted to know what the pilot had to say, but held back from asking. Dalton stood nearby, watching closely, keys clicking sharply on his cell phone as he tapped a message. My guess was that General Cutter would receive the message.

Corinne wasn't far away, so I turned toward her. She was pale, but not as frightened as one might think. Did she see this coming?

I wouldn't be surprised.

∾

Notes—Colonel Hunter

After the second chopper was gone over twice and declared free of explosives, the pilot was searched carefully for weapons. We loaded in four hours late. I had texts from one of the President's aides, telling me the meeting scheduled that morning was postponed.

Madam President really wanted Corinne and Rafe there for some reason. Corinne didn't like flying in a helicopter; that was easy enough to see when she sat between Rafe and James. Dalton reached over to help buckle her in when he saw her hands shaking, but she managed to get it fastened on her own. Rafe helped her adjust the headset so she wouldn't be deafened by the noise.

That's when I learned Rafe had my phone number. *She's not used to this,* he texted.

Then she'd better damn well get used to it, I texted back. *Lose my number or I'll get your phone privileges revoked.*

They all had special issue phones for this trip, but only for use within the group. All other numbers were blocked. I thought Corinne was the only one with my number. Obviously, I was wrong.

Dalton provided your number, at the behest of General Cutter, came the reply.

Then fuck off, unless it's important, I returned.

You got it.

∾

Corinne

Rafe and Auggie were having a textual tussle. I wanted to roll my eyes. I didn't—I was too busy trying to ward off a panic attack. Dr.

Shaw was on one of the first two helicopters and long gone before ours exploded on the lawn.

I wasn't looking forward to this trip, not least because the French Ambassador would be there. No doubt, an incident that happened six years earlier would be brought up, as it was a sore spot between him and the President.

Priceless paintings from the Louvre had been burned after a section of it was taken over by terrorists. Tourists—visitors to the Louvre on that fateful day—died while nations watched artwork that had survived for centuries turn to ashes in a matter of minutes.

One of the terrorists, who'd reportedly committed suicide with the rest of the attackers, was American. That was enough fuel for the French President and the French Ambassador to condemn the involvement of a U.S. citizen.

It didn't matter that twenty-six of the thirty-nine tourists' deaths were also American. French nationals, Swiss, German and British citizens died, too. Thirty-nine deaths attributed to eight terrorists, who'd committed suicide after killing the last of their hostages.

French forces stormed in shortly after.

Nothing has been the same, since.

I drew a shaky breath.

No need to bring up that debacle now—I'd likely hear enough about it after I arrived at Camp David.

Corinne, if you need help when we arrive, ask for it, August texted me. I didn't have the phone I'd been given in my hand, so I pulled it from the small purse I carried when I felt it vibrate.

If I get the help you're suggesting, I'll be out for the rest of the day, I texted back. *I'll deal with this the best I can.*

I'll have Shaw on standby.

Right.

What's wrong? That came from Rafe.

You know, I'd like to say mind your own business, but that will only intrigue you, I texted back.

Have you tried meditation?

With hopeless regularity.

I'm sure most of our conversation could have taken place verbally, if we didn't have the sounds of the helicopter vibrating our bones as well as our eardrums, and if our ears weren't covered in protective gear. Therefore, texting worked as the next best thing. I just had no desire to continue our conversation.

I was grateful when the chopper set down and we were allowed off it.

$\sim$

An hour later, after a quick lunch, we were ushered into the meeting room. In addition to the French Ambassador, the British Prime Minister was there with his interpreter, the German Chancellor had come with his interpreter, and the acting Russian Ambassador had also come.

All of them were frowning.

I wanted to hold up my hand and say "all my fault," after which I would be escorted from the building and allowed to write in quiet confinement.

That didn't happen.

Several things concerned me about that meeting—it was an extension of what had been discussed at a recent G-8 conference. Terrorist threat levels were on the rise for some reason, and everyone wanted everybody else's information.

All of them discussed potential targets—public transportation, water supplies, government facilities and so on. The French Ambassador brought up the attack in Paris six years earlier, but the others considered that an anomaly.

Why would terrorists attack another museum?

During that meeting, which lasted four hours and would continue into the next day, I watched several people. I noticed Rafe watching the same people. I had four hours of rehashed conversations to mentally consider what—and how much—to tell August.

$\sim$

We met over dinner—all of us. I didn't want to tell everybody there what I knew. Rafe was holding back for the same reason. "I didn't get much," Maye offered. "Pretty much what they were thinking is what they were saying. They're all afraid they'll be targeted next."

"The French Ambassador is pissed; I could smell it all over him," Nick said.

"He's mad because of that stupid museum debacle. Who cares if a couple of paintings got burned?" Becker huffed.

"Thirty-nine people died there," Ken reminded Becker. "Most of them Americans."

"One of the terrorists was American. The French Ambassador tries to make it look as if he were in charge," Maye said. "I doubt that's the case. His profile points to his being a follower, not a leader."

"I believe he wanted to commit suicide and appear a hero to his adopted religion," Rafe said quietly. "Colonel Hunter, I'd like a private word with you when we're done, here."

"What about?" Dalton began.

"A private word," Rafe insisted.

"Can I be there?" I asked. "I think Rafe and I may have something similar to say."

"You think so?" Rafe lifted an eyebrow and gave me a skeptical frown.

"I think so," I said, toying with my fork. We had prime rib sitting in front of us; I'd barely touched mine, although it was quite good.

"Then we'll talk after dinner," August agreed. "The three of us. Privately." He challenged Dalton to disagree. Captain Dalton Parrish didn't argue with Colonel August Hunter. Sometimes, rank really did have its privileges.

"The British Ambassador's interpreter isn't who she says she is."

"She's a spy-for-hire."

Rafe and I attempted to speak at the same time the moment the door closed behind August. He'd chosen a small meeting room in our shared bungalow for the private conference. August didn't display shock often, but he wore a concerned expression now.

"What the hell are you talking about?" he sputtered.

"She's—well—she's wormed her way into that position for a reason," I said. Rafe stared at me as I offered that information.

"I was about to say the same thing, only I can say that I've seen her before, and disaster always follows close behind. Somebody wants information, and she's getting it for them," Rafe sighed.

"Let me talk to some of the others. You'll both be on call, tonight, in case I can get a meeting." August stalked from the room, slamming the door behind him.

"That went well," I muttered.

"You know we'll have to talk to the President tonight," Rafe said.

"Yeah."

"I don't know what her real name is," Rafe answered the President's question later. It was nearly midnight; Rafe's and my exposition of the interpreter in question had raised some eyebrows and caused a flurry of investigations. "I've never seen her use the same name twice."

"I'd doubt your information, if Corinne hadn't pointed her out as well," Madam President shook her head.

"I understand your reluctance to believe anything I say," Rafe acknowledged. "That doesn't alter the fact that this woman, who currently uses the name Mary Evans, is quite adept at changing identities and nationalities—as the situation requires."

"How do you know so much about her?" the President asked.

"Because she was hired by the Soviet government on at least two occasions. I have nothing but contempt for her."

"This changes things," the President flung up a hand. "Look, I've got several agencies investigating her background—photographs, information, you name it. What I have so far shows she's really good— otherwise, she'd never have been hired by the British government."

"As you see, other governments have hired her," Rafe said. He was suggesting that the British government hired her for their own purposes.

"I don't believe for a minute the Prime Minister knows about her," I snapped, causing Rafe to turn swiftly in my direction. "You said she was gathering information for somebody. It's not the British government."

"If we grab her now, we'll never know what she's up to, or who hired her," August pointed out. "Besides, what would we charge her with? All we have is information that we can't substantiate." He jerked a thumb in Rafe's and my direction.

"Look, I'm having her phone tapped, and we'll have someone checking phone calls, in and out. We'll set up somebody to follow her and report on every movement from now on. I don't want to alarm the Prime Minister if we can help it," the President said before turning to me.

"Corinne," she said, "Is there anything you can give me to get the French Ambassador and his President off my back?"

I froze. Rafe now stared at me. August shook his head and looked away. "No, Ma'am," I lied. The panic attack came immediately afterward.

I don't know how Rafe found his way into my bedroom the following morning, but he was there with a cup of coffee in his hands. Surprisingly enough, he offered the cup to me.

"You were there," he stated baldly as I worked my way into a sitting position and accepted the cup.

"Go away. Thanks for the coffee."

"I figure there are people out there who'd pay seven figures or more to know you survived that attack."

"Are you one of them? Plan on selling that information to the highest bidder?" I asked, handing the cup of coffee back to him. "Go away. I have enough worries without you adding more."

"I understand that. Perhaps better than you know," he said,

handing the coffee cup back to me and sitting on the bed. He ended up leaning against the headboard beside me and staring at the wall in front of us. "How much do you think someone might pay to have information on my continued existence?"

"Touché."

"Madam President, those panic attacks happen every time the subject comes up. I keep waiting for her to tell me—to get that burden off her shoulders. It's locked up so tightly within her, she may never let it go." Dr. Shaw shifted in his chair as the President studied the doctor across her temporary desk.

"Look, I know all about the forensics. About how the bodies showed signs of torture before they were killed—Corinne's included. I may know why they waited until the last to shoot her, but that's information I don't feel comfortable giving out." President Sanders raked fingers through dark hair turning gray at a rapid rate. The presidency tended to do that—make someone gray long before their time. Madam President refused to mask the signs of age or stress with hair color.

"You know that would be considered privileged," Doctor Shaw began.

"I and two others know. That's it, unless Corinne chooses to tell you herself."

"Of course, Madam President."

"Will you do me a favor, Shaw?"

"Of course, Madam President."

"I want information on Derik Thompson's parents. His upbringing. Anything you can find that might point to his reasons for becoming a terrorist and involving himself in that mess. I'm tired of being vilified in French."

"I'll get right on it."

Corinne

Becker made an effort to sneer at me as we walked toward the meeting room. I figured there'd be more of the same from all involved —posturing, withholding information, excuses, blame, all in several languages.

I wasn't disappointed. Rafe and I, though, made a point to watch everyone in the room and not just Mary Evans, AKA the spy to be named later.

CHAPTER 6

"Something's going on." Nick dropped his bag on the floor of his suite. Becker had followed Nick after the choppers left them at the Mansion. "Why are they talking to Corinne, all of a sudden?"

"I think Maye knows something, she's just not talking."

"Or just not talking to us."

"Too bad they stuck Corinne in the bungalow with Colonel Hunter, Captain Parrish and the Russian. I figure we could pound a reason out of her."

"You know you'll be in trouble if you touch her," Nick warned.

"Huh. What's a little punch, now and then?"

"Becker, you know your brain isn't your best asset. Let me think about this, all right?"

"Don't take too long. I really want to know what's going on."

"So do I. Patience is a virtue, remember?"

Notes—Colonel Hunter

"What was Captain Parrish's reaction when he wasn't included in the meeting with the President?" James asked. James hadn't been invited to the meetings either; he'd gone as my assistant and stayed in the bungalow, doing routine tasks and keeping me in the loop on the chopper explosion.

So far, the pilot hadn't cracked. That worried me, as he was military. Someone had gotten to him, and we were still attempting to determine the cause and what, if anything, he might know about the Program.

The explosive was on a timer—I'd figured that out early on. It made it easier for Corinne to delay all of us without getting herself involved. Too bad her hand was forced later on, with Mary Evans' appearance beside the British Ambassador.

We'd followed her trail—there really was a Mary Evans with all the appropriate documentation—from Northern Ireland. Dead, of course. That came as no surprise. If you dig far enough, eventually you'll see daylight.

The President still hadn't notified the Prime Minister of the doppelganger at his side. She wasn't scheduled to translate for him again until he made a visit to China in six weeks. That could give us enough time to watch her and determine her purpose.

"Dalton wasn't happy. I can't help that," I said, brushing past James and heading toward my office. Instead of sitting behind my desk, I stood at the window beyond it, studying the blackened patches of grass on the lawn and considering the bottle of bourbon in a bottom desk drawer. James brought me out of my musings by tapping on my open door.

"Colonel Hunter?"

"What is it, James?" I turned in his direction.

"Corinne is here to see you."

"Send her in."

Corinne

"That's an unusual request, but I'll see what I can do," he said.

I'd asked to see images of all the people Mary Evans had contact with. I had my reasons; August might guess at some of them. I didn't care about that. I wanted to see whomever she saw—it was important.

"Please, Auggie. I think this is important," I said.

"I could show them to Rafe, too," he mused.

"Then show them to Rafe, too. He might know something."

"He turned out to be useful at Camp David," August said.

"I think he's pissed enough at the Russians to be even more helpful. He's from Ukraine, you know."

"Back when Ukraine was still part of Soviet Russia, I know," August agreed.

"Then you know it was never a comfortable union. We're talking genocide, Auggie."

"I know that, too. Your Krav Maga lessons resume tomorrow. Be ready to run with the others at six."

"Yeah."

∾

"Chamomile." Rafe plunked the box of tea onto the counter two minutes after I got back to the kitchen. My visit with August hadn't gone as well as I'd like, but at least he was considering my request. Rafe wanted me to sleep instead of staying up half the night, going over what I knew and what might be done about it.

"Really?" I shook my head at him.

"Try it. It won't keep you awake—I know that much."

"You know, I want to bang my head against a wall. Then maybe bang yours against a wall."

"You won't be any good at all tomorrow if you don't sleep. I overheard your argument with Doctor Shaw at Camp David."

We'd had an argument, all right. I couldn't sleep most of the time I was there. He wanted to give me prescription sleep aids. I stopped just short of telling him where to put them.

"You need sleep. Have you looked at yourself in the mirror, lately? Those dark circles under your eyes tell me you're exhausted."

"If I drink this, will you get off my case?"

"If you drink this and attempt to meditate."

"Fine. Want to join me in a cup?"

"I will, if you'll drink it."

"Fine."

I didn't point out that he appeared amused—a slight curl at the corner of his mouth gave him away. Honestly, I wasn't sure why he worried about my sleeping habits. He'd just knock me to the floor during our lesson in the morning, after I wore myself out with a three-mile run.

Our grocery order was delivered while we were having breakfast the following morning. It was after our run and before Krav Maga. Rafe was delighted that his order was there and set about putting soup ingredients into my slow cooker.

"Real chicken noodle soup, instead of that tinned shit," he said, placing the lid on the cooker.

"Really? Tell me again who stole a bowl of that tinned shit the last time I ate it," I said.

"I've had worse during my lifetime."

"I'm sure you have. If you'll give me fifteen minutes, I'll get ingredients for fresh bread into the bread machine."

"You're kidding."

"No, I like fresh bread. Don't you?"

"I wondered if you actually used that thing, or if it would just sit on the counter collecting dust."

"I use it; I just can't eat an entire loaf by myself before it goes stale."

"You have fifteen minutes."

My hopes were dashed that the Five would lose interest in my Krav Maga beatings. All five were back and watching as Rafe did the usual

—showing me a move and then moving faster than I could in my attempt to employ the countermove.

"I suppose my strategy of wearing you out isn't working," I said, blinking up at him as he stood over my prone body. He threw back his head and laughed.

"How about a round or two with me?" Becker came off the bench and stretched while I peeled myself off the floor.

"Which one of us?" Rafe asked.

"You."

"Good. Corinne, go sit down."

I did, choosing a spot well away from the others. I had no desire to rub elbows with any of them.

In the next ten minutes, I learned that Rafe had been taking it easy on me. He beat the hell out of Becker, who barely had time to rise before Rafe put him down again. I wanted to cheer, but that might be considered bad taste. I did smile, though, once or twice.

∽

"Good bread." Rafe had another thick slice.

"Thanks. I like it, too. Chicken and noodles are outstanding." I lifted a spoonful of noodles and ate them with a smile.

It's funny how politics make strange bedfellows, and mutual enemies forge friendships. It didn't matter how many times Becker might shove me in the mud—it was all worth it just to see Rafe put him in his place.

I loaded the dishwasher while Rafe put leftovers away. I almost felt like hugging him. I didn't. If we even touched, it would be all over the Mansion in five minutes. That's why we didn't discuss Becker's beating, either.

That stayed in the gym, where it belonged.

∽

Notes—Colonel Hunter

"I thought you'd be interested in this." Shaw set his laptop in front of me. I listened and watched while a recording of Becker talking with Nick was displayed. He spoke about hitting Corinne to get information. At that moment, I wanted to teach him a lesson, but the Blacksmith had already done a good enough job.

"I hear Becker can barely move this morning," I said, attempting to hide the cheerfulness in my voice. "After Rafe handed his ass to him yesterday."

"Are you concerned at all that Rafe and Corinne seem to be getting along, now?"

"Why? I figure she sees the sense in it," I said. "He's growing on me, too."

"I think he and Corinne have things in common," Shaw said. "That may or may not be a good thing."

"Why do you say that?"

"I saw Safer this morning at breakfast. He thinks Rafe may have been the target in the explosion."

"Why? Has the pilot talked?"

"Not yet. If Rafe goes down, who knows what that could do to Corinne? Especially if she's beginning to see him as a friend."

"This is ridiculous. What evidence do we have that he was the target? Why not Corinne or me? James, perhaps?"

"Dalton Parrish?" Shaw quirked an eyebrow.

"That sounds more likely than the rest of us," I said. "You know Cutter has enemies everywhere."

"Then why not go directly after him?" Shaw asked.

"To make him sweat?"

"Colonel?" James appeared beside our coffee shop table.

"James?" He wouldn't have come if it weren't important.

"The pilot was found dead ten minutes ago. Hanged himself."

"There was no evidence he might be suicidal," Cutter stormed through the cafeteria where we'd called a quick meeting with Shaw and the handlers. I didn't say it and kept my expression neutral, but to me, it looked as if Cutter was blustering.

Shaw studied our new Director with interest. This was the first time the General had seen fit to come to the Mansion after taking the position, and it was after the pilot hanged himself with the belt they'd allowed him to keep.

I'd toyed with the idea of asking if Corinne might be allowed to visit the pilot, but discarded it. Now, I wish I'd gone ahead and asked. She might have been able to tell us something. That opportunity was now lost.

The worst part, perhaps, was that the pilot had a family who hadn't been notified that he was being held for questioning. The FBI was investigating them, too, and they didn't have a clue.

Cutter continued to bluster about the ongoing investigation, and that it would continue and he wouldn't rest until we got to the bottom of this. All the usual platitudes. The truth, however, was that I wouldn't be where I was if Corinne hadn't held all of us up.

Turning my head in Dalton Parrish's direction, I watched him instead of Cutter. He wore a frown as Cutter made promises he likely couldn't keep. Corinne had saved Parrish, too, and I think he knew that.

Corinne

"Here's his photograph. It's the best James could do." August handed the photograph of the dead pilot to me. I made a face as I studied his military picture. Rafe, who sat nearby with his handler, watched as I blew out a breath.

"He didn't want to. He was ordered to," I said, handing the photograph back to August.

"Corinne, you can't say that with any certainty."

"I can say it with certainty. You just can't believe it with certainty."

"Who paid him?" Rafe asked.

"I don't know. I'd have to see the one who paid him," I said.

"Is that how this works?" August asked.

"As nearly as I can explain it," I shrugged.

"Corinne, how long have you been able to do this?" August asked. I hugged myself.

"For a while," I said. "But who'd believe me?"

"I'm starting to believe you now," August muttered.

Dalton Parrish called Dr. Shaw when the panic attack came.

Notes—Colonel Hunter

"I think we should call a meeting with the President. I want the others to know what we know, and I need her permission to do that. I don't want to see another episode of Becker threatening to hit Corinne," Shaw fumed.

"There's still no guarantee he won't make an attempt," I said.

"At the moment, Corinne is of more use to us than Becker ever was."

"That's true, and I never thought it could happen. Becker's only gift is muscle, and the President is reluctant to let that out often."

"Because Becker is stupid enough to get captured," Shaw said. "If his captors do any medical workup on him, we're screwed."

"And that's why he's only sent out with Nick or some of the others," I agreed. "When they know muscle is needed. After that little showdown with Rafe, though, he may not be the first choice for muscle from now on."

"He may realize that, even if Nick hasn't pointed it out, yet," Shaw shook his head. "Before, it was the Five against one. That dynamic may have changed. Becker won't like being replaced; you know that."

"Is he stupid enough to take it out on the weakest one—like always?" I toyed with a file on my desk—James had collected my notes from the Camp David meetings and sent an electronic copy to the President. Corinne was featured prominently in those notes. This was my copy—for my private files.

"I think we should pay special attention to Becker from now on. If he's about to retaliate for any reason, I want to know about it."

"Then give the order. You have the authority."

"I want backup. You're the logical choice."

"Then you have it."

Corinne

Our bedrooms were bugged, except on sex nights. I think it had something to do with the list, but I sure didn't want to ask. Sex between partners was off-limits for the Mansion's collective entertainment. Our bathrooms were the only rooms not bugged, and let's face it, bathrooms should just be private, period.

Rafe had done the usual in Krav Maga. He sent an e-mail to me afterward; I found it when I made my way to the computer, cup of coffee in hand, to sit down and write.

You're getting stronger, he said. *You might consider lifting weights with me.*

Got any five-pound weights? I shot back.

Yes, but those are for sissies.

Really? What do you think I am?

You can lift more than five pounds. I saw you manhandle that bag of flour.

Right. Lifting that weight, however, had a purpose. All-purpose, if I remember correctly.

Lifting weights has a purpose, too. You can do weights with me after Krav Maga lessons, three days a week.

Joy.

James spots me.

Really?

He does. He likes to look at my crotch.

TMI. Besides, there's nothing wrong with wishful thinking.

Understood. I told him from the beginning I was straight, but there's nothing wrong with window shopping.

I'm glad you have a good attitude about that. James is pretty awesome.

He's probably reading this right now.

That wasn't why I said it.

I know.

Fifteen seconds later, I got an e-mail from James.

Thank you! When are you baking cookies again?

How about the weekend?

We may be busy on the weekend.

Joy.

Fifteen minutes later, Auggie was on my doorstep, with James, Dalton and Rafe. We had a meeting in my kitchen. It involved a two-week trip to London and Paris with the Secretary of State, Maye, Kevin, Ken and our respective handlers. I wanted to have a panic attack. I didn't.

"You've been outfitted and packed. All you need is pajamas and underwear," James informed me when August and Dalton left. Rafe and James had stayed behind with me in the kitchen.

"Somebody bought for me again?" I squeaked.

"One of the President's assistants. Bought for Rafe and the others, too, so don't hyperventilate."

"James, this is two trips in less than two weeks."

"Think how the Secretary of State feels."

"He wanted that job, remember? Please tell me I won't be squeezed into something too small and require oxygen."

"Too small?" Rafe huffed.

"Shut up, you. You're annoying."

"I thought I was conveying incredulity. My mistake."

"James, can I pay you to drop weights on his head?"

"How much?" James grinned.

"No one will be dropping weights. I'd send you out the door, except that would do me no good at all," Rafe grumbled.

"I'm teasing. James knows that," I said. "Besides, it's my door."

"As I said, it would do me no good at all. You'd only come right back."

"I don't have anywhere else to go, since I'm an orphan and all."

"Cori, were you? Really?" James asked.

"I can't answer that."

At least we weren't on a commercial flight when we left two days later—on a Friday. The Secretary of State had a function to attend with the Prime Minister on Saturday, so we were going. The President didn't trust the woman posing as Mary Evans, and worried that she'd be there with the Prime Minister and a few non-English-speaking dignitaries.

Rafe said she was fluent in too many languages to count, and he was right. August was on the list of intended recipients if any new information was gathered on her, and promised to share photographs with me. I hoped I'd see the one I wanted to see.

Meanwhile, I was asked to advise August, who would then advise the Secretary of State, at the President's behest. We didn't need an incident. I couldn't agree more, but I couldn't say at the moment who was in the most danger.

"August, what's the Vice President's schedule while we're gone?" I asked. The flight had been smooth for the most part, but chose that moment to buck us around. I hate turbulence, but there isn't anything I can do about it.

"No idea—I don't usually get that information," he said, turning a curious glance in my direction. He sat beside me, while James sat on the other side with Rafe. Dalton sat behind Rafe, with Maye's handler, Jeff, beside him. Maye and Kevin took up another row, while Ken and his handler sat across the aisle. Kevin's handler was stretched out, taking an entire row for himself while he napped. The Secretary of State and his entourage took up the office and better seating toward the rear of the plane.

"Can you pass a message along that the VP needs to be careful?" I said.

"I can try."

"Thanks." I turned my attention toward the front of the plane—the pilots were locked inside their cubicle while two flight attendants filled drink cups for some of the others.

"Cori?"

"What?"

"You scare me."

"Auggie, I scare myself, sometimes."

The Connaught Hotel was our destination after we landed Saturday morning. I was ready to do a faceplant on a bed; that wasn't to be. We showered, changed and loaded into three limousines for a visit with the Prime Minister.

"This is why I never ran for office," I joked as our vehicles were allowed inside a gated entrance by armed guards on our way to 10 Downing Street.

"You're not locked in, now?" Dalton asked.

"You know, we haven't had a discussion yet, have we?" I made a face at him.

"Whatever you do, don't have a discussion with her," Rafe said. "You'll lose, I promise."

"Be nice, Corinne," August warned.

"I am nice. All the time. You just don't see it that way."

"We're here," he announced, curtailing our conversation. I sighed and slid out of the car when my door was opened.

The door to 10 Downing Street is rather modest, considering it houses much of the British government behind its unassuming frame. Designed by Christopher Wren in the late 1600s, the huge building is connected to 11 and 12 Downing Street, which house the Chancellor of the Exchequer and the Prime Minister's Press Office, among other things.

I felt it when I walked across the threshold, where a guard greeted us.

Trouble was on the way.

~

The meeting only lasted an hour; the rest of us kicked our heels in an antechamber while the Prime Minister and the Secretary of State had their private meeting. The state dinner would be held later—in the evening and in another part of the building, after we had some rest.

Too many things were in motion, however, so our rest might be short, if we got any at all.

~

Notes—Colonel Hunter

I didn't pass along Corinne's message. How do you tell the Vice President to be careful, anyway?

He'd gone to a suburb of Detroit, where cars were still made—an island in a former sea of continental industry, now dead. The Mayor invited him to a local ice-cream shop afterward.

A sniper killed both of them, plus two of their bodyguards.

CHAPTER 7

Corinne

News of the assassination was on every British television station. My hopes that the state dinner would be canceled were dashed—August walked into my hotel room while I huddled against the headboard, watching the latest reports.

"The Secretary wants to attend the dinner tonight, then fly back to the U.S. tomorrow," August said. He sounded guilty. "Normally, the VP wouldn't take a side trip like that, but the Mayor talked him into it," he added.

I didn't say anything.

Rafe and Dalton walked through my door, just as August had. Without a word, Rafe sat on the side of the bed, took one of my hands and held it tightly while watching the news with me. He knew I was shaking.

This could have been prevented.

Things were so much worse, now.

"General Cutter said the Detroit Mayor had the ice-cream place checked out beforehand, and plenty of police around. It shouldn't have been a big deal," Dalton said, taking a seat on the end of my bed and watching the news with us.

The journalist on television repeated what Dalton said, adding that nobody had seen the sniper—before or afterward, and there were currently no leads. News crews were held back from the small dessert shop, so they'd set up as close as they could, like hungry vultures waiting for their turn at the corpse.

"The VP has a family. I hope they're not watching this," I quavered.

"Corinne, I need you to be steady for tonight," August said.

"I know."

Ilya

For perhaps the hundredth time, I wondered about Corinne's past. Yes, I knew about the terrorist attack in France, now, but what about before then? Did she have a family? Was her orphan comment to James misleading? I didn't even know how old she was when the drug was administered.

The Mansion has a library, and I'd visited it twice—once to research the names of those who'd died in the Louvre attack. None of them appeared to be Corinne. That meant that she was either not reported among the deaths, or it had been covered up, somehow. My guess was the latter, but I had no way to prove it.

Everything I did was scrutinized, but I couldn't say they watched me any closer than they did Corinne. We were the wild cards, she and I. How she'd managed to escape them for more than five years and live outside the Mansion still astounded me, and why she'd allowed them to pull her back in by displaying a bit of her talent astounded me more.

Corinne wasn't stupid. Not by a far shot. She was vulnerable, though, and she knew that better than anyone. Perhaps she realized—more than any of us—what was coming and decided to do something about it. I gripped her hand tighter for a moment before patting it and letting go.

"We have to get dressed, cabbage," I told her. "We'll get through this."

~

Corinne

I decided not to read anything into the cabbage comment. Wearily, I climbed off the bed and went to find the black dress I was supposed to wear for the evening. Rafe and Dalton left, leaving August standing near the foot of my bed.

"Corinne, someone will be taking care of the VP's family," he sighed before following the others out the door.

"Too bad somebody can't take care of us, too," I muttered, slipping the black evening dress off its hanger with shaking hands.

~

Nobody spoke to the Secretary's entourage—they all spoke to him, offering their condolences on the loss of the Vice President. In multiple languages. Another interpreter stood beside the Prime Minister as he and the Secretary shook hands, but I wasn't surprised.

Mary Evans likely had other places to be when the shit hit.

All I had to do was control my shaking and the panic attack that threatened.

Ilya, I thought, *please be everything I think you are.*

~

Ilya

I heard her. I always hear her. A part of me wanted to tell her that. Another part waited to hear everything, in case she told me something I really wanted to know. I wasn't sure how to interpret what she'd said, however.

Was it related to my taking her hand, earlier, or for my other talents? I nodded and smiled, just as the others did while we followed in the wake of the Secretary of State. Did I know that Maye watched me, ready to defend the Secretary in case I went wild?

Of course.

She had no idea that I meant him—and all the others—no harm. There were some I did want to harm, however, but they were far away and of no concern to her.

"Rafe?" Corinne was beside me.

"Cabbage?"

"Exits?"

"Got them."

"Gonna need 'em. *Now.*"

Notes—Colonel Hunter

The lights flashed and a few female guests screamed when an outside wall was hit by an explosive. The loud boom was accompanied by the entire building shaking, as if we were having an earthquake. This sort of thing had happened only once before—that's why the gate had been erected at the entrance years ago.

That didn't matter now—someone, somehow, had gotten around that safeguard. Maye, Kevin and Ken surrounded the Secretary of State while two guards stepped up beside the Prime Minister, ready to herd both to safety. I didn't have time to look for Corinne, Dalton or Rafe.

I shouldn't have worried.

Corinne grasped Dalton by the hand and led him toward one of the exits; he'd wanted to run in the opposite direction. Rafe ran behind them, clearing a space for the rest of us.

The emergency lights came on, affording us enough illumination to see. The Prime Minister and his guards weren't arguing with our impromptu escape route, so I realized Corinne was heading in the proper direction.

I shouldn't have been surprised. The second blast hit, shaking the floor beneath us, knocking furniture over and dropping light fixtures onto a screaming, fleeing crowd. Yes, I knew they were running in the wrong direction, but you generally can't stop a frightened mob; you'll get run over if you try. Attempting to shout into the din as walls fell and glass shattered would be equally pointless. I didn't try.

I only recall seeing a small sign next to a narrow stairway leading downward after traversing several halls. The image stuck in my mind, however, as the last thing I read in the dim light when the third blast hit, vibrating the floor beneath our feet.

The green, rectangular sign, roughly the size of my hand, proclaimed in white letters, *To Bomb Shelter Area*, with an arrow pointing down the stairs.

That's where we went.

I knew people behind us were dead as we raced down the steps as quickly as we could, Corinne and Rafe still in the lead, the Prime Minister, his guards and the Secretary of State right behind. Dalton had dropped back to the middle; I brought up the rear, with Ken beside me. A bit of smoke billowed behind us, telling me the building was on fire.

In the distance, I heard sirens, but they wouldn't arrive in time for some. I hoped they'd arrive in time for us.

Corinne

If Rafe hadn't been beside me, I might not have fought off the panic attack. People's lives depended on me, and I couldn't let my fear take over. The screams we'd heard at first stopped after the third blast. Reminding myself that I'd have to worry about that later, I continued my race down the steps, Rafe a half-step behind.

At the bottom of the steps lay another door. The Prime Minister likely had the combination for the keypad beside it. I didn't wait for him. Flipping the cover down, I lifted my hand to punch in numbers.

"Wait," he shouted. "You only get two tries."

I got it on the first try. If I survived the night, I might not be welcome back in England again, but that wasn't my biggest worry. My biggest worry was getting the people with me out of this fiasco alive.

I'd been in a similar situation before, and was powerless to do anything.

This time, I hoped things would be different.

Once we were through the door, it shut behind us, rearming itself. At least that was one barrier between us.

Yes, we had followers. I just didn't know how far back they were.

A musty, concrete tunnel and another set of stairs lay beyond us. We fled down those steps the moment we heard gunshots. They were shooting at the doorknob behind us, attempting to gain access that way and bypassing the alarm. Not good.

"This tunnel will lead us to the Waterloo exit," the Prime Minister said, breaking into a trot and attempting to take control of our exodus.

"They're waiting for you at the Waterloo exit," I said, stopping him short, his guards sliding to a stop beside him.

"You don't know a thing about any of this," the Prime Minister huffed.

"If I were you, I'd listen to Corinne," Rafe warned.

"Sir, it would be better if we all paid attention to her," August said from somewhere behind. From the sound of things, our pursuers had broken through the door. We didn't have much time.

"Then what do you suggest? There's a warren of offices and shelters beyond this door and throughout this space. We can lock ourselves in and wait for rescue," the Prime Minister pointed out.

"They won't get here in time," I said. "It's your choice, obviously—I can't force you to believe me or do anything I say. I'm just trying to get us out of here alive."

"Then get us out of here alive. I warn you, if you're in on this, England will prosecute you to the fullest extent of the law."

"I have no doubt," I said dryly. "Let's go."

I punched in a second code to get us through the door, which August shut behind us. We already heard running footsteps; it wouldn't be long before this door would be treated to the same abuse as the last one.

I knew where the door leading to the Waterloo exit was. We

weren't going near it. Instead, I led our group in the opposite direction, stopping in front of an air vent.

"No," the PM shook his head as I knelt to open it.

"Yeah. We're going a different way. This shaft leads to another vent, connected to the Citadel beneath the Ministry of Defense. After that, we'll change course again."

"Madam President, I hate to interrupt," President Sanders' Chief of Staff knocked softly on the Oval Office door.

"Hal?" the President looked up from the papers on her desk. She no longer saw them; they were merely an excuse—a decoy, to make it look as if she were busy. While she and the Vice President hadn't been close friends, they respected one another. The VP's loss was a terrible blow—to her and to the country.

"I've had word from Britain," Hal Prentice said. "Ten Downing has been attacked. They're pulling bodies out of the building—it was hit three times by rockets and partially burned. There's no word on the Secretary of State or the Prime Minister. It's all over the media, in addition to the Vice President's death. The Joint Chiefs and your cabinet are on the way."

"Dear God." The President dropped her face in her hands.

Corinne

At least the vent was large enough to crawl through, and I was grateful the PM and the Secretary were still limber enough to do so. August and Ken made sure the vent cover was closed behind us—I didn't want our pursuers to guess right away where we'd gone.

"Corinne," Maye hissed, "How long is this fucking vent?"

"Probably half as long as a fucking football field," I said.

"What's your beef?" Dalton asked—he was crawling behind her.

"I don't have enough room to protect anyone in this tight space," she complained.

"I hope you won't have to," I said, ignoring the panicky timbre of her voice. It told me she was slightly claustrophobic. I wasn't about to yell at her about that. "I hate crawling anywhere in an evening dress," I added. "It sort of sucks."

"This isn't the time for chitchat," August reminded us. We shut up and kept crawling. Somewhere, far behind us, I heard the clang of the vent cover being ripped away. We crawled faster.

~

Ignoring the cramps in my back and legs, I lay flat on my belly while Rafe crawled over me to punch the vent cover off. I cringed at the sound it made as the metal clattered against tile. Rafe somersaulted out of the vent gracefully, while I crawled out like a wounded lizard dressed in an evening gown.

I moved aside so Rafe could help the PM and the others out of the ventilation shaft, while I leaned against the wall and attempted to even my breathing.

"They're coming," August said when he dropped out of the vent last. That's when Rafe and the PM's guards took stock of the hallway around us—there wasn't any furniture or anything heavy to shove against the vent and slow our pursuers.

"Which way, cabbage?" Rafe asked softly. I peeled myself away from the wall, lifted the skirts of my evening dress and took off at a run. The others ran behind me.

~

President Sanders blinked in disbelief. Another news report interrupted the one she and her cabinet watched concerning the Secretary of State and the British Prime Minister.

"It is now confirmed that the Tower of London was breached during the confusion after the attack on 10 Downing Street, and an anonymous source reports that the Imperial State Crown and other valuables have been taken. It is not known as yet whether the two incidents are connected."

"Holy fucking hell," the Secretary of Homeland Security cursed.

~

Corinne

The Pindar Citadel beneath the Ministry of Defence might have been worth the enormous price paid when it was finished in the '90s. The facility housed a huge warren of rooms, bomb shelters, sleeping quarters and everything else one might require in the event of a siege. We didn't have time to stop and appreciate it—our pursuers were catching up.

I hoped the door we ran toward would hold them back for a few minutes; it was nearly a foot thick and surrounded by concrete. The problem? It wasn't meant to hold off a direct attack—it was meant to keep government officials safe in a bombing crisis.

We raced through it, and August and one of the PM's bodyguards manned the spokes of the locking mechanism, turning them as quickly as they could.

"Go on," August snapped while he and the guard worked. "We'll catch up."

I took off again, while Rafe and the others followed. They probably weren't going to like what lay ahead of us, but it might give our pursuers pause and I hoped they'd think we'd gone another way.

The passage was beyond a service door, which was locked. Rafe and Maye managed to kick the steel door down, since we didn't have a key and it didn't have a keypad. The small, square room was for maintenance workers only—containing a six-foot, round airshaft in the floor, with a huge fan whirling inside the shaft. Why did I take them that way?

Beyond the airshaft lay another door that hadn't been used in a very long time. It led to the abandoned site once known as the Chancery Lane deep shelter and Kingsway telephone exchange.

"We have to cross the shaft and get to that other door," I shouted over the noise of the fan and pointing at the door beyond. "Rafe, we need the door placed over the shaft so we can cross, then we need to carry it through that other door when Auggie and the guard get here."

"His name is Dave," the PM said.

"Dave and Auggie," I corrected myself.

"I'll make sure it happens," Rafe nodded.

Carefully, he and Kevin lifted the door and laid it across the shaft. Blocking the air caused newly created winds to swirl about us, lifting my skirts and attempting to blow my dress over my head. Grabbing expensive fabric, I tied it in a makeshift knot so I wouldn't endanger myself or the others.

The door barely fit over the shaft, and the PM's second guard made the first trip to test its safety before allowing the PM across.

The Secretary came next, with Ken, Dalton and Maye close behind. I could hear running footsteps in the hall outside by that time.

"Go, Corinne," Rafe urged.

I pulled Kevin with me, and halfway across the door, with forced air whipping hair and clothing, I heard muted gunshots outside.

Hurry, Auggie, I thought at him before Kevin leapt off the door, sending it scraping across the opening and almost dislodging it with me still on it.

Rafe shouted before grabbing the door and keeping it from sliding off the shaft. I fell to my knees and teetered for a moment on the door's edge, almost coming face to face with whirling fan blades.

August ran in, supporting a bleeding Dave—he had a shoulder wound where an enemy's bullet had hit its mark. Standing as quickly as I could, I took two steps and almost fell off the end of the door, leaving it empty for the others to cross.

Dave had managed to kill two of our pursuers, but he'd been wounded in the process. It didn't matter that two were dead; more were on the way. Dave had to be helped across the chasm by Rafe and August—he'd already lost a lot of blood and was far too unsteady on his own.

"Maye, we need this door down, too," I gasped for breath as I came to a stop at the second door.

"We'll get it," Kevin and Ken said together. I moved aside to allow them room. In unison, they kicked, sending a not-so-heavy door crashing into a round tunnel beyond.

"I hope you know where you're going," the PM said. "I have no working knowledge of these tunnels."

"I think she knows," Rafe said, grabbing my arm and pulling me through the door. "Buck up, cabbage. We need you to get us out of this. We still have eight behind us, and they're armed to the teeth."

I took off, Rafe beside me, with the others following. Ken dropped back to help August support Dave; we didn't have time to stop and give the poor man first aid. At least the wound was in his right shoulder, but it had to hurt and he was bleeding badly. Ken had a hand over the wound, attempting to slow the blood loss.

"This is a nightmare," I panted as I ran. I hoped we could get through the tunnels without the enemy sighting us well enough to take more shots. "This way," I called, turning to the right and running through another tunnel.

The tunnels were round and sturdily built, with regular, curved steel ribs supporting the structure. A rumble over our heads sent a ripple through the group, until we realized it was a tube train rolling past. One of those tunnels lay above us at some point. "Charing Cross," the PM mumbled. At least he knew where we were.

Lighting was quite dim, too—there wasn't any need to fully illuminate a tunnel system that was only used for storage at times. Our footsteps echoed—it couldn't be helped—everyone ran in dress shoes; Maye and I in heels.

Once, these tunnels housed government records, followed by the trunk exchange run by the Post Office, where calls could be routed throughout Britain. Its claim to fame was that the hotline between the Kremlin and the White House passed through the exchange. Who knew that one day, the Prime Minister and the U.S. Secretary of State would be running through to escape assassins?

We raced past generators bolted to the floor in round tunnels at least fifteen feet in diameter. A bullet pinged off one of the metal behemoths somewhere behind us. "Are you armed?" Rafe asked the PM's second guard. That drew our momentum to a temporary halt.

"He is," the PM answered.

"Give me your gun. I'll hold them off," Rafe said.

"I don't think that's a good idea," the guard snapped.

"Edward, give him your gun," the PM ordered.

"You can have mine, too," Dave panted as August and Ken carried him forward. Rafe took Dave's gun and ejected the clip. "I only fired twice," Dave explained. He'd hit a target with both shots.

"Mine's fully loaded," Edward handed his gun to Rafe.

"I'll stay with Rafe," Maye offered.

"Do it," August nodded curtly. "Get them off our backs until Corinne can get us out of here."

"Save your shots," Rafe handed Edward's gun to Maye.

"I'm not stupid," Maye hissed.

"Good. I don't need stupid," Rafe said. "I need a good shot."

"Come on," August nodded at me while I blinked at Rafe.

Heaving a sigh, I turned and led our party toward the next branch in the tunnels. That passage would take us upward and to another door, which I hoped to hell the PM could get us through. I also hoped that Rafe and Maye would make it out as well.

Ilya

I positioned myself behind a huge generator that hadn't seen operation in more than a decade. Maye settled behind a bulkhead fifteen feet behind, after I'd told her to take two shots from that location when our pursuers reached a point ten feet from where I knelt.

Giving me a nod she settled in, preparing to get two shots off as requested. Likely, she'd make them count, too. We had standard British issue Glock 17s, and I had fifteen rounds to her full seventeen.

They came after us, boots hitting the tunnel floor in a regular rhythm. They weren't expecting any of their quarry to stage an ambush—they assumed all of us would keep running.

Maye hit the first target in the head three feet ahead of me, as requested. The second target was hit in the leg. He shouted at the others and jumped toward my hiding spot.

That was a mistake.

Grabbing him by the neck of his body armor, I flung him into a steel rib, crushing his skull. He was dead when his body slid to the floor. Maye fired again, hitting a third pursuer in the throat. He fell, gurgling and gasping for breath before he died. Jerking the Glock from my belt, I fired at two more, wounding one and forcing the other to take cover behind another generator farther back.

They hadn't anticipated our ambush, and I now had two dead men near enough to filch their weapons.

We had Glocks—they had submachine guns. Two of those would be useful during a brief siege. One of their remaining five was wounded, and if we waited long enough, he'd bleed out from the wound to his leg. If we waited long enough, perhaps Corinne would get the PM to a phone where he could call for backup.

Corinne

I did my best not to jerk every time a gun was fired in the tunnel behind us. Dave looked extremely pale and August and Ken were now carrying him. I'd gotten a good look—he'd kept August from getting shot, taking the bullet in his own shoulder and getting two shots off in the bargain.

I was determined to get him out of this mess so he could get the help he needed. The tunnel we needed next was feet away, now, and we'd take another right. We'd be going up flights of stairs past that, and I hoped we had enough strength left to make it.

"This isn't the Furnival Street exit," the PM said, reading the sign we passed as we made the right turn into the adjoining tunnel. "It's the Tooks Court exit. That's blocked."

"Says you," I said, my breathing ragged. I was tiring and worried I wouldn't make it up the steps toward the surface. Those steps were wide and made of concrete as we began to ascend. Ken and Auggie began breathing hard halfway up—they still carried Dave, who was now unconscious.

～

Ilya

The one I'd wounded likely realized he was dying, and decided to go out fighting. He intended to open a path for the four behind him by emptying his submachine gun in our direction. He was successful up to a point—I hit him in the head the moment he ran out of ammunition, but his efforts had given the others a chance to move forward.

They still outnumbered us, and one of them shouted that information at us as his fellow assassin dropped to the floor.

"Fuck off. I don't care how many of you there are," Maye shouted back.

"Stop being an American," I hissed in her direction.

～

Corinne

I imagined that a heart attack awaited as I struggled up endless steps. *Keep going*, I chastised myself. I only carried myself. August and Ken carried a wounded man between them. Even the Secretary was doing better than I was, and he was in his sixties. When we reached the door, I almost collapsed next to the doorframe.

"Prime Minister?" Edward turned to the PM. The door was there, and it was armed. Not just with a keypad, either. This one had a retina scanner, too.

"Try your radio, Edward," the PM nodded at his guard.

"Still not working, sir," Edward said after making the attempt. I figured the tunnels had stymied the technology, but here, we were close to the surface. The PM turned to the apparatus next to the door.

"Keeping secrets, eh?" the PM sighed and shook his head. "Well, I have an eyeball and a code. Let's hope both work."

Ilya

Two minutes passed before another assassin made the attempt. He leapt from his hiding place, firing his weapon indiscriminately while his three fellows moved forward behind him. By the time his weapon was empty, they were much closer than they had been.

I took him down the moment his ammunition ran out, but had to duck behind the generator again when the others fired at me. If they continued to do this, they'd be on me before the last man went down.

Corinne

A part of my mind knew, even as tired as I was, that the PM could get through the door. I just hoped the rest of us would also be allowed through. The moment the door swung open, six men, armed with semiautomatic weapons, waited for us.

The PM was not happy.

Ilya

Two more committed suicide, leaving one in a position very close to mine. I'd taken down his predecessors when their ammunition was depleted, but every time, this one moved forward.

I figured he was the best of the lot—or the worst, where I was concerned. He intended to kill Maye and me, no matter what it took. He fired several rounds in my direction, just to see what I'd do.

Bullets hitting metal from that close is always a frightening experience. I preferred to be farther away, as any one of those bullets could kill me instantly if they struck my head. I had plans for the future, and they certainly didn't include dying in an abandoned tunnel in Britain.

Another round of bullets hit around me. Maye shouted—one ricocheted, hitting her in the arm. Leaping up, I fired at the assassin's position with the Glock, emptying it before lifting one of the semiautomatics and firing it as I walked forward. He was four feet away from me and I dared him to fire back. I'd waited for the last one; they'd instructed me to hold back unless there was no other option. I grinned as I emptied the gun and he rose from his hiding place.

Time to employ the shield.

Corinne

"Sir, there's gunfire in the tunnel," one of the armed guards informed the Prime Minister. "Ours are on the way, but they may not arrive in time."

I held my breath.

Dave was receiving medical care nearby while an ambulance was en route. We'd ended up in the Government Actuary Department, which had been built over the old Tooks Court entrance into the tunnels. All records indicated the shaft to the surface had been sealed off.

All those records lied. I assumed the lie held a purpose; I was too terrified for Rafe to consider the reasons.

We'd been led to a comfortable office after the Prime Minister threatened to have all six armed men sacked if they didn't allow us passage, once he got the door open. They couldn't help us fast enough after that.

"Corinne, he and Maye are very good. If there's any way," August sat heavily beside me.

"August, don't give me platitudes," I whispered, attempting to shove down the panic attack.

"Water, mum," a bottle was placed in my hands.

"Drink it, Corinne," August said, taking the cap off the bottle he was given and emptying it in six swallows.

"This is insane," I mumbled, struggling to remove the cap on my bottle. August took it and did it for me. I drank. Until that moment, I hadn't realized how thirsty I was—or how shaky. I could barely hold the bottle steady to drink.

"Save any for me?" Rafe knelt beside my chair.

I spilled water on him, giving him a grateful hug.

CHAPTER 8

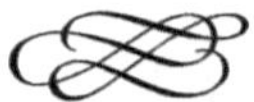

orinne

We heard about the theft of the Imperial State Crown, the Orb and the Sceptre from the Tower of London on the drive to our hotel. The Secretary was with us; the PM had an appointment at Buckingham Palace.

What did it matter that it was after two in the morning? Maye's wound was a graze, and the ambulance crew that arrived to take charge of Dave had patched her up. "Do you think the two incidents were connected?" Kevin asked.

I was much too tired to speak, and almost too tired to listen. I huddled into my corner of the limousine and listened while the others talked.

"We can't rule that out," August said. He and the Secretary of State had been on the phone almost from the moment we'd gotten out of the tunnel. Rafe dispatched the last of the assassins after Maye was wounded, so all eight were dead.

The PM could sort all that out; I wanted a shower. Crawling through a vent in an evening dress, followed by a lengthy run through abandoned tunnels hadn't done much for me or my clothing. I was covered in dust, grime and had at least three long rips in my dress.

The others didn't look much better.

August also reported on the assassins waiting at the Waterloo exit for the PM—of the four of those, one was dead and three managed to escape. A manhunt was ongoing, but I didn't hold much hope that they'd be caught.

When Mary Evans' name was mentioned, however, I did perk up. "She's missing. We had someone following her, and she just disappeared," August shrugged.

That was a problem. A really big problem.

"We'll have a meeting in the morning, before we fly back to the States," August said. "The PM is providing guards at the hotel. Try to get as much rest as possible. Everybody should be up by oh-eight-hundred. Cori, I want to talk to you tonight."

"No, Auggie," I moaned. I wanted a shower and bed. August wanted to talk.

"You, too, Rafe."

~

"The Secretary of State will see to it that none of you will be mentioned in the rescue operation," August paced in front of us. He'd hauled us inside his suite for the talk while the others were herded to their bedrooms by their handlers.

August sent Dalton to his room, too. I wondered how he felt about the exclusion. "While Dave really is a hero for saving my ass in those tunnels, he'll get the bulk of the credit. Neither of you can mention this incident outside the Mansion."

"You don't let me outside the Mansion anymore—who am I gonna talk to?" I muttered. I was exhausted and shaking.

"I know the drill, Colonel," Rafe said. "We need sleep, not a lecture."

"Then you can go. Corinne has to stay."

Rafe mumbled something in his native language. I got the idea he was telling Auggie to go fuck himself. He stalked out of the suite, leaving me alone with Colonel August Hunter.

"Corinne, I want to talk to you about your transfer. I heard you as plain as day in my head. Now, I'm not talented, so there's no way I can send a message back, but that talent alone could make you invaluable to the Program. There are no bugs in this room, so you can speak freely about what happened tonight."

"I don't want to talk about it," I said, wrapping arms about myself tightly. The shaking was getting worse.

"Look, I have to put this in my report to the President."

"Then do what you have to do. It could get us both killed."

"What the fuck are you talking about?" August exploded.

"Cutter," I whispered, my voice trembling. "He'll be first in line for the VP's job. That would be a major mistake."

"What the hell does that have to do with this?" August was angry and on the verge of violence.

"Do you have Dalton's phone conversations tapped?" I lifted my eyes to watch August as he went still.

"Corinne, that's classified," he began.

"Then listen to them for the next two days. I think you'll get an answer, Auggie, and you may not like it when you hear it."

I was barely out of the shower when Rafe walked into my room. "Are you all right?" he asked. I was wrapped in the robe supplied by the hotel and my hair was hanging in wet strings down my back. Not my most attractive moment.

"I'm fine," I lied. "How about you?"

"Look, I've done this all my life," he said, raking fingers through his hair and looking away for a moment. "It really doesn't bother me. I know it bothers you."

"There's nothing we can do about it," I said. "I'm sure Dr. Shaw will be waiting the moment I get back to the Mansion."

"Someday, cabbage, we should have a talk," Rafe said.

"Fine, as long as it isn't tonight."

"Agreed. Go to bed and try to sleep." He walked out of my room, closing the door softly behind him.

Notes—Colonel Hunter

I was resolved to listen to Corinne's warnings from now on. I was prepared to act on them, too—to the best of my ability. I left a message for James, in code. He'd pay attention to Dalton's phone conversations until I asked him to stop.

Sleep hadn't come for a while, so a third cup of coffee was in my hand while I waited for the others to gather in the hotel lobby. We had vans coming to transport us to the airport, and I had notes to write during the flight back to the States.

Corinne—I needed to see the President about her. Rafe performed to expectations, but Corinne continued to puzzle me. Why had she chosen to reveal talents now, instead of after she'd received the drug?

I'd have to consider that later—after I was rested and better focused. Rafe arrived first, closely followed by Dalton. The others, Corinne included, arrived less than five minutes later. I caught Maye and the others staring at Cori from time to time, but they quickly looked away when she turned in their direction.

They were speculating, just as I was. The President's hand could be forced on this—there wasn't any way Corinne's performance the night before could be erased from all their minds. Our two wild cards— Corinne and Rafe—had saved our lives last night.

The vans arrived, forcing my thoughts away from them and onto the task at hand. We rode to Heathrow, too tired to have anything other than necessary conversation.

Corinne

My eyes felt as if they had sand in them, and an unusually bright morning in Britain made them water in pain. Maye and the brothers watched me whenever they could, attempting to figure out what had happened the night before. I might have been of less interest to them if I'd grown an extra head.

The ride to Heathrow seemed to take forever—London is a huge city, after all. August squeezed between Dalton and me on a back seat in our van, and I appreciated his attempts to protect me. Rafe sat in the row in front of mine, and I hadn't failed to notice that Dalton didn't want to be near the former spy if he could help it.

Rafe got Ken's company instead, with Maye and her handler in the first row. The others rode in the second van, and theirs followed ours as we made our way through London traffic to the airport.

I didn't care where I sat on the jet, as long as I could close my eyes and sleep. On the trip from the States, I hadn't been offered anything. This time, I had a pillow, a blanket and bottles of water and juice.

Who knew?

Rafe took the seat next to mine, leaned back, closed his eyes and was asleep in minutes. I stayed awake for half the trip.

"You have a meeting with the President tomorrow," Dr. Shaw informed me when I walked into my kitchen. Rafe and August were right behind, so the message was meant for them, too.

"What time?" August asked.

"Three. She has an hour to give you. She wants a report, and has a few questions."

"Great." I shuffled toward the fridge and pulled out the carton of milk. I offered a glass to Rafe, who shook his head and pulled the dusty bottle of bourbon off the top of the fridge before he went looking for a suitable glass. August and Dr. Shaw sat at the island to have a drink with Rafe and me. I was the only one having milk.

The good news, I suppose, was that Rafe and I had two days off, so he wouldn't be pounding me in Krav Maga lessons. "The Vice President's funeral is scheduled next week," Dr. Shaw said, emptying his glass and pushing it toward Rafe, who poured more bourbon.

"The White House is keeping the lid on the incident in London. The reporters only have information on the Prime Minister's two guards. The one who was shot was interviewed earlier from his hospital bed."

"As far as I'm concerned, he can take all the credit." I hunched my shoulders and stared at the patterns in the granite island. "He saved Auggie's life; that's all I care about."

"And I thought you didn't care," August quipped.

"Shut up," I mumbled as good-naturedly as I could.

"Corinne, I cleared some time for you tomorrow morning at ten," Dr. Shaw said. "I'll be here then, whether you're dressed or not. We'll talk."

"Say it ain't so," I moaned and dropped my forehead on the island.

Rafe stayed when August and Dr. Shaw left. "Corinne, what's wrong?" he asked. By mutual, silent agreement, we didn't touch.

"Everything," I breathed.

As promised, Dr. Shaw arrived in the kitchen at ten the following morning. I had a bad-hair day going, following a bad-hair night. I brushed it and my teeth, at least, before sitting down with Dr. Shaw.

"Now, what would you like to talk about?" Dr. Shaw said, first thing. "I suggest the events in London as a starting place."

"Dr. Shaw," I began.

"Call me Leo. You've earned that right."

"Seriously? What about the stationery I ordered for all our communications?"

"Corinne, be serious, please," he said.

"I'll have to get used to it first," I said. "It just seems unnatural to say Leo to your face."

He laughed. That didn't happen often.

"There's one thing I ought to tell you," I said. "And believe me, I had a good reason for not saying it before."

"What reason is that?" he asked.

"Because we don't need a war with a certain Asian dictator to be named later."

~

Notes—Colonel Hunter

"Do you mean to tell me those burned paintings were fakes? That Louis the Fifteenth's crown at the Louvre is also fake?" I stared at Shaw in disbelief.

"Corinne said, and I quote, *we don't need a war with an Asian dictator to be named later.*"

"Holy fucking hell," I blurted. My meeting with the President just became much more complicated.

~

Corinne

"So," the President steepled her fingers and studied me with unblinking scrutiny, "The crown in the Louvre is a fake. Do you suspect that the ones behind the theft of Britain's crown jewels are also behind that attack and theft?"

"Yes, but I can't get a handle on who's responsible," I said, doing my best to sit up straight instead of sinking into my chair.

"Is that what you're doing—searching for the ones responsible?"

"Or the one," I said, happy that my voice only shook a little. "He, she, it or they have lives to pay for. I intend to see that they pay."

"I should have brought her to you in the beginning," Dr. Shaw muttered. He'd insisted on coming to the meeting with August, Rafe and me. "You've gotten more information in five minutes than she's given me in five years."

"Don't get all upset, Leo," I said. "I had my reasons. I told you those reasons earlier. Heads have been hot over that whole incident. What could have happened if they had a specific target?"

"I see your point," the President leaned back in her chair. "With the information coming out now and only to a select few, we may be able to employ—shall we say classified measures—to retrieve these items?"

"I think we have agents in other departments who might be able to track them," August suggested.

"Then I'll look into who might be able to handle this. Someone who speaks the language fluently and can fit in," the President said. "I'll let you know. Corinne, are you working on the other part of this, still—the part of making the ones responsible for that massacre pay?"

"I am," I said. "I just need more cooperation from a few people."

"Then you can have anything you want, within reason."

"I just want photographs," I said. "Colonel Hunter knows which ones."

"See to it," she nodded to Auggie.

"What about the Secretary of State and the Prime Minister?" Rafe asked. "Are they still targets?"

"Possibly," President Sanders replied. "Security has been increased and all departments here and in Britain are on alert."

"Any word on the one who called herself Mary Evans?" Rafe asked his follow-up question.

"None. Vanished like a puff of smoke in a high wind. We currently have nothing on her location, but our resources are working on that now."

"I believe she's our go-between," Rafe said.

"Do you have any idea who is directing her movements?"

"None at the moment, but if I can see those photographs Corinne mentioned, I may recognize someone."

"Then you have my permission to contact the necessary departments. Look, I hate to end this meeting—it has been more than productive," the President said. "But I have another meeting. I'll have someone show you out. Thank you—all of you, for your exemplary service in London."

Notes—Colonel Hunter

James brought information to me the moment I arrived in my office—a flash drive containing phone conversations between Dalton Parrish and General Cutter was placed in my hand as James offered a silent frown. He and I listened as Dalton informed Cutter of

Corinne's performance in the tunnels beneath London. I cursed the moment I heard Cutter refer to her as a witch.

$\sim$

Corinne

I owed Auggie cookies; he didn't mention my transfer to the President. Not while I was there, anyway. If they held a private conversation at another time, I didn't care, as long as they kept it to themselves.

Usually, I don't bake on Tuesdays. As I had the day off, aside from meetings, I baked cookies for August and James. Rafe showed up after I took the first batch out of the oven, so the intended recipients got the second and third batches. I figured they could live with a dozen apiece.

"Do you have a washer and dryer?" Rafe asked as he stuffed the rest of a cookie in his mouth.

"Yes—in a closet outside my office," I said. "Why?"

"I like to wash my own jeans. The service here puts starch in them. I prefer to keep them soft. It allows me easier movement."

"Fine. You can borrow my washer and dryer."

"I'll make gumbo tomorrow for dinner."

"Really? What kind?"

"Seafood gumbo."

"You're my hero," I said. "Do we have crackers left?"

"I'd prefer fresh bread."

Rafe brought six pairs of jeans over, stuffed them in my washer, then made himself comfortable on a nearby chair while I went through the most recent chapter in the book. Taking days away from a manuscript requires that I go through the last two or three chapters, just to get back in the groove.

"I've read it already. It's good," Rafe said when I finished reading.

"It needs editing. I'll send out the first half soon, so my editor can start working on it."

"Want to invite James to dinner tomorrow night? I tend to make enough gumbo to feed an army."

My inter-Mansion phone rang beside my desk. I couldn't call out on it, but anyone inside the Mansion could call me. "Hello?" I said after picking up.

"I want to come," James said immediately.

"We really need to find you a date," I informed him dryly. "But your cookies are here waiting. You probably already know that."

"Can I come get them now?"

"You're always welcome here, unless I'm asleep or in the shower."

"On my way." The line went dead.

"What shall we name our adopted child?" I asked Rafe. He laughed.

I had no idea we'd have uninvited guests. Thank goodness Rafe did make enough for an army. All of the Five showed, with Carol, Kevin's handler, and Jeff, Maye's handler. James had a great time—he probably hadn't been to a party since college.

"Why didn't we know you could—you know," Maye said to me as Rafe handed her a glass of wine.

"I can't explain it, really. August would probably kill me."

"He wouldn't, he'd just be pissed," James grinned. "This gumbo is awesome."

"I guess it's a good thing I made extra bread," I said dryly.

"It goes great with the gumbo," Ken said, dumping more gumbo in his bowl. Everybody was in my kitchen. Extra chairs had been dragged in from somewhere, and several were eating around my dining table while the rest took seats at the island.

"Why didn't we think of this before?" Kevin asked. "I want to grill burgers on the back patio."

"I haven't been to a cookout in a long time," Nick said. "I vote for steaks, though."

"I think we could accommodate that—I enjoy cooking steaks," Rafe responded.

"I'll buy the grill, if they'll allow it," I said.

"What's this about a grill?" August and Leo walked in.

"Ask them. I'm just funding it, if it's approved."

"I think the new VP might approve it," August grinned. "Cori, the President asked me what I thought. The former Secretary of State will be the new Vice President." My mouth dropped open—I know it did—because Rafe tipped it closed with a finger beneath my chin.

"You saw who took off the minute we started cleaning the kitchen," I said, flopping onto a barstool with a cup of chamomile.

"No surprise. I'd have bet money on Becker leaving first, and I'd have won."

"Hah. No way I'd take that bet."

"I'm surprised Dr. Shaw stayed to help. Not surprised that James did."

"Here's to good gumbo." I held up my cup.

"I'll second that."

Thursday, it was back to running, followed by Krav Maga and weight training. Becker was the only one to show up for Krav Maga. I'm sure it was for pointers. At least he hadn't shoved me in the mud, because it was raining during the six a.m. torture. Springtime in the D.C. area. Lovely.

August waited in our kitchen for Rafe and me when the weight-lifting torture was over. By that time, I was ready for a shower and lunch. *Auggie,* I thought at him, *why is Dalton even here, except as a spy?*

"This won't take but a minute, and we can talk on our way to the former Vice President's funeral. The President wants both of you to ride with her and the First Gentleman," Auggie didn't bat an eyelash at the mental communication.

"Who's taking the Secretary of State's spot?" I asked.

"No idea, yet, but the moment they're brought on board and the schedule is cleared, that trip to France is in the offing."

"Auggie, I don't want to go there," I slumped my shoulders.

"Cori, it'll be all right."

It wasn't the first time I'd heard those words. They made me sad. "Corinne, I don't have a specific time for next Tuesday, but I expect both of you to be ready at nine. We'll be updated sometime after that, as to when we have to leave. The President doesn't want to take any chances."

"I understand. I'll be ready."

"I'm giving you permission to go out with James and Rafe tomorrow, to buy something to wear. Make sure it's tasteful and discreet."

"Does it have to be a dress?"

"That's preferable, yes."

"Damn," I sighed.

≈

Notes—Colonel Hunter

"I'm just waiting for him to make his move," Shaw said.

"What move?"

"With Corinne."

"Has he said anything to you?"

"No, but it doesn't take a genius to see it."

"Neither one has any names on their list."

"Do you think for a minute they'll be that obvious about it—face it, placing a single name on that list is the same as announcing to the entire Mansion that they're a couple."

"Look, I know he has a big beef with the Russian government right now—a lot of Ukrainians do. You think we can trust him with Corinne?"

"Do you think Corinne would trust him, if he wasn't trustworthy?"

"I don't know. People have been blinded by love or lust in the past."

"Corinne isn't acting like a Chihuahua in heat, you know. Neither of them are young and stupid."

"Then let's keep an eye on them while they're out with James tomorrow. We'll see where this goes."

~

Corinne

You'd think I'd been let out of prison. Nice jeans, low-heeled short boots, a blue, boat-necked top and earrings were what I wore. The day was overcast, but I didn't care. I was going *outside*.

With Rafe.

What did it matter that they'd have an entire SWAT team discreetly following us? Somebody, somewhere, wanted to know whom the target was when the helicopter exploded, so they were watching us like hawks. It made me wonder if they were watching Auggie and Dalton, too.

"Stay on your toes, cabbage," Rafe breathed next to my ear as we walked out of the Mansion's side door toward a waiting car. We'd have a driver and James as a personal escort. I made a point to make eye contact with the driver.

No problem there.

Alexandria, Virginia, was our destination; an upscale department store waited there. It wasn't far away, but traffic made the drive longer. Our destination was quite close to the Pentagon, actually, in Pentagon City. When we arrived, I stared—the adjoining mall was huge.

The driver found a spot in a parking garage, and we walked from there. Just as Rafe asked, I watched everything around us—he did, too. James appeared to be more watchful than I'd ever seen him be, and together the three of us strolled into the mall area and headed toward the department store.

I knew we were followed discreetly; that was also a concern. Someone had gotten to a helicopter pilot; what might keep them from getting to one of those who followed us now?

"Stop being obvious, cabbage," Rafe rumbled at my side.

"Okay." I attempted to breathe out the tension gathering inside me. "This is supposed to be fun. Relaxing," I reminded myself. After my confinement at the Mansion, the mall and its many shops overloaded my senses, especially since my fear was waking and shoving everything else aside. I found I couldn't focus on anything except that.

Rafe's hand went to my neck, gently swept my hair aside and massaged my skin. I wanted to moan at the contact—it felt wonderful. Too soon, we arrived at the department store and he took his hand away.

"Dresses or suits first?" James asked.

"Let's do suits," I said. "I'm too shaky to pick an outfit right now."

"Cori?" James turned his full attention on me.

"It's nothing," I lied and waved away his concern. "Nothing imminent, anyway."

"You sure?"

"Yeah, it's just the usual," I said.

"Let's look at suits, then," Rafe took charge of the situation as well as my hand and led me toward the nearest escalator.

"Get what you want; we can get it altered faster than they can do it here," James advised as Rafe and I studied the selection of suits. For a funeral, it had to be dark, tasteful and discreet. I forced my mind to focus on Rafe and his selections.

"I like the dark gray and the navy pinstripe," I said after Rafe slipped into several suit coats.

"We'll get both," James said.

"We have to hurry," I said. "They're getting closer. We may have time to run through the dress department, but that's it."

"Who?" Rafe turned to me, then.

"I don't know. I just feel them coming closer."

"To the dress department, then." James led the way downstairs, where the women's clothing was.

I felt as if I were suffocating as I lifted skirts, blouses and jackets off racks and raced toward the checkout. James paid and we headed toward the mall entrance.

"In here," I grabbed Rafe and James' hands and led them into a tiny shop not far away that sold women's lingerie. Pulling them behind a large display sign hanging in a window, we watched as three men walked past. They looked as if they were ready for a golf outing. Two of the three appeared to be identical twins. I released a shaky breath.

Right behind them came some of those who were guarding us. They knew, just as I did, that these three were looking for us. "Go," I hissed. We took off, moving as quickly as we could out of the store without being obvious. Two of our discreet guards caught up with us near the entrance to the parking garage, and they stayed with us until we were safely inside the car.

The driver took off without a word, the screech of the vehicle's tires scraping against my nerves as he drove us away from customer parking. James received a call on his cell halfway back to the Mansion; August was on the line. James put the call on speaker. "We have one of them in custody," August said. "The other two are dead."

"Who?" Rafe asked.

"We have no information, and we're having trouble with identification at the moment," August replied. "Did you get a look at them? Recognize anyone?"

"No, but that's no surprise," Rafe responded. "If I'm the target, they wouldn't want me to recognize a potential shooter. Two of them were twins; I could see that clearly."

"What about you, Cori? Did you see any of them? Know anything about them?"

"One wanted me. The twins wanted Rafe," I said.

"Are you holding up?" August asked—he'd noticed the quaver in my voice.

"I didn't collapse on the floor, but it may be because Rafe and James were holding me up."

"I can have Dr. Shaw waiting for you," August offered.

"No, Auggie. I'll get through this, I think."

~

Shopping bags were dumped inside Auggie's office as we walked in. He already had photographs spread across his desk. I lifted one of them—it was of two bodies, both shot from close range. The twins were obviously dead.

"These two were after Rafe," I repeated, handing the photograph to a frowning August. "The other one was definitely after me."

"What can you tell me about him?" He handed a photograph of the third man to me.

"Auggie, his mind is a mess," I said. "I'm not getting much at all from him. It's like he had orders, and that's all he could remember."

CHAPTER 9

*N*otes—*Colonel Hunter*

James and Rafe took Corinne back to her suite while I examined the photographs again. I had information from our team, too, concerning the shootings. They'd occurred in a maintenance area between the department store and a nearby hotel; the two dead men got off several rounds before ours took them down.

Getting the third man was a fluke—he'd stumbled and lost his footing. It was easy to take him after that. The incident was handled discreetly, with locals guarding the area until vans arrived to remove the prisoner and the bodies.

Forensics was working on the bodies while the prisoner sat in an interrogation room. I hoped he wouldn't end up like the pilot—dead in an apparent suicide. What I'd discussed two hours earlier with the President and General Safer was that I was being followed, too, so my wife had been sent out of town to visit her mother.

Most of us scheduled to ride in that helicopter were targeted. What we didn't know was why. I suspected the Russians were after Rafe, but how had they learned of his existence, or what he even looked like now?

Corinne? How could anyone know about Corinne? She was only now showing her talents, after all. It led me to believe that information was leaking from the Mansion, but how, and through whom?

"Colonel?" James was back.

"James?"

"I want to do anything I can to find out who's doing this."

"Doing what?"

"Releasing information on Cori and Rafe."

"Add me to that list," I said. "They're following me, too."

"What about Dalton? He was supposed to be on that chopper."

"No idea," I shrugged. "But it bears a closer look."

Corinne

"I was hoping we'd have time to do lunch while we were out," Rafe said, opening the fridge and searching for the package of sliced roast beef.

"Lunch out may not be on the itinerary anytime soon," I said.

"Want a sandwich?" he asked, setting the roast beef, mayonnaise and a tomato on the island.

"Maybe half a sandwich. More than that might make me sick. I feel queasy."

"Then I'll make half a sandwich for you."

Ilya, I thought at him, *we have to start paying attention to the ones who refuse to show me their face.*

"Want lettuce, too?"

"Yeah."

Ilya

Things were quiet around the Mansion for the rest of the day and into the following morning, when Nick and Maye, who were scheduled to go with the new Vice President to the former Vice President's funeral, went out to buy clothing.

Nick was hit in the arm with a bullet, while Maye barely escaped injury. We had a meeting Sunday night, after Nick was released by the medical unit upstairs. Corinne's and my shared kitchen was the venue of choice.

"It appears that the entire Program is targeted, and not just parts of it," General Safer announced. I wondered that he was here instead of Cutter for this meeting, but didn't comment. It was on my list of things to inquire discreetly about, however.

Cutter was furious that the President hadn't moved him into the VP's slot, and I imagined that we had Corinne to thank for that. Cutter would have been a huge mistake in that position, and would likely hurt Amelia Sanders' bid for reelection the following year. I didn't want to speculate on what might happen if the President was killed or incapacitated with Cutter in the Vice President's position. That could become extremely dangerous.

I wasn't about to ask Dalton about any of this—he attended the meeting reluctantly and sat at the table next to Kevin, with little expression on his face as he listened to Safer with the rest of us.

I figured that Corinne would let August know if anyone in our kitchen was involved in the leak of information, so I wasn't overly concerned at the moment. The other thing I surmised was that all cameras and listening devices in the kitchen had been blocked or deactivated temporarily, so the meeting was as private as any meeting inside the Mansion could be.

"Both our attackers are dead," Maye said. "Is there anything new on their identification?"

"We have nothing so far, and that concerns me," Safer acknowledged. "How can five unidentifiable gunmen show up so quickly? They carried no ID, no credit cards or anything else that might help, and their fingerprints aren't in any database."

"Has the one in custody talked, yet?" Nick asked.

"No. Hasn't spoken a word, as far as I know. Wrote a note, asking for an attorney."

"So he's taking the fifth to the extreme?" August asked.

"Looks that way."

"Did you take his belt away?" Corinne asked.

James snorted at Corinne's question.

"Yes. He no longer has anything left to hang himself, unless he gets creative with his clothing."

"Are we still set to attend the funeral next week with the President and Vice President?"

"Yes," Safer confirmed. "I don't believe I need to tell you how vital it is that both come away safely."

"You don't have to tell me that," Maye huffed. "Will there be plenty of protection surrounding the chapel?"

"We've increased it as of today," Safer said. "Every man checked out beforehand, and Secret Service is guarding all doors."

"You don't think it's only the Program being targeted, do you?" August observed.

"Not after the Vice President's assassination, no," Safer said. "We had no rumblings on that one. We've been digging deeper and listening more carefully since then."

That meant the NSA and every other agency was on high alert. So far, the Vice President had been assassinated, the British Prime Minister and the U.S. Secretary of State targeted, and possibly other officials in foreign countries. That's what the meeting at Camp David was about—potential terrorist attacks in multiple countries.

"What about the G-8?" I asked. "Are all those countries potential targets?"

"We're looking into that, and other agencies are busy with all the information that's been supplied so far. That's not our concern. Our concern is keeping the Program safe, and then keeping the President, Vice President and other highly-placed officials safe."

"What will you do if the Program is exposed?" Nick asked.

"Likely move it; send it underground and let it sit dormant for a while, to throw off conspiracy theorists," Safer said. "We don't need that. Now, we may have a leak already; that's what concerns the President and me. If you see any unusual activity, or if anyone asks questions better left unanswered, let August know. He'll contact me, and we'll make sure the President gets the information."

"Since when did Hunter get to take point?" Gene Little, Becker's handler, demanded.

"Since he's been more useful than you ever were," Safer snapped. "He does investigative research and stays in contact with me and the White House continually, while you twiddle your thumbs and watch Becker play basketball. It's your job to listen and take orders, just as Colonel Hunter is expected to do."

The division in the ranks is widening, I heard Corinne's voice plainly in my mind.

She was right, and likely knew it wasn't a good thing. Since I had no knowledge of Safer's previous interactions with the Five, I didn't know if Becker's handler had gotten dressed down before. I'd have to investigate that, in addition to the other things on my list.

Corinne sat next to Colonel Hunter, while I'd taken a position against the wall near the door. I wanted to watch all of them. Study them. I was in danger, just as they were, but I wondered if we were being targeted as a whole or individually, from different directions. Corinne and I needed a private place to talk; I just wasn't sure where that might be.

Corinne

I wanted that talk Rafe suggested once—in a safe, non-bugged place. I'd have to go looking for it. He might know things I didn't, and vice-versa. August, too, was on my list of private conversations, and that might be another problem.

Safer had painted a target on Auggie's back, by snapping at Gene. Gene let Becker do whatever he wanted—consequently, Becker would be on Gene's side if Gene wanted somebody pounded or embarrassed.

Auggie, we have to talk, I sent in his direction. He dropped his chin in a half-nod, indicating he'd heard me. *Do we have those photographs of Mary Evans? I really want to look at them*, I added.

We hadn't gotten anything yet—the agencies who'd taken the photographs were busy tying them up with bureaucratic red tape, to keep them out of anyone else's hands. Maybe the President ought to get in on that. I needed those photographs and soon.

"If there are no other questions?" General Safer asked. He was done and ready to leave.

Nobody raised their hands, so Safer left with three handlers—Vance, Preston and Carol—hot on his heels. They wanted a private word I could tell, and didn't want to talk in front of the rest of us. Gene, a sour expression on his face, pulled Becker out of the room shortly after.

"Cori, I want you and Rafe in my office. Now," August said and headed toward the door. Rafe waited while the others, Dalton included, shuffled out of the kitchen before he shut the door and hauled me toward Auggie's office.

"We're having trouble getting the photographs you wanted," August said immediately when Rafe and I took seats inside his office. James was outside at his station, making sure we weren't interrupted. "The President may have to cut through this bureaucratic bullshit," he went on. "Nothing I've done has moved those assholes any faster."

August was cursing—that meant he was really pissed. He wanted answers just as I did, and neither of us were having any luck. He couldn't come out and tell them why he wanted the information, so his requests were going through channels. It also told me that Cutter hadn't asked for the information on Auggie's behalf—his requests wouldn't have met with brick walls.

"You may be wondering why I haven't involved the Program Director in these requests," August said, echoing my thoughts. "I have an answer. Corinne, I feel you need this information, although it may upset you."

"What information?" Rafe asked.

"It's on this flash drive," he pulled a small drive from a locked drawer and slipped it into his computer. "This is a recorded phone conversation from a few days ago."

Rafe and I listened—it wasn't difficult to determine that the conversation was between Dalton and General Cutter. I thought Rafe might explode when Cutter called me a witch. He wasn't talking in generalities, either. He meant a bona-fide, spell-weaving broom-rider. In his few, ultra-conservative brain cells, that meant one thing.

Thou shalt not suffer a witch to live. When he actually said those words to Dalton during their conversation, I drew a shaky breath.

It mattered not that the King James Version of the Bible was written after the Inquisition was in full swing, or that the term witch was misinterpreted and may have meant a poisoner of either sex. For those like Cutter, the Bible was God's word, spoken directly into King James' printed verses.

"I've already discussed this with the President," August said.

It didn't matter; I was shaking anyway. Cutter wanted me dead. Was that why he hadn't shown his face to me—afraid I might be able to tell?

Fucker.

"Corinne, the President is removing Dalton as Rafe's handler. I'm taking over for him until another handler can be found, if it proves necessary. I figure Safer is handing him his walking papers now. We don't need a handler spying on somebody else's ward with the intention to harm, and we certainly don't need a Program Director who wants a member of the Program dead."

"What does the President intend to do?" Rafe asked, a chill in his voice.

"Cutter will be asked—discreetly of course—to step aside and retire permanently."

"When will that happen?"

"Next week, after the funeral. We don't need more than one thing at a time cluttering up the media."

"Who's in line to take his place?" I asked. While the word *witch* and the threat that followed sent a chill through me, the fact that Cutter would be asked to step aside sent a bigger chill down my spine. This wasn't a man who'd happily accept a request to step aside and retire. Trouble would come of it—I just wasn't sure what form it would take. Cutter was more than dangerous—to all of us.

"I don't have an answer," August replied. "I think the President intends to be much more careful choosing the next Director. She wanted to throw Cutter a bone, since he has so much support throughout the country."

"And perhaps turn Cutter aside from running against her in the next election?" Rafe asked.

"It has happened before," August agreed. "If she'd stopped at naming him Secretary of Defense, then we wouldn't be having this conversation. Since Hugh, his predecessor, was also Director of the Program, the President thought it made sense. It didn't, and most people involved in the Program understood that. We need someone a little more open-minded than Paul Cutter."

"Auggie, you know there'll be trouble to come of this," I said.

"I'm afraid of that, too, but we can't let him keep the job. Not with that attitude. The President was really pissed when she heard this conversation, and it took place right after the two of you saved the Prime Minister and the Secretary of State. Dalton contacted Cutter to spill everything he knew about that rescue, and Cutter responded to your act of heroism by calling you an offensive name and making implied threats."

"He's not getting a Christmas card," I muttered. "I think Dalton was only following orders," I added.

"Dalton took an oath when he came aboard, to protect the Program and all involved. He didn't do that. He knew what Cutter's response would be. He'll be reassigned, so stop worrying about his sorry ass." August shook his head at me, as if he couldn't believe I'd stoop to defend Dalton Parrish.

"I think he meant well; he just got caught up with the wrong person," I said.

"Corinne, stop giving that bastard any sympathy," Rafe muttered.

"There's something else," August said.

"What?"

"I'm leaving the bugs and cameras inside your suite—including the kitchen—turned off, Cori. They'll be active outside your windows and the outside door, but you'll have privacy inside your suite. I know that having no privacy bothers you, so the President ordered it done. From now on, you'll have to contact James through traditional means to tell him the cookies are ready."

"Are you kidding?" I stared at August in disbelief.

"Not kidding. The President appreciates what you've done for the country, and this is her way of rewarding you."

"Then please tell her thank you for me," I whispered.

I felt numb as Rafe and I walked out of Auggie's office. No bugs inside my suite? I didn't know how to react. That meant, perhaps, that Rafe and I could have a private conversation.

First, though, I needed a drink.

"Want wine or the hard stuff?" I asked the moment we walked inside our kitchen and shut the door.

"Scotch?" he lifted an eyebrow.

"I have some Macallan here somewhere," I said, scooting my step stool toward the fridge. I always kept the good stuff in the cabinet over the refrigerator. "Here." I handed the bottle down to him. "Twenty-five year. I love Macallan. It's hard to find Macallan Amber, though. I like it, too."

"Someday, we'll go to Scotland and get all we want," Rafe grinned as he pulled two glasses from the cabinet. "Plain or rocks?"

"I want ginger ale with mine, and a couple of ice cubes."

"Wimp."

"I keep telling you that. You never listen." I hopped off the stool and went in search of a bottle of ginger ale in the fridge.

He poured Scotch; I added ginger ale and ice to my glass. "Here's to private conversations," he held his up in a toast. I clinked my glass against his. He leaned in to kiss me.

I forgot to breathe.

I'll never forget our night. He didn't push me, or even attempt to convince me to get naked with him. He was content to wait for that. Instead, he herded me toward my sitting room, settled me onto the sofa and wrapped an arm about me, pulling me close.

"Tell me," he whispered against my ear, his breath warm and flavored with expensive Scotch. His accent had gone straight from American to Ukrainian, and I was sorry I couldn't understand his native language at that point—I figured his words would be delicious and something to savor.

"Rafe," I began. If he wanted my story, he had to understand how uncomfortable that was.

"When we're together like this and nobody watches or listens, call me Ilya. That is the name I want to hear you cry out when we make love."

"Ilya, I love that name, first off. Second, I want to tell you, but I have to prepare myself for it. Does that make sense? Something else you ought to know—I haven't had sex in a very, very, long time."

"First off, thank you. Second, I understand. Third, that will only make it sweeter."

"What simple question can I answer that will keep you for now?" I asked.

"How old?"

"Seventy-three."

"Perfect." He kissed me again.

While we worked on our second glasses of Scotch, we turned to business. "What trouble do you think might come from Cutter being relieved of his duties?" Ilya asked.

"He's connected to several organizations, some of whom find no difficulty in pumping money into campaigns," I said. "If he'd been named Vice President, that would have made things simpler for him to get the nomination."

"But that would mean the President," he began.

"I think that's tied up in all this," I said. "I have absolutely no proof that the President is a target, but it makes sense to me. Plus, if Cutter thinks I'm a witch, well, you can imagine what the people who back him think. As backward as he is, they're a hundred times worse. They'd like to unleash an inquisition here and now, to bring the country in line with their political and religious views."

"How do you know this?"

"I did some research in the past five years. I've been looking for the ones responsible for that attack in France. Sometimes the trails led in different directions. Somehow, there's a network out there, and I can't explain who's behind it or how it's connected, even."

"How did you do this research without Colonel Hunter or the others knowing?"

"Library computer system," I said. "I paid several people cash at the library to do research for me. My name isn't attached to any of it, and the people I hired thought I was doing research for a book. Printed photographs can be helpful, if the printer is good enough."

"Where is all the research?"

"I had to trash it, so nobody would know what I was doing. I really need those photographs of Mary Evans, or whatever her name is," I said, sipping my Scotch and ginger ale. "I think she may be connected somehow with the puppet masters who are stringing all of us along."

"This is more frightening than I thought," Ilya murmured.

"This government does business with those who can provide security services in Afghanistan and other Middle Eastern countries. They employ a lot of ex-military personnel. It's like the U.S. military is college, and the security services are the pro leagues."

"This I already knew," he nodded. "These are connected to those who want Cutter in office?"

"Yes. They have tons of money, and they can dump any amount they want into a campaign and barely feel it. Other business concerns are out there, willing to do the same thing."

"You think they want to control legislation and elected officials?"

"Yeah. They just don't want to get their hands dirty doing it, so they have to hire somebody else to do it for them. Somebody very,

very good. Somebody able to steal the crown jewels from the Tower of London good."

"And Mary Evans is connected to this?"

"I think so."

"I think so, too."

Rafe didn't allow me to slack off in running, Krav Maga or weight lifting. He did kiss me while we made breakfast, though. Then he proceeded to give me a solid trouncing in Krav Maga.

James spotted him in weight training, as he usually did, but gave me a wicked grin while I lifted ten and twenty-pound weights nearby. I wanted to tell him to save the grin—I hadn't done anything to warrant it.

Yet.

"Colonel Hunter wants a meeting with you two, Maye and Nick tonight. Dinner at seven in the restaurant downstairs," James said when we were done.

Auggie wanted to talk about the funeral scheduled for the following day.

"We'll be there," Rafe said. "Come on, you. You need a bath." Hooking an arm around my neck, he propelled me out of the weight room.

Lunch came after a nice shower. No, it wasn't together. Rafe went to his suite; I went to mine. We met in the kitchen, clean, hair damp and hungry for lunch.

"What are your plans this afternoon?" he asked. "Want an omelette?"

"Omelette sounds good," I agreed. "I need to work on the book."

"You need to stop worrying about tomorrow."

"I can do that by writing."

"I have a better idea."

"Checkers?"

"Fucking."

"Gets right to the point. I like that," I said. "Want me to chop onions and tomatoes?"

"Yes."

"Cool."

❧

"Cabbage, time to wake up."

"Hmmm?"

"Dinner in an hour. We have time to shower and dress."

"Do I have to move? I like it here."

Here was cuddled against Ilya's chest.

"Come along. You can't wallow in bed all day."

"I'll bet I can."

"You want Colonel Hunter to turn the bugs on again?"

"I'm up."

"You are so very fine," his fingers trailed down my ribs as I sat up in bed.

"I thought we were getting up."

"We are. I merely wanted to remind you that this is for me."

"Who else would it be for?"

"You make me laugh."

"Right. Are you getting out of bed first, or do I have to crawl over you?"

"You may do whatever you like. I will enjoy the sight of it, either way."

Forty-five minutes later, we were on our way to the restaurant downstairs and the meeting with Auggie, Maye and Nick.

❧

"You will be driven to the White House at oh-five-hundred tomorrow morning, where you'll be briefed by the Secret Service agents riding with you and the President. The First Gentleman isn't going," Auggie said when we took our seats at the round table he'd chosen inside the restaurant.

"Thank goodness," I slumped in my chair. Graye Sanders, the First Gentleman, was just another target and his absence would make things easier for Rafe and me.

"The same goes for you," August nodded to Maye and Nick, "only you'll meet with the VP's guards."

Nick didn't seem happy that he'd been assigned to the VP, but Rafe and I'd had nothing to do with the assignments.

"Why the time change?" Rafe asked. "I thought we'd be leaving at seven."

"I had a conversation with the President, that's why," August replied. "Only she and I are currently in the loop on this, so keep it to yourselves and be ready by the designated time. Corinne, did you get a message from Dr. Shaw?"

My appointment with Dr. Shaw had been rescheduled so I could do this assignment. He didn't seem to mind—I'd gotten an e-mail from him earlier, giving me the time for the rescheduled session. "Yeah. We're good," I said. I wasn't looking forward to rising at four in the morning for our drive to the White House, but there wasn't anything I could do about it.

"Dalton has left the Mansion," August went on. "He'll be reassigned next week."

"Will he keep the Program secret?" Maye asked. I suppose Jeff had given her the particulars on Dalton's exit.

"He'd better," August muttered. "His communications will be monitored anyway. He probably knows that."

"This is a snarled mess," I said, rubbing my forehead. Our food arrived, so the conversation slowed as we began to eat.

"I don't feel good about this," I mumbled as I joined Rafe in the kitchen early the following morning. We'd slept in our own suites, if you can call tossing and turning sleep.

"What's not right?" he asked.

"Everything. It just feels—weird."

"We have to be downstairs in ten," he pointed out. "Are you ready?"

"I'm dressed. I guess that's ready."

"Come, then." He took my hand and led me to the door. "What do you think is the problem?" he asked as we walked toward the center of the floor and the stairs leading downward.

"It's as if everything is in flux," I said. "Like somebody who can't make up their mind whether they want strawberry or vanilla ice cream."

"Is it that unimportant?" We took the steps together at a quick pace.

"I don't think so—well, that's not exactly true. It's like deciding on strawberry, when you know it's safer, or vanilla, because it holds danger."

"An unusual analogy." We reached the second floor landing and proceeded down the steps to the first floor.

"It's the best I have after little sleep and an early morning," I said.

"Perhaps they'll stop at Starbucks, then," Rafe grinned at me.

"I'd kill for a vanilla latte right now," I mumbled.

"Even though vanilla might be more dangerous?" he teased.

"Please stop. You're way too cheerful. Don't you know that cheerfulness at this hour is unconstitutional?"

"I will curtail that activity immediately."

"Please do. And don't start it up again until I've had more coffee."

"I will keep that under advisement."

"Ready?" August waited at the bottom of the steps for us. Maye had also arrived, but Nick hadn't shown up yet.

"He's on the way," Maye said when August turned to her. Thirty seconds later, Nick came trotting down the stairs.

"Let's go," August said. Until then, I had no idea he was coming with us. I didn't question, however. August was finally getting the authority he deserved, and that was a good thing.

We didn't get to stop at Starbucks. Instead, we drove directly to the White House. Halfway there, I shrieked as the images hit me, and I must have shouted at Auggie while mentally screaming at everyone left inside the Mansion to get out. August hit an alarm on his cell phone, but that early in the morning, few people were already up and time was short.

The Mansion exploded with more than a third of its inhabitants still inside.

CHAPTER 10

"Corinne, hold your head up. We're here with you," Rafe soothed as we walked toward the limousine carrying the President. "We'll know something soon."

I wanted to drop to my knees and weep. Yes, most of those inside the Mansion still held me in contempt, but that didn't mean I wanted them to die.

"We need you near the President," August said on my other side. "For the same reason. Cori, you saved a lot of people who would have died. We'll talk about that later. Dr. Shaw has already called in—he's on the scene and helping those who need it."

"James?" My voice quavered.

"He's fine, but got banged up saving some files. He's all right, Cori."

I'd been too afraid to use what I had to check on him. I almost wept in relief.

"Corinne, I realize this is difficult for you, but we need you. I need you," the President said as we loaded into her limousine. She was flanked by two Secret Service agents, who wore communication devices and looked tougher than chainsaws.

Rafe could take both of them easily.

"Will you do something for me, then?" I asked, blinking at the President and working to keep the quiver from my voice.

"Anything—within reason."

"I know this is disrespectful, but will you have someone—preferably a bomb squad—go over every inch of the Vice President's casket? I have a terrible feeling they're not done with us, yet."

"Oh, dear God," August muttered.

"See to it," the President nodded at one of her agents. We listened as he gave the order and the vehicle began to move. Twenty minutes later, we received a message that the bomb had been located and disarmed.

"How in the name of Hades did it get there?" The President's anger erupted.

She was in her sixties and looked every bit of it, her once-dark hair showing much gray. Her eyes were still a clear blue, indicating the intelligence behind them, however. I could read the level of her anger easily.

"We don't have that information yet, Madam President, but we're working on it," her agent replied before barking orders into his communicator.

"You can be assured the ones responsible are long gone," Rafe sighed.

The funeral was uneventful.

The ride back to the White House was anything but.

Rafe heard the missile approaching the limo the moment the images hit my brain. Both of us shouted at the driver to stop, but he ignored us and hit the gas.

Sure, the limo was bulletproof. It might have been rocket-proof, too, for all I know. What I remember is this—the vehicle sailing through the air as the blast lifted it and flung it forward. Both Secret Service agents were shielding Madam President as we tumbled end over end along the street.

Rafe kept me safe, somehow, inside the shield he created. My head snapped twice as we bounced along, but his arms kept me from being jolted too much.

The problems came when we came to a metal-scraping halt after what seemed forever. Six men surrounded the vehicle, their weapons drawn.

A firefight with more Secret Service ensued, while we cringed inside the vehicle. Bullets pinged and whizzed against every part of the car as assassins attempted to shoot their way inside. I shuddered when one of our attackers slid down the side, the bloody wound in his head creating a sickening squeak against glass and metal as he dropped.

Capitol Police were on their way; Madam President's agents in the car called for backup the moment we'd settled on the road in one piece, but we'd already lost six Secret Service agents outside the car.

One of our attackers hit the windshield with the butt of his gun, pounding in a hard, regular rhythm while attempting to break reinforced glass to get to us. He died, dropping where he stood as Capitol Police arrived and began shooting.

Once the immediate threat was eliminated, Rafe loosened his grip on me. It wasn't until then I realized I'd been holding my breath during most of the ordeal. "We're all right," he whispered against my ear when things looked to return to normal. I offered a silent nod of agreement.

It took an hour of checking the streets and nearby neighborhoods before we were allowed outside the car and escorted back to the White House in a second vehicle by more Secret Service. I was a wreck by that time, but we still had a meeting with the President about the destruction of the Mansion, the bomb in the casket and the attack on her vehicle.

I sat on a sofa in a room near the Oval Office, listening while August and the President were updated on the Mansion's casualties.

The luxury of our surroundings felt like decorative punctuation marks at the end of a poorly worded and awkward sentence. It didn't fit. Shouldn't have been. I wanted to deny it when August read names off a list he'd received on his cell phone.

Kevin and Ken, plus their handlers—dead.

"You won't find Becker or Gene," I said flatly, my lips numbed and unfeeling as I spoke. "Tell the crew to stop looking for them."

"Why?" August turned to me.

"Because they brought the bomb inside the Mansion to begin with. I saw it, right there at the last. They didn't know Rafe, Maye, Nick and I were already gone. They dumped it in Dalton's empty suite."

"Why didn't you see this earlier?" The President asked.

"Because they couldn't make up their minds to do it until then," I said. Yes, I was giving the people present better insight into my talent, but it wasn't anything they couldn't already determine for themselves.

"She did say something this morning as we were walking downstairs at the Mansion," Rafe acknowledged. "That things seemed to be in flux."

"Madam President?" An aide knocked softly on the outside door.

"Come in," the President said.

"We just received word," the young man reported. "Captain Dalton was found dead inside his quarters and General Cutter has disappeared."

"Thanks, Greg," the President said.

"This is the best we can do at the moment," August said as we arrived at a building in Arlington. "It's scheduled for renovation, but for now, it's ours until they can find something else for us."

Sometime in the past, the four-story, square brick building had been used as upscale apartments. That was in the eighties, judging by the décor.

Every suite held a kitchenette—dated, of course, but still functional.

Rafe lifted an eyebrow at me. I shrugged. It didn't matter. We'd lost so many. The latest death toll was twenty-two, plus the six Secret Service agents. We only had the clothes we wore. Those things no longer mattered. So many families would receive bad news, and there was no comfort we could give them.

"This location isn't on anybody's radar," August said, taking a seat on a floral-patterned chair in the common area downstairs. "Those responsible for the bombing don't know about it, and the information won't be given to anyone else for a while. Cori, did you get anything on Preston? Did he leave with Becker and Gene?"

"No—to the last question."

"Dead then." August shook his head.

Nick, who sat nearby, wore a stone-faced expression. Preston was his handler.

"We heard from Jeff; he's on the way now with James," August said. "There's an office upstairs, but the equipment is outdated. That'll either be fixed in the next week or we'll be moved again before then. Safer's talking with the President now—he says he should have waited to send Dalton out of the Mansion. This likely put Cutter on alert."

"Cutter's involved in this?" Maye asked.

"It's likely. All his personal files and belongings are gone—his home was searched earlier. It's suspected that he was involved in Dalton's death, too."

"Why would he do that?" Nick asked.

"Because Dalton wouldn't cooperate, most likely, so Cutter convinced Becker and Gene to do his dirty work instead."

"What does that do to the Program?" Rafe asked quietly.

"It could blow up in our faces," August said. "Only one or two know everything there is to know about it. The rest of us only know what we need to know to do our jobs. With Becker in enemy hands and available for testing, somebody could backtrack and produce the same results in others."

"He was pissed because he wasn't going on assignments like he was before," Nick offered. "Becker, that is."

"He's placed all of us in danger," August said. "He was

presented with what he saw as a better deal after Safer told Gene the other night that he was useless. That set the wheels in motion."

"Where does that leave us?" Nick asked. "We're two men down, and those two men could help track enemy movements through cyberspace."

"Auggie, I know you may not think this is important right now, but we still need those photographs I asked for," I said. My fingers twisted nervously together as I asked, and I wouldn't have asked if I didn't feel it was important.

"I'll see what I can do," August sighed. "You understand that the President's mind is on other things, right now."

"Yeah."

"Cabbage?" Rafe's arms were around me the moment the door shut behind us. We stood inside his new apartment, both of us feeling as if we'd been dropped onto an alien landscape. Nothing there belonged to us, and the day's events had ensured that we were on unsteady ground.

"Oh, God, Ilya," I mumbled against his chest. The chessboard was shifting around us, in movements too swift and blurred for us to comprehend or counter.

"Corinne?" Dr. Shaw's voice came after the knock on Ilya's door. I moved away from him and Rafe called for him to come in.

"She could use a sedative, I think," Rafe said before I could stop him. "She's been shaking for hours."

"Corinne, I do have something with me. It'll relax you, that's all," Leo Shaw said. "You can eat something while it takes effect, then lie down and rest. There's pizza on the way," he added.

"But what if I," I began.

"Cabbage, trust me. Nothing will happen while you rest. I promise," Rafe said.

"Fine."

"Yes, it will be fine. Doctor, please proceed." Rafe waved Leo forward.

James walked in with a box of pizza two minutes after Dr. Shaw gave me the sedative. I think I fell asleep before I finished my second slice.

∼

Ilya

She fell asleep against my shoulder, a half-eaten slice of sausage pizza still in her hand. "Thank you," I nodded at Leo Shaw, who'd joined James, Corinne and me for pizza. James and Leo looked exhausted to me, but I didn't want to point that out. Corinne was my primary concern.

"No problem. James, take enough pizza with you to fill you up—I believe we have bedrooms waiting across the hall." Shaw nodded to James, who rose stiffly.

"I have pain medication," James waved off Shaw's offer of more. "I'll take it before I lie down."

"Good. Good-night, Rafe." Shaw led James out of my room and shut the door.

"Now, let's get you to bed," I whispered against Corinne's hair. "We will worry about these bastards tomorrow."

∼

Corinne

One of the reasons I hate sedatives so much is that I always wake feeling groggy, with a foggy slime confusing my brain. It takes hours to dissipate, while I wander about like a zombie shopping for groceries; nothing looks familiar or seems appropriate.

"Coffee." Rafe placed a paper cup in my hands. It took half the cup to realize I was drinking a Starbucks vanilla latte.

"Uh, thanks," I mumbled eventually. He led me toward a seat in the common area, where August, James and Leo waited for us. Maye, Nick and Jeff arrived moments later.

"We'll be moving tomorrow," August announced, once everyone was present. "I have people working on our new residence, now. They won't know anything about who's moving in, they're just making it habitable. The old staff—what's left of it—will arrive just before we do. While I don't have to worry about clothing or personal items, the rest of you do. James will be helping with that. Corinne, I hope you had your books backed up somewhere. Everything in your suite was destroyed."

"I have everything backed up," I said.

"I have her things backed up, too," James said.

"Look, at the moment, the enemy doesn't know that any of you survived. We're going to keep it that way," August said. "In fact, Safer and the President are the only ones who know for sure that you survived the attack at the Mansion. We'll let the enemy believe that they killed the Program for now."

"How will we explain our presence at the funeral yesterday?" Maye asked.

"We banned cameras inside the chapel, and your entrance and exit with the President and Vice President was under cover and not recorded. Only those inside the chapel may have seen you, and it's likely they thought you were a part of the Secret Service."

"Let's hope it stays that way for a while," Rafe said.

"James has a laptop; give him lists of personal items you'll need in the next three days, including clothing sizes. We'll have someone take care of that until we can do a better job. There's a food delivery on the way, so start making your lists now."

"I already ordered replacements for a lot of your stuff," James whispered to me as the others rose to walk to their apartments. "Since all the requests and orders have to go through me for approval anyway. Got stuff for Rafe, too."

"Lotion, underwear, mascara, bath soap and jeans?" I asked.

"All that and more, in the brands you like."

"Good. I didn't have any lotion after my shower," I sighed. "Thanks, James. You're awesome."

∽

We weren't informed of our destination when we walked out a back door and climbed into dark vans for the drive to our new residence the following morning. Rafe insisted that I stay with him both nights, but we used our time together to sleep. Neither of us felt up to sex, and I was grateful he didn't ask.

Virginia Beach, away from the water and in a wooded area, was where we ended up, at a huge, Mediterranean-style villa that would house all of us easily. While it wasn't as large as the Mansion, the grounds were smaller, gated, and would be easier to patrol.

There was only one large kitchen on the first floor, however, which disappointed Rafe and me. Our assigned suite was on the second floor, with a balcony. Yes, Auggie put us together. At least there was a sitting area and a study, so I could have space to write.

"You don't mind this?" Rafe asked as we walked through the suite together, deciding where we wanted things.

"No. Do you?"

"No. I want this. I would complain if they separated us." Those words came with a tight embrace and warm breath against my neck. I love his accent when he sets it free. Then, he is Ilya and not Rafe, just as he wants it.

"They'll set up a cafeteria kitchen in the apartment over the garages," James walked in, breaking up the embrace. "Sorry," he apologized.

"Where will they set up the common dining area?" Rafe asked, pulling away.

"Probably in the library downstairs. It's empty. Colonel Hunter says you can cook downstairs in the kitchen if you want, but others will probably use the space, too. At least until the kitchen over the garage is operational."

"James, what about Kevin and Ken?" I asked.

"They'll uh, be buried in Arlington. By order of the President."

"Oh."

"We're not allowed to go," he added. "For safety reasons. They're officially burying you, Rafe, Maye and Nick, too."

"In case Cutter and his associates come looking?"

"That's the idea. From now on, if you go with the President or any other official, you'll be disguised."

"Joy."

"It'll probably be a wig, contacts and dark glasses, but you never know," August walked in and stood by the large window in the sitting area. "This is a nicer view than the one I have."

"August, does your wife know?" I began.

"The President says she can live here if she wants. If she doesn't, she'll have to stay with her mother. It's too dangerous for her at the house."

"This is ridiculous," I shook my head. "You shouldn't be chased out of your house."

"It's fine—I can visit her now and then. She'll still see me about as often as before," August shrugged. "That's if she doesn't come."

"You think she won't?"

"She's not fond of how the government rules my life," August grimaced. "If she comes, she'll be confined to the building unless we can get her out secretly. She likes to shop, so there's a big negative, right there."

"Sorry."

"Not your fault. I signed up for this, you know."

"Someday, you'll have to tell me that story," I said.

"I'll consider it. Furniture is on the way. Hopefully we'll have beds by nightfall."

"I hope so, too. I'm not fond of sleeping on the floor."

"We need a new Secretary of Defense," the President pushed a list of names across her desk toward the Vice President. "Anybody you want to add to this list?"

The Vice President, who'd formerly been the Secretary of State, studied the names. Five were listed. "Where do you think Cutter is? Are you going ahead with the plan to say he left the position for personal reasons?"

"For now. We know why he's on the run, but the country doesn't. He still has plenty of supporters, and if we cry foul without him there, they'll accuse us of all sorts of trickery."

"Or worse. He was hoping for the VP slot, wasn't he?"

"I believe that's true. We dodged a bullet on that one."

"We paid for it, too."

"Yes, we did."

"Too bad Safer is retiring. He's the best fit, but he doesn't want it."

"He wants to go fishing and spend time with his family."

"I have no problem with that. Look, Amelia, will we be able to keep them safe—the ones who saved my ass in London?"

"Two of them are dead, Jon. In the bombing."

"Fucking hell. Which ones?"

"Kevin and Ken. To keep the others safe, including the ones with you yesterday, we're officially burying all of them except Becker in Arlington."

"They're in that much danger?"

"We're in that much danger, too. Think about it—get us and them out of the way, the country is ripe for the picking. Somebody tried to kill me yesterday, remember? If Cutter wasn't in on that, I'll eat my desk with salt and pepper."

"I know. The whole thing is preposterous. When did Cutter become such a liability? It happened right under our noses."

"Cutter's been on the fringe for a while. I hoped offering him the Secretary of Defense position would settle things and bring him around. That didn't happen."

"So, he has Becker, now?"

"And his handler. I have no idea what he intends to do with both of them, but we're already preparing for the worst."

Corinne

Our beds arrived sometime after midnight. Until then, Rafe and I had settled in a corner of our bedroom and tried to nap as comfortably as we could. That didn't really work so well.

When the furniture arrived, I was grateful for the army of government employees who unloaded and placed all of it while the villa's new residents watched in bleary-eyed satisfaction.

I just hoped none of them recalled us afterward, or broke their oaths not to disclose any of it.

"Now we go to bed," Rafe said after we'd placed clean sheets and a blanket on the mattress.

"Yeah. Please don't wake me up in the morning."

"I'll see what I can do."

I'd been waiting on the photographs of Mary Evans. I had mixed feelings about them the next day. Rafe was with me as we looked them over in August's new office. James had barely gotten the computer hooked up—at least he had a hook-up. Mine was scheduled for the following week.

"This one," Rafe and I pointed to the same man simultaneously. I had no idea he was looking, just as I was. Not only for a connection, but also for revenge.

This one wasn't pulling the strings, but he wanted something from the puppet master—through Mary Evans. "What does he want, and what is he willing to pay for it?" I blinked at August.

"This is the one I hunt. The one most dangerous to your government," Rafe informed our handler. "He will stop at nothing to get his way."

Notes—Colonel Hunter

"This was part of the deal," I told Shaw. "Rafe gave valuable information to us in exchange for medical care and the drug, and we agreed that we'd allow him to hunt this fucker down if he survived and the target was located. We didn't expect him to survive, or to be as useful as he is."

"A high-ranking officer in the Russian military is the target?" Shaw shook his head in disbelief. "This is a suicide mission for Rafe—admit it. It will kill Corinne to take him away."

"You think I don't know that? She's a hundred times better off if he's in the picture. The truth is, all the trouble we're having from the Russians? This guy may be behind it." I tapped the photograph lying on the table. "He's advising their President, and his advice isn't good for us or any of the surrounding countries."

"This places him in Ireland three weeks ago. What the hell was he doing there?" Shaw asked.

"Talking to Mary Evans. We know what happens if she's around."

"People are targeted and important things are stolen?"

"Exactly. I don't know who she's working for—Corinne was disappointed that we didn't have anything on that, but we do know that she's working on a deal with this asshole."

"Cori asked me to investigate whether Cutter may have had contact with this woman." I studied the image of Mary Evans—that was her name until we learned her real identity.

"That could explain a few things," Shaw muttered.

"It could. I'm sure he had his eye on the VP's office, so there's the possibility that he was involved in the former VP's death. It makes sense, especially when the bastard took off running after the Mansion was destroyed."

"If you can't get what you want one way, then look for an alternate route?" Shaw lifted his eyes to mine.

"That's what I'm worried about."

"I'm worried about what they all want. Do you think any of them are working together, or whether the one who's getting everybody else what they want has an agenda of his own, and isn't only interested in making money?"

"You're assuming it's only one person. What if it's more than that? We still don't have identification on those who attacked Corinne and the others. No fingerprints, no ID—these assassins didn't just drop from the sky."

"Still no leads on the one who killed the VP, either," Shaw pointed out. "We can't identify any of the men who attacked the President's limo. If others were there, they disappeared without a trace."

"Then, in the middle of all this, Rafe will be sent to track a Russian General; the President has already cleared it. I don't like this. He's walking into a trap."

Corinne

"When?" I hugged myself—I couldn't help it. Rafe was going to track a Russian General and get information if he could.

"I leave for Ireland in two days."

"No," I moaned.

"Cabbage," he began.

"I understand. I do. I just don't like being without you."

"You haven't had me that long."

"Honey, you're better than the best chocolate I ever had," I said. "And I'm addicted to chocolate."

"Ah. Where's my feisty, insulting cabbage?" His arms went around me and I closed my eyes with the pleasure of his warmth.

"In a depressed funk," I mumbled against his shoulder.

"Your appointment with Dr. Shaw is ten minutes away. Shall we go together?"

"That's scary."

"No. He will see both of us. You will tell things you have never said. He and I will hear those things."

"See previous statement."

"We have two days, cabbage. Let us make the most of them."

~

"You're both here?" Leo Shaw looked surprised. He should.

"Yes. Corinne will tell us a story," Rafe said, putting me on the spot. I wanted to kick his ankle. I didn't.

"What story is that?" Leo settled deeper into a new, leather chair behind a new, cherry-wood desk. His office was on the villa's first floor, in what should be a private study.

"Corinne will tell us things about the terrorist attack in France," Rafe pulled me onto the sofa and sat beside me. He'd wedged me between the sofa arm and his body, so I couldn't escape easily.

"What things?" Leo asked, his voice deep and even. He used the same voice to convince his patients that it was safe to tell him anything.

"Where do you want me to start?" I stalled. Any way you looked at this story, it would be painful.

"Start at the beginning," Leo said.

"The beginning? Well, when my husband and I walked into the Louvre that morning, it was the first time I saw the woman who calls herself Mary Evans."

Rafe stiffened beside me. "You saw her before?" Leo kept his voice even.

"Yes. She was going out the door, carrying a large plastic bag and a tote—both from the museum gift shop. I know now that original paintings and the crown were inside her bags."

"They'd already been replaced?" Rafe asked.

"Yes. I didn't know that then, of course. I know it now."

"You were married." Leo said it flatly.

"Yes."

"Will you tell us your name?"

"No. My name—and my husband's name—aren't on the list of victims."

"He is dead?"

"Yes. I watched him die. They killed him in front of me."

~

Notes—Colonel Hunter

"She didn't go into detail," Shaw said. "It was hard enough for her to tell us what she did."

"Where is she now?" I asked.

"I gave her something and Rafe is with her in their bedroom."

"So she was married."

"Yes. Still wouldn't give me her name. I don't know what she's protecting, but there's something there. The most horrible thing was the deaths of the children who were with some of the tourists. She said that five of the six terrorists were sociopaths and only wanted to cause pain and death. The sixth killed the other five at the end, then killed himself. I believe that was the plan all along, but the other five didn't know it. They thought their rescue was on the way."

"That's crazy," I shook my head. "No wonder she wouldn't talk about it. Nobody would want to talk about that."

"He thought she was dead, too, when he committed suicide."

"So she was forced to watch all of them die."

"Looks that way."

"Fuck."

"I think it's extremely important to Corinne that we find those who orchestrated that mess—as well as recent events. She and Rafe are convinced they're connected. You and I tend to agree with that assessment."

"They're connected, all right. We still don't have verification on the location of the items taken from the Louvre, or whether the British crown jewels are resting beside them, but I don't doubt for a moment that the same one paid for all of it."

"There's no lack of money to back Cutter's mad schemes, whatever those are," Shaw said.

"Billions," I agreed. "Enough to entice anyone with the resources to pull off this kind of larceny and assassination. Those people in the Louvre? Collateral damage, to provide an excuse for the robbery."

"And Corinne happened to be there. If she hadn't, we'd still believe that it was an act of terrorism only, and unconnected to the rest of this."

"Is Rafe set up with identification?"

"Several sets, with safe houses and drop box locations here and there. I think I'd worry more about him disappearing, except that he cares about Corinne."

"He cares about Corinne. That's not a lie. He'd do anything for her, I think. I just worry about separating them."

"She can't go—she'd be a liability."

"They both know that. What I suggest, however, is to get any information or photographs we receive from him to Corinne, so she can tell us what she knows."

"We've learned our lesson on that, I think. The President was shocked when she and Rafe pointed out General Baikov."

"She'd be wise to allow Corinne to vet anyone who comes close to her for any reason."

"I'll make that suggestion. All she needs is a photograph, after all."

∼

Ilya

Disturbing—her story. No wonder she was so reluctant to tell any of it. It opened wounds and she was ill prepared to deal with so much pain. I watch her sleep, now, surprised there have been so few tears through it all.

No—Corinne shakes instead of weeping, as if she has decided that those who brought this evil upon her are not worthy of her tears.

I agree.

Like me, she has a score to settle. It may turn out to be that our scores are with the same one—or ones. Both of us, in our own ways, have promised ourselves that the guilty shall not go unpunished. There is too much blood and too many deaths to avenge.

I love you, I murmur to her in my native language. She is asleep and cannot hear.

It is the truth, however. Yes, I loved another in the past, just as she did. They are gone, now, and we have each other. We understand one another. Perhaps it is fate. Who knows? She moves beneath my hand. I soothe.

∾

Corinne

I slept eight hours. Eight hours I could have spent with Ilya. We skirted the issue of our visit with Dr. Shaw, unwilling to bring that pain back into our lives. Instead, by mutual, unspoken consent, we went downstairs to the kitchen and proceeded to cook.

Somehow, James had performed a miracle and replaced most of what I'd had in my kitchen, including a bread machine. We had fresh bread baking, cookies in the oven, pot roast on the stove and were working on fresh green beans when people started wandering in.

Fried chicken was added to the menu—we didn't have enough pot roast for all who showed up, but we ended up serving just about everybody at the villa that night.

"Why didn't you invite me to dinner before?" August asked. He'd gone through a plate full of pot roast, mashed potatoes, gravy and green beans.

"Uh, you're married, remember?"

"Oh. That."

"She's not coming, is she? Auggie, are you sure you're okay with that?"

"Yeah. This is my work. Both of us get that."

"But," I said.

"No buts. This job is important, and I don't want to do anything else. End of story."

"All right. I just hope it doesn't put a strain on the relationship."

"What if I were stationed overseas? She wouldn't go there, either."

"Okay." I patted his shoulder.

"Want more bread?" Rafe carried a plate of fresh bread.

"I'll take a slice." August helped himself. "I like home-cooked meals."

"Me, too. That's why I wanted a kitchen," I said.

"That's why I wanted a kitchen—and Corinne," Rafe grinned and put an arm around my shoulders.

"Is that right?" I leaned back to look up at him. He kissed me in front of everybody.

CHAPTER 11

"General, this is quite unusual—the blood chemistry."

Paul Cutter watched the biochemist hired to examine Becker's blood as he tapped the computer screen. The molecular biologist standing nearby nodded at the biochemist's words —Cutter knew he'd never seen anything like it, either.

"You know I'm not interested in how different it is. I'm interested in separating the part of it that kills most other hosts. For research purposes, you understand. My colleagues and I are willing to pay handsomely for the results, and there's a bonus if we get those results within three months."

"That may be difficult to achieve," the molecular biologist said. "Although we're willing to do our best."

"I'd appreciate your best. Let me know if you need assistants or equipment. We have full funding for this project."

Corinne

Rafe didn't want me to go to the airbase with him. I didn't want to cry in front of him. I ended up only sniffling a time or two as I watched him climb into the standard-issue, dark van. We'd said our good-byes in private earlier. James and August stood with me as the van drove away.

"James will take over your self-defense instruction," August said as we turned to go back inside the villa. "Beginning tomorrow."

"James?" I blinked at him. He shrugged and grinned.

"He knows he won't get cookies if he's too harsh," August smiled. I hadn't seen him smile in days. "I expect him to be thorough, Corinne. I won't settle for pretending."

"Yeah? I still have bruises from Rafe. He never took it easy on me."

"He wants what I want, and that's you capable of fending off an attack."

"You worry too much," I muttered.

"I'll be waiting in the new workout room at ten tomorrow morning. That'll give you time for running and breakfast," James said.

"Yes, drill sergeant," I said. "Am I supposed to salute, too?"

"No. I'd have to teach you that, and I doubt you'd take it seriously anyway."

"True." I hunched my shoulders. They were trying to take my mind off Rafe's departure. I sighed.

∼

Two days later, after my self-defense class, running and weight lifting, my new computer arrived. James arrived with it, to hook it up for me.

"I got a two-terabyte hard drive, the same wireless keyboard and mouse you had before and a huge, non-glare monitor that's easy on your eyes."

That wasn't all—he'd ordered a new workstation, a comfortable chair and anything else I wanted, including a tablet, a laptop and a second monitor. I also had file cabinets for hard copies and research files.

"You know I could have paid for this," I said while he hooked up cables.

"I know. We didn't pay for the stuff that got blown up, so consider this your insurance payment. Besides, you need these new monitors for the photographs we'll be sending to you. All Colonel Hunter asks is that you study the photographs as soon as you can after we send them, and let us know if there's anything about them we should watch for."

"I'll certainly do that. Will we get anything from Rafe?"

"That's the plan, but it may be sporadic."

I couldn't send messages; August already said that. I found myself hoping that Rafe wouldn't be gone long, but that was unlikely and impractical. *Stay safe*, I sent in Rafe's direction as I watched James work on my computer.

～

Ilya

The streets of Dublin, narrow and crowded at night in the Temple Bar district, was where I stood when I received her message. *Corinne*. I missed her and found myself shoving the ache away. I had a lead on Mary Evans and was determined to track her down. If she didn't want to reveal what she knew, I think Corinne might be useful in that respect. The American President did say that she'd provide anything needed in my search.

My needs could include Corinne and her talents.

My lead was a man—one who'd barely been in the photograph I'd seen of Mary Evans speaking with Baikov. The man looked to be a stranger. Corinne never pointed him out—she couldn't see his full face. I was learning things about her, although we'd never discussed them.

She had to see their faces clearly to do what she did and to know what she knew.

This face was blurred and partially visible. I recognized the location in the photograph—a hotel near Temple Bar on Fleet Street. While I didn't expect to find Mary Evans standing on a sidewalk again, I could track down the man in the photograph who, as it turns out, drove a cab. He'd driven Mary Evans to the designated meeting place and then waited nearby to take her away again.

Armed with a computer-enhanced image, I intended to track him and his cab down. Ignoring brick-paved streets and square-cut, stone sidewalks between shops and buildings, I cautiously looked about me, studying every cab that drove past.

~

"I'm not sure why we're here, actually."

President Amelia Sanders studied the one who'd spoken. Three scientists sat in chairs before her, wearing expressions of curiosity and confusion.

"Because I couldn't reach Richard Farrell," the President said.

"He's probably in a tent at the South Pole," another spoke. "That's what I heard three weeks ago. You realize we only have partial information. Richard is the only one," he stopped speaking when the President raised her hand.

"One of the recipients is, shall we say, running amok on the outside," the President began. "I want to know—as much as you can tell me, anyway—what the full liability of that might be."

"Not good," the neurobiologist mumbled. "It depends upon whose hands he falls into, and what their goals may be."

"Think worst-case scenario," President Sanders replied. "While Dr. Farrell won't appreciate having his vacation with the penguins interrupted, I'm sending someone after him."

~

Corinne

"Cori," August laid a folder on the kitchen island next to me. I was making a grilled cheese sandwich for dinner, with tomato soup. Everybody else was lined up at the makeshift cafeteria over the garages.

"I thought you were going to send me digital images."

"This is how these arrived, and it was faster to run them down here than to wait for James to scan them."

"Gotcha. Where did they come from?" I dumped my grilled cheese onto a plate and lifted a photograph.

"Rafe."

"I'll look now. Want a sandwich?"

"Got ham?"

"Yeah."

He ate a club sandwich while I studied photographs Rafe had taken in Dublin.

"This looks familiar," I said, selecting one of the eight-by-tens and holding it up.

"He says it's a cab driver."

"Yeah. I can see that. This guy was only partially in that last photograph, wasn't he?"

"I wondered if you'd notice that."

"I'm noticing now."

"What can you tell me? Anything?"

"He's not above taking money for not-so-legal activities."

"Will he tell where he picked up and dropped off Ms. Evans?"

"He'd better. Just be warned, he may not live long afterward."

"Will that be a bad thing?"

"Not necessarily. He has some blood on his hands."

"You think someone is watching him?"

"I can't say for sure without seeing them."

"Got it. I'll make sure the information is passed along."

"Thanks."

Ilya

"I don't squeal."

The cabbie spoke through swollen and split lips. I'd had to work him over after catching him—he didn't want to cooperate.

"Fair enough. I'll just kill you and toss your body into the Liffey. I'm sure nobody will be surprised that you ended up there."

"Wait," he mumbled. "If I tell you, will you let me go?"

"Sure. I'll let you go," I said. "Just tell me about the woman."

Corinne

"Cori, can you give me a reason to arrest this guy and keep him in jail?" August was back, only this time, he stood behind me as I sat at my computer and scanned the latest chapter in my book.

"He killed his wife. She's buried in a wooded area," I said.

"Can you tell me where?" August suddenly held his breath—hoping, I'm sure, that I could tell him exactly what he wanted to know.

"Let me pull up a map on my other monitor—may as well justify the expense, huh?" I said and typed in the information needed. It only took a few seconds, after which I pointed to a spot not far from the American Ambassador's residence.

"Are you fucking kidding?" he hissed.

I switched to a satellite version of the map and enlarged it as much as I could. "There, in these trees," I said.

"Can you print that map for me?" August was all business, suddenly.

"Yeah." I printed the image, made a circle on it and handed it to him.

"I'll get on the phone right away. If this is true," August walked out of my suite, mumbling to himself.

Ilya

The cabbie was arrested by the locals the moment he walked out of the old warehouse. I'd let him go, as promised. The Garda was instructed to ignore the rope burns on his wrists and ankles, and the bruises and swelling on his face.

Corinne had come through for us, in a way I couldn't begin to understand. The body of the man's wife was found almost immediately; he hadn't hidden it very well. She'd been missing for five months. He said she was visiting relatives in Northern Ireland.

Somehow, my Cori had seen right through that. The information I received from the cabbie would send me to Edinburgh, and I had a flight scheduled the following morning, with a short layover in Manchester. That left little time to gather my things and get out of the safe house.

"Look, we need something to divert attention from our camp," Cutter explained.

"I have a target in mind already." Ted Ryan was more than pleased that Cutter approached him, and even happier that Cutter offered to provide funding and equipment for the endeavor. His militia needed new weapons and ammunition; working for Cutter provided a way to get those things.

"What's the target? I need to inform my associates."

"How about the capitol building in Sacramento?"

"You think you can pull that off? That would certainly be a coup," Cutter nodded with enthusiasm. "You have no idea how much I despise those people."

"We'll get it done. I'll need two million up front, though, and a quick trip for me and my boys to Canada immediately after."

"You got it."

Ilya

Half of Edinburgh Castle was destroyed by several bombs while I was in the air over Scotland. The news that the crown, first worn by

James V and housed at the castle, had been taken during the bombing greeted me upon landing.

Nearly a hundred tourists were dead. More were wounded. I cursed the fact that I hadn't gotten on Mary Evans' trail earlier, and cursed those in the American government who'd held the photographs back from Corinne and me. If we'd been given that information only a few days earlier, this might have been avoided.

Cutter was tied to this somehow and that only reinforced my idea —and Corinne's, that everything was connected. Someone was at the heart of all this, handing out favors in exchange for huge price tags or other favors in return.

I had to get to Mary Evans, if she were still in Scotland. Grabbing the duffel I'd brought with me, I made my way out of the airport. The first thing on my list was to contact those I knew in the states to see if they'd gotten information on Mary Evans when she landed in Edinburgh two weeks earlier, and whether there were any hits at hotels or on public cameras. The second thing on my agenda was to enlist Corinne's help. If anyone employed at the castle were in on the bombing, she'd be able to tell from their photographs. I merely needed the photographs to begin with. Therefore, I contacted Colonel Hunter to begin the process.

❧

Corinne

Ninety-six people were dead, most of them tourists, in the Edinburgh Castle bombing. More than sixty others were in local hospitals. Rafe was somewhere in the city; August brought photographs of castle employees and many of the tourists who'd died.

The CIA was working to get other photographs from Scottish authorities. It was my duty to look through those August brought to me on a flash drive.

"Auggie, do you know how awful it is to see photographs of people who've died?" I asked, forcing my way through photograph after photograph.

"I'd think you wouldn't see much," August said. I sat at my computer, going through information while August sat next to me, watching the images go by as I examined them.

"I see how they died," I said. "It's not pretty."

"Cori, that's disturbing."

"Tell me about it. This one—not an employee but in on it," I pointed at the screen.

"Registered as a Spanish citizen," August entered information onto a tablet.

"He was responsible for some of the explosives," I said. "Not all of them, though. Three others were recruited."

"That explains four separate explosions," he nodded. "Can you tell if all the others posed as tourists, or if any employees were involved? We need live ones to question."

"This one didn't know what was going on with the others. He only had his assignment. He was fooled, though. He had instructions to wait in the area that eventually got bombed, and then make his way to another room in the castle at a designated time. Someone detonated the bomb he carried while he waited for the proper moment."

"Fuck. Never mind," Auggie waved me back to my task as I stared at him. "Let's get through the rest and see if there's anyone else involved."

We found two of the three remaining bombers. That meant one was not identified as yet, or had gotten out alive. "You think he may have been the one who detonated the others?" August speculated.

"I don't know," I said, allowing my shoulders to slump as I sat at my computer. "These three didn't really know what was going on. They were tricked into believing they could get away after dropping their bombs off in toilets and such."

"One bomb did go off in a toilet," August blinked at me. "The explosives were portable, potent and likely hidden in clothing, on their person or in bags. Certainly not visible or apparent, unless you had dogs or some other form of detection. The toilet bomber walked right into a bathroom and left his package there. Probably locked the door behind him, so nobody else would find it before he could get away."

"Then he either got spooked or coordinated everything," I said. Auggie muttered *fuck* again. I shook my head as I stared at the photo of the third bomber. He was young—barely seventeen. I wanted to throw up.

"I'll send this information to Rafe and our departmental contacts," August rose from his seat. "I'll let you know if I get more, later."

"Thanks, Auggie."

"Cori, I should be saying that to you."

"Yeah."

~

"Look, I'll get the information to the proper authorities," the British Prime Minister promised the President. "If I hadn't had firsthand experience with what she can do, I wouldn't believe it myself."

"You'll find it accurate," President Sanders agreed. "We don't have the fourth bomber because we didn't have complete information from our sources."

"Understood. If I have anything else, I'll send it your way. We want these people caught quickly. It's a black eye against my government."

"It isn't just yours," the President admitted. "Trust me, others have been hit; they're just not aware of it yet."

"That's alarming."

"It is. Let me know if there's anything else we can do."

"I certainly will. Thank you for the information."

~

Ilya

I was met by a CIA operative working in the UK. The location chosen was a pub on the Royal Mile, far enough away that we could get in and out without drawing interest from guards and local authorities scattered behind numerous barricades. Nobody was allowed to approach the castle without permission.

With help from the Prime Minister through the President, I was about to have permission. I would also have a companion—the CIA wanted in, too. My contact identified himself as Gerald Nelson and didn't suspect I was anything except an American who worked for a separate agency.

He watched me with cautious scrutiny while I finished my coffee. I was resolved to send a photograph of my CIA confederate to Corinne soon. I'd learned early never to trust anyone.

That's when the text came. Pulling out my phone, I read the message. The cabbie in Dublin had been shot dead in his cell. Nobody had seen anything, or so they'd claimed.

Hunter had told me what Corinne said about the man—that he might not live long. Likely, someone didn't fancy him talking about some of his activities. Too bad he'd already talked to me; it just wasn't on record. It made me wonder if Mary Evans had returned to Dublin after her assignment in Edinburgh was completed.

"Ready?" I asked, standing abruptly.

"Whenever you are," Nelson rose from his seat. "Let's take a look at bombed rubble, shall we?"

Corinne

"What can you tell me about this one?"

"Auggie?" I took the printed photograph from him.

"Just curious."

"Okay." I studied the man. "He isn't using his real name. Works for a government agency. Somebody wants info from him bad." I stood in alarm. "Auggie, get Rafe away from this guy. He's connected to Cutter."

August was on the phone so fast he was a blur.

"The President wants us on a plane to Scotland tonight," August said. He'd run out of my office earlier to report his findings to the President. He was back, now, James right behind him. "Pack your bags, Cori. We'll be out of here the minute you're done."

~

I remembered the last time I'd been on a flight to Europe. My ankles had swollen, I hadn't been able to sleep and I felt miserable from jet lag for two days. Back then, I hadn't been to Scotland. It wasn't on the itinerary.

Now it was, only I didn't think for a moment that any touristy things were on the agenda. I was going there to study the one currently known as Gerald Nelson, CIA. This time, Dr. Leo Shaw sat next to me on a military jet, while James sat across the aisle and Auggie had a row to himself farther back so he could work on his laptop. None of that happened during my last trip, either.

"Are you all right?" Leo asked. "Do you need anything?"

"I'm fine," I assured him. "Will Maye and Nick be okay while we're gone?" Jeff, Maye's handler, was doing double duty, taking Nick on after Preston's death. He had his hands full—Nick liked Preston—a lot. He was so angry with Becker and Gene for causing Preston's death that he might explode, too. He and Maye needed a distraction—in the worst way.

"The President has a function—they'll be there in the background and away from cameras," Leo replied. "We'll be in contact with the President and Vice President if there's anything you should see."

"Good enough," I sighed.

"Corinne, what troubles you the most in all this?"

"That we won't find the one behind all this in time," I said.

"Will you tell me why you were reluctant to come to us with your abilities earlier?"

"I wasn't needed by the Program before. Living on the outside let me get research done that I can't do inside the walls."

"I think we might be able to lift restrictions on much of that, now. I'll speak with Colonel Hunter and the President."

"That would be nice, as long as I know the people who will be checking on my research."

"You need to see them?"

"Yes."

"I see. Is there anything you might tell me about Becker?"

"Becker is being brainwashed and Gene is being paid. Becker is a tool in the hand of the enemy, now. Even killing him won't mitigate the harm he can do. They'll just preserve his body to get what they want."

Leo stared at me for several seconds, as if he were considering how I knew what I did. "I'll go speak with Colonel Hunter immediately." He unbuckled the seatbelt and heaved himself out of the narrow chair beside mine.

Notes—Colonel Hunter

"Shaw?" I moved my laptop bag so he could sit beside me.

"Corinne says Becker is a tool in the hands of the enemy, now."

"That's what the President and the rest of us are afraid of."

"I believe her. She says it doesn't matter if he dies—they'll preserve his body to get what they want."

"Fuck. I didn't realize Cutter knew so much."

"He likely has spies everywhere. Gene probably spilled everything he knew."

"Do you remember the nurse who gave Corinne too much medication the first night she was at the Mansion?"

"She died in the explosion."

"I think we should research her background—bank accounts and such."

"Can we do it from here?"

"I'll start the process now. James!"

~

Corinne

The moment Auggie yelled for James, I pulled the jacket I'd brought with me around my shoulders, leaned back and closed my eyes. They could do part of my research for me while I slept.

~

Notes—Colonel Hunter

"Look what we have here." James handed his tablet to me. A photograph was displayed. I recognized both people in the picture. Nurse Shelbi Oaks and Gerald Nelson, CIA—having dinner at an upscale restaurant two months earlier. She'd posted it on social media, probably without Gerald's knowledge or consent.

Corinne said Nelson was connected to Cutter. Now, Shelbi Oaks was likely connected to both. Too bad she was dead—I wanted to question her myself.

"Deposits from us and from another source were found in her bank accounts—regular deposits."

"James, I want to know if she was ever responsible for drawing blood from anyone in the Program." Shoving down the panic that threatened, I waited for James to search medical records. At least we still had those—the database wasn't kept at the Mansion for security reasons.

"Twice," James confirmed. "The first time eight months ago, the second, four months ago."

"Fuck. Cutter may have had information long before he came on board as Secretary of Defense."

"It's likely they only had a small amount—an attending would notice if too much blood was drawn. They might have stolen enough to get a taste, but not enough to do research. Until they got their hands on Becker, anyway," Shaw said.

"What are they hoping to do, Colonel?" James looked worried.

"It could be any number of things. Don't panic until we have a better handle on this, all right?"

"Perhaps we should send Maye and Nick after Becker," Shaw suggested. "It would have been better with Kevin and Ken, but we may be able to find someone nearly as good to track information for them."

"It's a thought. Maye is decent, but she lacks the intuition the brothers had. I'll get this to the President, and she'll make the final decision."

∼

Corinne

The trip to the designated hotel didn't take long after we landed. Jet lag affected all of us, but there was some hope I might see Rafe. That kept me going. What I didn't expect was that Rafe had the one calling himself Gerald Nelson tied up in his hotel room.

I studied him while August pulled up a photograph of Gerald and nurse Shelbi on his tablet. "Recognize this?" he said pleasantly, shoving the tablet in Gerald's face.

"I don't know what you're talking about," he snapped.

"It's difficult to deny involvement when the evidence is right in front of you. We've checked this for authenticity. The waiter remembers taking the photograph for your girlfriend, Shelbi. You didn't want a photograph taken; she had him do this from a distance so you wouldn't know. Too bad you didn't tell her why she shouldn't take pictures and post them on the Internet. We also have reliable information that places you in General Cutter's camp. Would you like to discuss why that's a problem?"

"He won't, because he arranged to have the Vice President killed and the bomb stuffed inside his casket," I said.

"Who the fuck are you?" Gerald turned to me and hissed. Rafe, who stood close by, backhanded him. Hard.

Four hours later, I studied the men chosen to escort Gerald back to the U.S. Gerald chose not to implicate anyone else, and wanted a lawyer. The money trail wasn't pretty, though. Some of it was traced through business concerns, all of which were against the current U.S. government.

The guards were all right—at least for the trip back, but like the cabbie from Dublin, I didn't have high hopes for Gerald's continued survival.

Anybody who had any connection to any of this died after their arrest. "Enjoy your flight," I nodded to Gerald as he was escorted toward the plane we'd brought to Edinburgh.

"Corinne, what will happen to him?" August asked as Gerald's shackles were checked before he was loaded onto the plane.

"They'll kill him," I said. "After he lands."

"Do you know who?"

"I haven't seen them, yet."

"Cabbage?" Rafe's arms came around me as we watched the plane begin to taxi down the runway.

"Honey?" I turned my head to look at him.

"Thank you for coming." He leaned down to kiss me.

CHAPTER 12

*C*orinne

We were allowed to sleep for seven hours before rising. A trip to the bombed castle was on our agenda for the day. Rafe and I spent the night together, and we'd probably slept for five hours. Maybe five and a quarter; I wasn't looking at the clock. We met Auggie, James and Leo for breakfast before our departure. We received the news while we ate.

Gerald was shot in the head during his transfer to a designated holding facility. The gunman shot himself immediately after. The assassin had no identification on him, and like those who'd tracked Rafe and me at the mall, nobody could figure out who he was.

The problem? He was identical in every way to the twins who'd tracked Rafe at the mall, right down to the fingerprints. It's as if someone made a photocopy of the first one to make the second and then a third. Sadly, all three were dead. "Auggie, have they run tests on these people?" I asked.

"I believe someone is working on that," he hedged.

"What are they finding?"

"That's classified, Cori. Even I don't know."

"But you know something's up, don't you?"

"That is the indication," he agreed. "Eat. We have to leave in ten minutes." I went back to my scrambled eggs and grilled tomatoes.

~

"We're attempting to save as much as we can to rebuild," our guide informed us as we walked around a pile of mangled cannons. The cannons used to line a stone wall. That wall was now rubble, barely guarding a precipice that someone could tumble over easily and fall to the courtyard far below.

Past that and below the castle remains lay Edinburgh, which was clouded in a light mist. Fog lay over the water in the distance. I could see a clock tower rising at the side of a tall, stone building below the castle and in between, a dark church spire surrounded by other buildings—many built centuries earlier. The castle walls still standing were built of pale and dark-gray stones intermingled with browns and near-blacks. I wished I could have seen it whole.

Rafe placed himself between me and the edge of the blasted wall. "I don't plan to jump, honey," I mumbled.

"I wouldn't let you," he replied. "Let's go. It's wet and you're cold. Besides, there are other things to do and people to see."

A meeting of guards and employees had been arranged to discuss the rebuilding efforts, memorial services and the theft of the crown jewels. I was there to study the people attending.

Auggie—that one. The young woman in the gray trench on the third row, I sent to him. I'd quickly scanned the crowd after they'd taken their seats. August nodded to me before pulling our guide toward the door for a private discussion. She had no idea what was in store for her.

~

Ilya

"I sneaked her into a private wedding party held at the castle a week before the bombing," she wept. "I thought she cared about me. She visited with me several times in the last four months."

"I believe she led you on," Colonel Hunter said. We sat in a private office near the castle gate while the young woman, identified as Alynne Nicholls, was questioned.

I'd insisted that Corinne wait outside with Dr. Shaw and James—in case the woman didn't cooperate. "This woman was also connected to the thefts in London, when the Tower was breached," Colonel Hunter continued.

"I'm so sorry," fresh tears fell. "I had no idea she wanted to destroy the castle. I love my job here."

That job had already evaporated. "Where is she now? Have you had contact with her?" I demanded.

"No. She broke up with me."

I wanted to curse. I didn't. Mary Evans wasn't above using anything at her disposal to get what she wanted, including emotional attachments with others.

"What information did you get from her—anything personal? Did she say where she was from?"

"She said Amsterdam, but she traveled a lot for her work."

"And what was that?"

"She said she was a magazine photographer. She had a nice camera and equipment."

"I'll bet she did," Alynne's supervisor exploded. "She took fucking photos of the castle so she could bomb the hell out of it. And you let her, without notifying me or anyone else."

"She gave me this," Alynne pulled a business card from her purse. "I carry it with me all the time."

"Did you ever call this number?" Colonel Hunter examined the business card. It had a name and contact information on it—Denna Philpot with TravelGlobe Magazine.

"Yes, but I always had to leave a message."

"Good. We'll take this. Is there anything else you can tell me about her?"

"She likes Mexican food."

"Favorite restaurants?" I asked.

"The one on Cockburn street—I can't remember the name. She

always paid cash. I never saw her use a credit card."

"We'll talk to the staff there, then." I was done with her. She'd be arrested, but I had no idea what would happen to her. It wouldn't hurt to have her watched, however.

"I'll have the President's office communicate with local authorities," Colonel Hunter nodded to Alynne's supervisor. "This woman is likely in danger, just because she spoke with us."

"I'll be waiting for that call," he said. We walked out. I wanted to pull Corinne close—I felt we were being watched but could find no overt evidence of it.

Ilya, I don't feel safe. I heard her message clearly as I walked toward her.

"Get us out of here," I barked at Colonel Hunter while grasping Corinne's hand. The office building blew up behind us as we raced through the door.

∾

Corinne

The fifth explosion at the castle was all over the news, but there were only two casualties—Alynne and her supervisor. Our presence in the same building was carefully edited from any newsfeeds, via instructions from London.

Somehow, the bomb had been strategically planted in the lining of Alynne's purse to take care of her if she were caught and questioned. The information we had was quickly transferred to London and then to the U.S., while the source of the bomb was identified. Alynne, who was mostly innocent, would take the blame for everything. That news was already splashed across televisions worldwide.

Copies of the business card was passed to other departments for further study while we piled into Rafe's latest safe house. It only had two bedrooms, so that could pose a problem.

Yes, I was shaky. I hated that, but we'd had too close a call. Neither person in that office knew of the bomb, leaving me mostly blind to its presence. Rafe felt uneasy eventually, just as I did, so he acted quickly, shoving us out the door and onto the stone courtyard, where we were knocked flat from the blast behind us.

"Cabbage, your nose is bloody and there are bruises everywhere," Rafe pointed out when we walked wearily into the safe house.

"You didn't come out of it unscathed," I pointed out. "Nobody did."

"Look, there are two bathrooms; who wants to go first? First-aid kits are in both," Rafe said.

"James, why don't you go?" I said, offering one of the bathrooms. James had a nasty cut on his chin and his shirt was hanging in shreds from his right arm. "I can help with the cuts after you clean up if you want."

"I'll take the help," he nodded.

"Auggie, take the other one. You don't look so good," I said, nodding to him. "I still think you ought to have that cut on your arm sutured."

"I'll find bandages," Leo offered. Of all of us, he'd been in the front and gotten the least of the blast. "Corinne, I'll take care of James after he showers; I'm worried about his wrist. Meanwhile, you and Rafe should let me know if anything needs attention."

"I'm okay, I think," I replied. "Just shaky as usual. Rafe?" I turned to him, then.

"I'm as well off as you—probably better," he said. "I just want a shower soon, that's all."

Ilya

I'd landed atop Corinne, so she'd hit her head on the courtyard stones. That's where the bloody nose had come from. I'd shielded our backs, therefore it was our fronts that received the damage.

"Cabbage, come into the kitchen; I'll clean your face," I offered.

"Well, since you can see it and I can't," she shrugged.

"Let me know if you need help," Dr. Shaw said as I led Corinne toward the small kitchen sink.

"Now," I said, pulling a clean kitchen towel from a drawer and turning on the taps. "Let's see how bad this nose is."

"I can't feel it," she said. "I'm too scared, I think."

"Then I'll make an assessment and determine whether Dr. Shaw should take a look. You may not feel the full extent of your injuries until later, anyway." Placing my hands beneath her arms, I set her on the kitchen counter. When the water was warm enough, I wet the towel and began cleaning her face.

"It's still bleeding," I said, wiping fresh blood away from her nose. "Here," I pulled a paper towel from the nearby roll and handed it to her. "Apply pressure while I clean the rest of this."

"Okay, boss."

"Yes," I nodded at her statement. "I am the boss right now. If you hurt anywhere, I expect you to tell me."

"Do I get to be the boss when I clean you up?"

"You can be as bossy as you like. Whether I listen or not is another thing."

"Typical."

"If typical involves my anger and concern after my cabbage is hurt, then yes, I am typical."

"I feel the same way, you know," she pointed out. "I want to slap somebody down for what they did to you, James and the others."

"Then I appreciate your concern and anger on my behalf," I said. "There is a terrible bruise on your forehead. I thought it might be mostly dirt. It is mostly bruise, instead."

"I don't really feel it," she shook her head at me.

"Hold still, my darling. Let me clean the rest of this. Then we'll let Dr. Shaw have a look."

I wasn't expecting what happened next—her eyes filled with tears. "What is wrong? Did I hurt you?" I asked, pulling the cloth away.

"Oh, God, Ilya, where have you been all this time?" She wrapped her arms around my neck and sobbed.

∾

Corinne

Why can one gentle word of endearment make you fall apart? "I'm so sorry," I sniffled and attempted to pull away.

"No," he said, running a hand down my back in a soothing caress. "Don't be sorry. We've had too many brushes with death lately. Your reaction is understandable."

"This is such a horrible mess." I leaned away successfully, then. "Come on, let's look at you, now. Any particular place to start?"

His left elbow was bruised where he'd landed on the stone courtyard, and ought to be X-rayed. I didn't say that as I cleaned dirt and grit away from his skin. Both of us looked as if we'd been tossed off a moving motorcycle, front-first.

"The President is shutting down this operation for now," August walked into the kitchen holding up his cell phone. "She's calling us back. Nick has disappeared."

The flight home wasn't comfortable—even cleaned up we looked as if we'd been in a brawl and come out losers. "I'm sorry," I patted Rafe's hand.

"I will track him eventually. And her, too. I hope they know I'm on their trail," Rafe growled softly.

"Any idea where Nick is?" August settled onto the seat across the aisle and pointed his question at me.

"He's hunting Becker," I said.

"To join him?"

"To kill him."

"I thought they were friends."

"That was before Becker and Gene got Preston, Vance, Carol, Ken and Kevin killed. Every time I saw him after the Mansion bombing, he looked like a pressure cooker about to explode."

"So he's hunting on his own," August dropped his head against the seat back with a sigh. "This isn't good."

"He could get himself killed," Rafe said. "Cutter has too many resources at his disposal."

"Nick knows how to survive in the wild," August sighed. "I have no idea where he'd start looking for Cutter, though. We've received no intel on his whereabouts from the moment he started running."

"Is the President prepared to call him an outlaw yet?" I asked.

"I don't know. She wants a meeting when we get back."

"Auggie," I half rose in my seat. The only thing keeping me from crawling over the seat in front of me was the seatbelt and Rafe's hands. Cutter was watching the carnage; he wanted to see the capitol in Sacramento fall, so he'd arranged for a view nearby. The explosion happened on the lowest level, in the middle of a wedding reception, bringing the dome down on top of two hundred guests.

I'll watch you die with pleasure, you bastard, I sent to him just before I fainted.

～

"Cabbage, your nose bled while you were out."

I woke propped against Rafe's chest, a cold, wet cloth held against my face.

"Did Auggie get the news?"

"He did."

Rafe and I were in the back of the jet, near the bathroom. Rafe had taken the entire row of seats for us, so he could stretch out and hold onto me at the same time.

"How many?" I asked.

"Are you sure you want to know? Someone is already taking responsibility—he sent video to the national news organizations."

"Cutter's paid monkey, no doubt," I said. "Do we have photographs of him?"

"I believe Colonel Hunter is waiting for Dr. Shaw's approval before he shows you anything."

"Then his approval can't come soon enough."

~

"Ted Ryan," Auggie handed his tablet to me so I could watch the video. We drove toward the villa in the back of a limousine the President sent to pick us up at the air base.

"He's the one," I agreed, studying Ted Ryan's images. "Paid by Cutter and Cutter's allies to bring down the house, so to speak." I blinked as Ted Ryan, in front of a white wall, proclaimed that the United States belonged to him and his constituents. He'd watched too many terrorist videos, evidently, because he brandished an automatic weapon as he spoke to the camera.

"Good luck finding me, you fuckers," he said at the end. I got an unedited version of the recording—the news stations bleeped out his profanity.

"The whole nation is terrified and every statehouse, including the ones supposedly on Ted's list of approved bureaucratic vendors, is covered in security and nobody is going in or out without getting X-rayed and cavity-searched first," Auggie muttered.

"Do we have photographs of anyone else associated with Mr. Ted Ryan?" I asked.

"Here." James leaned forward and handed me a second tablet. I stared at three photographs.

"Yeah. All of these were in on this," I agreed, handing the tablet back to James.

"After our meeting with the President, we have scheduled appointments with medical personnel at the villa. Just to make sure nothing serious is going on," Auggie held up a hand.

He didn't mention my fainting, but I knew Leo Shaw wouldn't let that go without doing an MRI and who knew what other tests, just to make sure my head was in one piece.

"What about Maye?" I asked.

"She's upset about Nick, evidently. Jeff has been trying to calm her down, but she wants to go after him."

"Understandable," I said. "I have a question. If Nick were pitted against Becker, who'd win?"

"Becker is a bull, while Nick is a tiger," Auggie said. "I'd put my money on Nick."

"Rafe?" He'd been silent, listening to the conversation and watching the video with me. He'd know whether Nick might take Becker.

"Becker relies on brute strength. Nick uses his head," Rafe replied. "Perhaps you'll tell me later what this is about?"

"Sure."

"Good." He pushed a lock of hair behind my right ear and offered a smile.

"Madam President, they're here." We followed the President's aide into the Oval Office.

"Thank you, Will. That will be all," the President rose to greet us as we trooped in. Will shut the door behind him when he left.

"Good lord, you look like you've been hit by a truck," Amelia Sanders shook her head and pointed toward seats. We waited for her to sit first, then took our seats with grateful sighs.

She was right—all of us had facial bruises, scrapes and scratches, while I still nursed a bloody nose. James' wrist was probably broken, but he was toughing it out until he could get an X-ray.

"If Rafe hadn't protected our backs, we'd be in worse shape," August pointed out.

"Thank you," the President nodded toward Rafe.

"We wouldn't have the information we do if it hadn't been for Corinne," he added.

"We already have someone working on the information you sent on the woman, but so far, all we have is disconnected numbers, an abandoned website and an e-mail address that has been canceled. We're still doing research. Our attention, however, has turned to the disaster in Sacramento."

"Tell her, Corinne," August nodded to me.

"Cutter paid Ted Ryan for this," I said. "James has photographs of three others who were involved."

"Ted Ryan and his militia have been a problem for twenty years," the President leaned back in her chair with a frown. "Long before I took office. His biggest problem with me is that he thinks I should be in a kitchen somewhere, doing dishes and cooking. His is a male-dominated world," she added, "where women have no place in positions of authority. He backed Cutter when Cutter ran against me in the last primary. The FBI keeps track of his movements and his social presence online. He made no secret of the fact that he'd never want a woman in the White House."

"He's a murdering creep," I said. "And I'm only saying creep because saying what he really is involves the worst profanity I can come up with."

"I tend to agree," President Sanders said. "What can we do about Nick?" She turned back to Auggie.

"No idea. Corinne needs medical attention, as do Rafe and James. I'll discuss this problem with Maye and them afterward and get back with you, if that's all right."

"Absolutely. If you need resources you don't have at the moment, let me know. I'll do what I can."

"Thank you, Madam President."

"You're welcome."

Rafe insisted on waiting outside while they did the MRI. I'd never had one done of my entire body, but they were doing one now. I thought Auggie might have a stroke when somebody suggested taking a blood sample.

That was tabled, and I was glad.

A mild concussion was the diagnosis afterward, and I was given medication for the cuts, scrapes and pain.

Rafe's elbow was sprained, so he was outfitted with a sling and told not to use the arm for a few days. I didn't point out that he couldn't do Krav Maga lessons like that.

James had a hairline fracture on his wrist, so he was the only one who ended up in a cast. I felt sorry for him—it interfered with his typing.

"I'm not letting you have alcohol for a few days, although we need a drink," Rafe muttered as he followed me into our shared suite.

"That sucks."

"What would you like to do instead?"

"Stay away from mirrors. My whole face is purple."

"Let us rest and consider what we should do later, eh?"

"Yeah. I'd like to lie down."

Nick

I can remember clearly the times Becker and I belittled Corinne. Called her a worthless cunt—or worse. Becker's biggest problem with Corinne was she refused to go to bed with him. I could see why, now.

Corinne turned out to be better than both of us.

Her note was still inside the envelope I pulled from my jacket pocket. Also stuffed in the envelope was ten grand in small bills.

Just in case, her note read. The envelope had been shoved under my door at the villa the morning she left for the UK. Somehow, she suspected what I was thinking.

The money would allow me to do what was necessary to track Becker and his fucking handler, Gene. I had no qualms about naming Gene the instigator in this mess, but Becker knew better. He knew what giving his blood to enemies of the state might cause.

I cursed Cutter under my breath. As much as Gene was responsible, Cutter made it all possible.

They'd taken an oath, goddammit. All of them.

I'd sat in a booth at a truck stop, having dinner when the capitol in Sacramento fell. Somehow, I knew Cutter was behind it, I just couldn't prove anything to anybody. I was back on the road, now, my backpack hefted over a shoulder as I made my way into North Dakota. Rain pattered on the hood of my jacket as I trudged along soaked back roads.

Maye said Corinne was capable of transfer. I wasn't sure of that until now.

Nick, her voice sounded in my mind. *If you want Gene and Becker, they're with Cutter.* She even gave me a fucking address in Utah. *They have guards,* she added. *Call for backup, unless you want to commit suicide.*

I had no intention of committing suicide. I had friends, and I intended to ask them for help.

Notes—Colonel Hunter

Corinne and Rafe were still asleep when I received the news. Sometime during the early-morning hours, Ted Ryan and four others involved in the Sacramento bombing had driven off the Ship Canal Bridge in Seattle, killing all inside the white van. Two died when they hit the water 182 feet below the bridge; the other three drowned before a rescue crew could get to them.

They'd been driving toward Canada. I suspected they had someone waiting somewhere, to get them past the border. Ted Ryan wasn't the brightest of people for sending the video claiming responsibility for the bombing before he left the country, but Cutter had guaranteed safe passage, somehow. It made me wonder if Cutter had used Ryan, then cut him loose.

"James, see if there were cameras on that bridge. I want to know if this accident was no accident," I said.

"Right away, sir," James called from his desk. "Do you suppose Cutter was attempting to divert attention to someone else?" James asked after a few moments.

"Possible, but we know better."

"Because of Corinne," James walked into my office. "If she hadn't given us a heads-up, we might be in the dark on this."

"True."

"Here," he handed his tablet to me after tapping for a few seconds. "Camera images of the accident."

James and I watched as the van suddenly careened across four lanes of traffic at high speed. The vehicle's front wheels ran up and over the railing, with no braking evident. Then, the van teetered on the railing for a few more seconds while two other vehicles pulled over nearby. Before any of the other drivers could reach the van to help, Ted Ryan and his crew toppled over the side and the van dropped into the water below.

"Karma really is a bitch," James shook his head as we watched the video a second time. The video had been posted by a Seattle news station, and all the national news programs were showing it, along with photographs of the bombed capitol building in Sacramento.

"Too bad Cutter wasn't in the van with them," James mumbled as numbers of the dead in the Sacramento bombing rose from the estimate given the night before.

"Let me know when Corinne and Rafe show up in the kitchen for coffee. I want to speak with them," I said, handing the tablet back to James. "Get me a copy of that video, too, and put it in a file."

"Yes, Colonel."

~

Corinne

"We'll have coffee; that ought to wake you up," Ilya kissed my temple.

"Something needs to wake me up," I sighed. "I'm not sure I can move." All my aches and pains had come to call that morning—my body had stiffened and complained during a restless night.

"Come along, moving will help," Ilya claimed as he sat up on the edge of the bed.

"Right."

Dressing that morning turned into an agonizing chore, as arms refused to accommodate coordinating sleeves. Eventually we wore enough to walk downstairs, which became an uncomfortable trek of uncooperative muscles.

"Cori, didn't you take your pain medication?" James waited in the kitchen for us, a cup of coffee in his hand.

"Not on an empty stomach," I said. "I have it with me." I pulled the small bottle from my sweater pocket, the pills rattling against plastic as I shook it at him.

"I'll get milk," James offered and slid off his barstool to walk to the fridge.

"Thank you."

"I beeped Colonel Hunter; he wants to see both of you," James said, handing a small glass of milk to me. I took my pill while Rafe made two cups of coffee.

"Does he want eggs?" I asked, shuffling to the proper cabinet to get a skillet.

"He's had breakfast, but he might want coffee," James said as Auggie walked into the kitchen.

"I do want coffee," he said, sliding onto a barstool next to James'. Rafe made a third cup and placed it in front of him.

"Ted Ryan and his bombing buddies died after driving off a bridge in Seattle last night," August said pleasantly, as if he were describing the weather instead of five deaths.

"Gee, that's too bad," I muttered, setting the skillet on the stove and heading toward the fridge for eggs. "Honey, do you want eggs and bacon or an omelette?" I asked Rafe.

"Omelette. Let me help."

He chopped ham, onions, tomatoes and mushrooms while I beat eggs and added milk. *Honey*, I sent in his direction, *you are amazing. I've never had a man who knew his way around the kitchen before.*

I poured eggs into the skillet, and he followed shortly with enough meat and vegetables to make a nice omelette. Two omelettes turned out to be enough for all four of us—Auggie decided he was hungry after all.

"How's the pain?" Dr. Shaw asked as he wandered into the kitchen twenty minutes later.

"Okay," James answered first, holding up his cast-covered wrist.

"Medication's helping," I said. "Want anything to eat?"

"Just coffee. I had breakfast earlier," he said, turning the coffee pod carousel and choosing the coffee he wanted.

"Coffee?" Maye walked in.

"Have a seat, I'll get it," Leo offered.

"You guys don't look so good," Maye said, nodding to us.

"You should see the other guys," Rafe grinned.

"Will we be sent after Nick?" Maye asked Auggie, her frustration over his absence evident in her voice and expression.

"I haven't gotten a call from the White House yet," August said. "This is a tough decision, Maye. Surely you realize that."

"I know. I just feel powerless and angry. Angry that Kevin and Ken are dead. Angry that Becker is more of an asshole than anybody suspected. That Gene is leading him down the wrong path. That Nick felt he had to take matters into his own hands."

"We all feel that way," Leo said. "It's understandable. Would you like an appointment this afternoon, so we can talk about it?"

"Yeah. Colonel Hunter, will you let me know the minute you get an answer from the President?" A silent plea clouded Maye's blue eyes as she blinked at August.

"I'll come to you first," he promised.

"Thank you."

CHAPTER 13

*C*orinne

We heard the helicopter approaching from a distance. I'm sure half the villa's population was staring out windows as the chopper landed on the helipad behind the house.

The Vice President and two guards stepped out of it and met August, Jeff, Leo and several others on the back patio. They were locked inside Auggie's office for an hour.

The Vice President flew away again after that. Then, the knock came on our door. James was outside when Rafe answered. "Colonel Hunter wants to see you in his office," he said. Rafe turned and motioned for me to follow.

"I've been named Director of the Program, or what's left of it," August announced when Rafe, Maye and I were called to his office for a short meeting. What he didn't say was that he'd be appointed Secretary of Defense in a few days, too, following Congressional approval.

That wouldn't make Cutter happy at all.

"Congratulations," I said. "You deserve that and more."

"Corinne, that means a lot to me," he said, his dark eyes shining. "Would you mind having dinner with me tonight, so we can discuss what to do about Nick? The President can't make up her mind on this, so I'd like your help."

"If you want. Just me, or Rafe, too?"

"Just you, if you don't mind."

"All right."

"I didn't know they did this," I said, turning in a circle to take in the private dining room located over the sunroom at the back of the villa.

"Started just before we left for Scotland. Isn't completely finished yet, but it makes sense, doesn't it?" Auggie said. "People can have private dinners without the noise of the cafeteria and everybody else listening in."

"Yeah."

We waited to begin our conversation after drinks were served. Champagne flutes were set in front of us, along with water goblets and a basket of bread.

"I didn't know you liked champagne," I said as it was poured for both of us. "I can only have a sip—concussion, you know."

"I know. This is in celebration of my new job," he said. "Since my wife can't be here," he lifted his glass in a toast.

"More power to you, Auggie," I clinked my glass against his.

"Now," he said when food was placed in front of us and our waiter left. "What do you know about Nick, and what should we do about it?"

"Nick is doing just fine," I said. "He wants Becker and Gene, but if Cutter happens to be in the way, it'll be too bad for him, too."

"This isn't something he can do alone, even if he does manage to find them."

"Auggie, sometimes things aren't what they seem on the surface. You know that."

"I sure know you turned out to be more than a pretty face."

"I don't know whether that's a compliment or not."

"It's neither, and it's a little insensitive," he acknowledged. "Will you tell me what you know about Nick, or is that something I don't need to know right now? I'm worried about the fact that he has no cash or credit cards."

"Auggie, he has money," I admitted.

"How?"

"I gave it to him."

"What the hell?" August dropped his butter knife and stared at me.

"He was about to explode. I knew that. I slipped an envelope of cash beneath his door before we flew to Scotland. I worry about him feeding himself, just as much as you do."

"He still has to find Gene and Becker."

"He'll find them. He knows what to do, too, when he does."

"He can't do this alone."

"Auggie, this is where you'll have to trust me, okay? I think Nick will be all right. You know," I watched as he lifted his butter knife, then frowned at the smear of butter on the white tablecloth for a moment.

"I know what?" He turned his eyes to me, then.

"I think Maye needs a project to keep her mind off Nick," I said, although that wasn't what I'd been about to say.

"Shaw says the same thing." He took another pat of butter and placed it on his roll.

"Do you think she could work at the Smithsonian without drawing too much attention or punching too many people?"

"Why?"

"I think somebody may target it, next."

Auggie thought for a few seconds before speaking. "Somebody wants the Hope Diamond, then?"

"Possibly."

"I don't need possibly, Cori. I need facts."

"They want it. I know that for sure."

"You think Mary Evans may be here in the States?"

"It's possible."

"Then I'll talk to the President and see if we can't get Maye into the Natural History Museum at the Smithsonian."

~

"What did you talk about?" Ilya asked when I got back to our suite after my dinner with Auggie.

"About Maye and the Hope Diamond. I think that's Mary Evans' next target. I'm amazed that she can get into the country with every department in existence looking for her, right now."

"She's done this before," Ilya frowned. "Many times. Perhaps she will arrive via Canada. Or Mexico. Or by private yacht."

"I just want her caught," I said. "I'm hoping Maye can do that. Ilya, I'm worried about Auggie."

"Why?"

"Well, first off, Cutter will be pissed. That'll paint a bigger target on Auggie's back. Second, I don't think his wife is gonna like being married to the next Secretary of Defense."

"He will receive that promotion as well?"

"I think that's the plan," I said dryly. "He's not telling anybody, but I figured it out. Keep it quiet, please, until the official announcement is made."

"I will."

"I really, really want a drink right now," I said, flopping onto the sofa in our sitting room. "I only got a sip of Auggie's champagne at dinner, to celebrate his promotion."

"How about a trip to the hot tub instead? For your muscle aches?"

"That would be nice."

~

We found James sitting in the hot tub when we arrived, his cast-covered wrist held out of the water and propped on the slate floor surrounding the spa.

"So, found a way around not getting it wet?" I smiled at him.

"Yeah."

"Want a towel beneath your wrist before I get in?" I asked.

"Would you?"

"Sure." I grabbed a towel from a stack next to the door and brought it to him. He lifted his arm while I placed the folded towel beneath it.

"Much better," he sighed as Rafe held out a hand to help me into the spa.

"Those stones are hard," I agreed and took a seat between James and Rafe. "Water is nice, though. I think I ache all over."

"Did Colonel Hunter talk to you about your pay?"

"What pay?"

"He wants to set up an account for you—the others draw a paycheck that they spend through me or through finance. Until now, you didn't get anything—you've supported yourself for the most part, except for a few expenditures here and there."

"I know. I really don't need more money, James," I said.

"But that's not right. Colonel Hunter wants to name you as a special consult, with an official pay grade and everything."

"But," I said.

"I've already set up the paperwork and the President signed off on it."

"Wonderful. Can I build a separate residence in the backyard of this behemoth, too?" I asked. "I really want a beach house, but that's not in the cards."

"That probably won't happen. Colonel Hunter has asked for a new facility somewhere to house the Program."

"He's probably right to do that," I agreed with a sigh. "But I hate being fenced in and confined."

"Thank you for being here so late," President Sanders offered Dr. Richard Farrell a seat in the Oval Office.

"I didn't have much choice. Your minions were particularly persuasive, Madam President," he replied. "Which one is on the loose?"

"There are two on the loose, but only one of them is with my less than savory opposition," Amelia Sanders responded. "Becker has defected, and Nick has taken it upon himself to track him."

"What do you want to know?"

"What Becker in the hands of an enemy might do to us."

"That depends."

"On what?"

"On whether they want to reproduce the Program, or if they merely want to kill ninety-five percent of the population instead."

"How quickly could they do both?" President Sanders did her best to mask her growing alarm.

"Not long, if they get on the right track. The drug is dangerous. You read the dossier when you took this office, I assume?"

"Yes. If the Program had begun during my term, I would have canceled it early on. The risks were just too great."

"I understand that. I also understand that Cutter may have been informed of this long before you offered him the position of Secretary of Defense."

"Because he was friends with the previous President?"

"Yes."

"Then why did they appear to butt heads at every turn?" the President asked.

"For obvious reasons. I was never fooled. If you'd contacted me beforehand, I could have told you that."

"I have one in the Program who could have told me the same thing, I think," she muttered. "I just didn't know to ask at the time."

"Who? I wasn't aware of any of them having that sort of talent."

"Then you should update your files. Corinne Watson can probably tell you what you had for breakfast yesterday, and what you'll have for breakfast tomorrow, most likely. All she has to do is see your face."

"Corinne Watson? Are you sure?"

"She's been one hundred percent accurate so far," President Sanders said.

"A latent talent," Dr. Farrell mused. "Interesting. I'd like to see her, if you don't mind."

"I can arrange it whenever you like."

"Tomorrow?"

"Yes. I'll see to it."

Corinne

"We're having visitors," August announced as Rafe and I walked into the kitchen. It was Thursday morning—I only knew that because the calendar on my desktop said so.

"Your food order arrived half an hour ago. James put it away for you," August added. "What is the likelihood of getting a fresh breakfast? I'll help."

"That depends on what you want," I said, covering a yawn. "Coffee, first."

"You should probably repeat your message about the visitors in ten minutes," Rafe said behind me. He steered me toward the coffeepot, just so I wouldn't be confused as to my original destination.

After I got started on my first cup of coffee, we put eggs, sausage, toast and juice together. "Who's coming?" I asked.

"Dr. Richard Farrell," August said. "He has at least six degrees listed after his name. I don't remember half of them."

"Makes it hard to print business cards," I said. "Maybe he should have stopped at three. To save money and paper. Why is he coming?"

"To talk to you. The President gave permission."

"Really?" Yes, the word was flat and sarcastic as opposed to upbeat and excited.

"Corinne, I'd appreciate it if you wouldn't revert to old habits," August said. "He'll be here with a military escort in two hours."

"My outfit for meeting people with at least six degrees is in the laundry."

"Cori."

"Yeah."

Notes—Colonel Hunter

"She writes the Sarah Fox novels," James explained to Dr. Farrell as we walked toward the sunroom at the back of the villa. I'd instructed Corinne to wait there for our arrival.

Dr. Farrell's escorts—two Navy men, were standing guard near the helicopter.

"A novelist? I admit I don't read fiction," Farrell confessed.

"That's all right," James said. "You asked about her; that's what you haven't heard yet."

"I'll be interested in what she has to tell me," Dr. Farrell said.

"It would be wise not to push too hard in that respect," I said.

"For what reason?"

"There are two possible outcomes. She could have a panic attack, or she could attack you verbally. Either way, you won't win the fight."

"Interesting."

Corinne

They wouldn't allow Rafe to be with me. I had to meet this man on my own. I'd hoped Auggie and James might stay for the questioning. I knew that wasn't to be the moment he entered the sunroom.

Dr. Richard Farrell studied me for a moment while August nodded in my direction before turning James around and marching away.

"Corinne?" He lifted an eyebrow at me.

"Well, I see the Program had eight survivors before two were killed," I said.

"Tell me," he took a seat on one of the cushioned rattan chairs decorating the sunroom, "why you didn't display that talent early on?"

"I was in mourning. Do you not understand that concept?" The other eyebrow lifted to join the first. "Besides," I added, "nobody needed to know six years ago. They need to know, now."

"They never told me who you were, before. It's the only hole in my knowledge of the Program."

"It will remain a hole. I'm not telling you or anyone else."

"You sound so defensive."

"I have a right to be. I didn't volunteer. You knew that and administered the drug anyway."

"You were dying."

"I know. Somebody wanted information, or they wouldn't have ordered you to give it to a potentially unwilling participant. They had six days to get you to Paris. They were waiting to see if anybody needed it, weren't they?"

"That was the previous administration's decision."

"Yes it was, wasn't it?"

"You don't trust them. The previous administration."

"Not even a little."

"Good. I don't trust them, either. That's why I was in Antarctica, until the President sent someone to collect me."

"I'm not surprised that the opposition wants you," I said. "You ought to be careful."

"I was. Still intend to be."

Can you hear me? I sent in his direction.

"I hear you fine," he said. "I didn't think it was possible," he breathed.

"Good," I said. "If I send a message and tell you to get the hell away from wherever you are, will you listen?"

"I will after today."

"Awesome. We don't need anybody else dying at the hands of those fuckers."

"Corinne, I admit that I would love to study you now, although I doubt you'd cooperate."

"True. I wouldn't. You might regret it, too."

"Why would I regret it?"

"Because I would beat you into a greasy stain on the carpet," Rafe released the shield about himself and sat next to me with a grin.

"Holy fucking shit," Richard Farrell muttered.

"When did you discover you could make yourself invisible?" Richard Farrell walked with us around the perimeter of the villa grounds.

"When Corinne told me it was possible," Rafe replied. "I had no idea."

He hadn't—I'd told him before he left for Dublin. I didn't want him hurt if I could help it. The shield might not hide him from thermal cameras, but that remained to be seen.

"You think I'm safer here at the moment?" Richard asked.

"For now. I'm not sure you can avoid captivity," I said. "At the moment, they're not sure where we are. You leave, they'll pick up your trail somewhere unless you're very careful."

I watched him as he processed the information. If he hadn't tested the drug on himself, first, years ago, he'd probably be dead. He was one-hundred-six years old and looked seventy-five years younger than that. His face and hair bore the wind-burned look of someone who'd been working in Antarctica until a few days before, but he still appeared too young to have numerous degrees behind his name.

Seeing him had given me information on the drug itself, and it was frightening. I shoved it aside—if I thought too much about it, I'd have the mother of all panic attacks. Even he didn't know everything about it, and that in itself was frightening enough.

"I hope you know that I wanted to halt the Program after the first volunteers died. That was taken out of my hands."

"You don't have much love for the previous occupant of the White House, do you?" I asked.

"None. I begged him to stop, but he already had the product and ordered the study to continue, with or without me. The only reason I stayed with it was to protect the ones I could—the ones who survived. When President Sanders was elected, I didn't feel quite as obligated— she wanted to protect the survivors as well. That's why I went on my Antarctic expedition—to clear my mind."

"Any luck with that?" Rafe asked.

"Not much."

"You thought that since the animal trials were successful, and your first human recipient—you—was a success, you felt it was safe to give to others," I said.

"Yes. That turned out to be the biggest mistake of my life. You have no idea how much I regret that. It was simple enough—we found by trial and error, almost, that an older animal would become young again. When I tested the drug on myself, I discovered it had other benefits."

"What benefits?"

"I can heal many illnesses. Sadly, I cannot heal anyone who is destined to die after taking the drug. I tried that. It didn't work."

"Has Colonel Hunter given you information on those sent to eliminate us?" Rafe asked. "Several of them appear to be clones—exact replicas, down to their fingerprints."

"That is frightening," Richard murmured. "Do we still have the bodies? Might I have a look?"

"I believe you should ask," I said.

～

Notes—Colonel Hunter

"I'd be more than happy to let you examine them. The President ordered that the bodies be held without further examination until she found someone she trusted," I said. Richard Farrell sat in my office, asking questions after having a conversation with Corinne.

I shouldn't have been surprised.

"We have one other we captured alive, but he refuses to talk," I said. "We can't identify him, either, but so far we haven't found any replicas of him."

"I'd like to take a look," Dr. Farrell said. "At all of them."

"You're hired," I said. "How soon can you start?"

"Immediately, although I'll need equipment and supplies to run tests."

"If you can solve this riddle for us, I think you can have anything you want."

∼

Corinne

It's amazing what can be accomplished in a short time with sufficient motivation. Dr. Farrell had a makeshift lab built in the villa's garages in less than a week. During that time, I knew Nick was closing in on Becker and Gene.

I hoped he'd call for help if he needed it. Auggie hadn't asked me for a report in the last six hours, although I could tell he was getting fidgety. After a brief training session, Maye had been sent to work at the Smithsonian.

She was equipped with tiny cameras and a wire, which several people at the villa monitored. She was posing as a staff photographer, who would be looking for ideal candidates among visitors to include in a brochure. She'd be backed up by several agents, too, who'd come running if she spotted the quarry. I had the idea that Mary Evans would show up, I just didn't know how or when at the moment.

"Bodies just arrived," Ilya said, pulling a curtain back and peeking through the blinds on one of our windows.

"Great. I really don't want to see them, but if it's necessary," I shrugged and kept typing. Yes, I was back to writing the book, but I'd hit the backspace key more than I'd typed words in the past three days.

More than anything, I wanted answers to the puzzles we'd been handed to solve, but without the proper people, I couldn't get to them.

Dr. Farrell agreed to keep Ilya's invisibility trick secret—for now. If the enemy learned of it, they'd know to look for ways around it.

"Ilya?" I stopped typing.

"Cabbage?"

"I think Auggie's about to be hit with divorce papers."

"Not good."

"Very not good. I understand how his wife might be tired of being alone all the time, but this isn't the best time for him to have that pain in his life."

"Should we tell him?"

"Honey, that's a terrible idea."

"What about Dr. Shaw?"

"I don't know," I leaned my head back and moaned.

"I know this troubles you, but it is not your difficulty to sort."

"But if Auggie is distracted, we have a problem."

"Possibly," he agreed. "What about Nick?"

"I think tonight's the night."

"I will be quite interested to see if he survives this."

"That makes two of us."

"How long before we can couple again?" His fingers dropped to my temples and rubbed them gently.

"I don't know. Maybe you should e-mail Leo. I don't have a headache at the moment."

"I don't wish to be the reason you get one."

"Who do you think is sending assassins after you?" I asked. He pulled his hand away.

"Baikov. If he suspects I still live, he will do his best to kill me."

"That means that some of those dead guys could have been sent by him?"

"Yes, although it would be difficult to say how he received the information that I live."

"What if Cutter managed to get a message to him—through Mary Evans and her boss?"

"Such information would command a very high price. I suspect that the Ambassador's death is tied to the same information. He paid guards and cleared the way for my escape from prison."

"He was a friend?"

"Yes. Unlike others I have been forced to associate with, he was trustworthy."

"I'm sorry your friend is dead."

"Many others have died searching for the truth of this, and even with your formidable talents, we have not found an answer," Ilya said. "We have the secondary players, but the primary? We have no clues. We do not know what he wants, other than to create fear and panic."

"What will Cutter's backers do with the information locked in

Becker's blood?" I asked. "If Nick gets to him tonight, will it be too late? I worry that they have a large enough sample to do whatever they want and no longer need him or Gene."

"Gene should have realized that he was worthless to them, except to convince Becker to defect from the Program. He is no longer useful." Ilya's hands were back and lifting my top. His fingers went to my breasts, where they tweaked my nipples through the thin fabric of my bra.

"Wow, espionage and foreplay at the same time," I said.

"Shhh," he whispered and pinched my nipples carefully while kissing my neck. "You will let me know if your head hurts. Immediately."

"Are you the boss again?"

"Very much so."

~

Notes—Colonel Hunter

I'd been worried that it could happen for a while, but now the evidence was presented in a private e-mail from her hired attorney. Laci wanted a divorce, citing incompatibility.

I realized that a spouse should expect their partner to be a partner. A part of me felt relief—we'd been growing apart for a while. Another part felt anger—I always provided for her. She never wanted children, so we didn't have any.

I needed a lawyer.

I didn't mind letting her have the house or most of the other things, but it needed to be as civil as we could make it.

Divorces are always messy.

A friend told me that, once.

I didn't have time for this.

I'm sure Corinne could have told me how many complications swirled about us, and I'd never told Laci how close we'd come to getting killed in London and Edinburgh. She only knew that she'd been forced out of the house and sent to her mother's in Pittsburgh.

Maybe she didn't care that my life was in danger. I wanted to pick up the phone and ask her if she still loved me.

I couldn't do that.

"Fuck," I muttered and started a new file on my computer, simply labeled *Divorce*.

~

Nick

The house was on fire. Gene and Becker were dead inside it. Cutter and two guards managed to shoot their way out and escape in a bulletproof SUV. I had a graze on my shoulder to show for it.

The problem? Cutter knew I was alive. Probably guessed that reports of my death, along with the others, was just a sham—an attempt to fool him and his cronies. I watched as the roof caved in with a crash and another, lower-level window blew out, raining glass on the lawn.

I smiled grimly. The property was located far from any town, didn't have a fire hydrant close and would burn to the ground before anyone could arrive to help. Gene and Becker would be blackened, useless corpses when they were pulled from the debris.

"Ready?" Davis gave me a nod when I spoke. We loaded into his Range Rover and took off in the opposite direction. I figured we'd need Corinne's help to get Cutter, and I didn't want to place my friends in more danger than they already were by trying to track him myself.

I'd call Jeff first, to see whether I'd be welcomed back to the villa or if a cell waited for me, instead.

~

Corinne

I knew the minute he showed up in the downstairs kitchen for dinner, instead of going to the one over the garages.

Auggie's wife had asked for a divorce.

"Here," I set a plate of spaghetti in front of him and went to get another plate for myself. Rafe gave me a slight nod and placed a generous slice of garlic cheese bread on Auggie's plate.

We ate in silence for the most part. I didn't tell Auggie that the house where Becker, Gene and Cutter had been staying in a remote area of Utah was burning, or that Cutter managed to escape but Gene and Becker never made it out. That could wait until later.

Actually, I expected Nick to give Jeff a call, which would be transferred to Auggie afterward. Nick would tell Auggie that most of the job was finished and then ask if he could come home.

I figured Auggie would say yes, with the promise of a stern talking-to when Nick got back. Nick probably expected that much at the very least.

Ilya, I thought at him, *Cutter just became more of a liability.*

CHAPTER 14

otes—Colonel Hunter

"Nick, are you sure they're dead?" I asked.

"Yes, Colonel Hunter. I made sure of it. The guards there protected Cutter and got him out of the house, but I think I winged him before they drove off."

"Then I'll have the FBI take charge of the bodies—they'll be brought here," I said. "How long will it take for you to get back?"

"Not long, if you arrange for transport."

"Where are you now?"

"Outside Provo."

"Then I'll make arrangements. I hope you don't mind driving instead of flying. Will you be at this number when I call you back?"

"Yes, sir."

"Good. I'll call you back in fifteen." After ending the call, I shouted for James.

"Sir?" He appeared in my doorway.

"Get Corinne and Rafe in here."

"Right away."

Corinne

I felt sorry for James—Auggie was working late, therefore James was also working late. Rafe and I walked in after James called us, and took seats in Auggie's office.

"I got a call from Nick," Auggie said immediately. "Becker and Gene are dead and probably pretty toasty by now. Nick burned the house down around them, but Cutter got away. Any idea where he might be, Cori?"

"On his way to Canada in a small plane, if he isn't already over the border," I shrugged.

"Tell me why we ought to keep him alive." Auggie's words surprised me.

"The only reason for him to still be breathing is that he may know how to contact the one who's orchestrating all of these things," I said.

"I want him dead," August huffed. "I don't care where he dies, I want him dead."

"Will the President implicate him in the Sacramento bombing?" Rafe asked.

"I don't know." Auggie dropped his face in his hands. "She should, but we still don't know who's funding his activities. We've hit a wall on the money—it's likely coming from offshore accounts."

"Not good," Rafe said.

"There are other complications, too," August sighed and dropped his hands to blink at us. "The President is scheduling a trip to Sacramento for a memorial service. She intends to speak at the service, then meet privately with the Governor afterward. I'm going, too, and I want both of you with us when we go."

~

Notes—Colonel Hunter

"Shaw, I'm naming you my second-in-command," I said. I'd asked him to meet me for a drink in what we'd come to think of as Corinne's kitchen. She had some fine Scotch there, so I poured for both of us. "If anything happens to me, then you're in charge of the Program until the President says otherwise."

"If anyone else asked, I'd refuse," Shaw said, lifting his glass in a toast. "Cheers."

"Why?" I asked after downing my first shot and pouring another.

"Because I haven't trusted anyone before you who's been in charge of the Program."

"Even Safer?"

"Come on, Safer never intended to be in charge. He liked where he was. Did you talk to him about this?"

"I did. He said he'd be happy to step aside now, as he has full confidence in you."

"That's good to know." Shaw emptied his glass and held it out for more. "Corinne has good taste in Scotch."

"And the money to buy the good stuff," I agreed. "She asked James to order a case of this right after we moved in here. Probably realized we'd need it."

"How much would a case of twenty-five-year Macallan cost, anyway?"

"Corinne doesn't seem to care about that."

"Right now, I'm glad. This is really good."

"I sent a list to you already, of things I'd like for you to do in certain circumstances if you find yourself in charge," I said. "Let me know if you have a problem with any of them."

"I will."

Corinne

"I hate packing," I said. "I hate dresses more." Our suitcases were spread across the bed, both in various stages of packing.

"You look good in them, cabbage."

"Right. I hope we won't need this thing," I shook my head after stuffing the dress bag into my suitcase. Heels followed, as did a new wig, a contacts case and a makeup kit. I'd have to wear the wig and contacts while appearing in public with Madam President, but I hoped there were no events requiring a dress.

Sacramento would be warm enough in late spring so I wouldn't need a heavier jacket. Ilya had to pack his dark suit and tie.

"Too bad we can't stay a few nights in San Francisco—I love it there," Ilya said.

"Why, you little spy, you," I turned and tickled his ribs.

"What's not to love about clam chowder in a sourdough bread bowl?" he grinned.

"I wish we could go, too. By ourselves. Just to do touristy things and eat and sleep late in a nice hotel."

"Someday, we will do those things."

"Honey, I hope you're right."

Six o'clock comes early, when you have to get up at five and get ready to drive to the White House, after which you have to take a helicopter to an airbase and fly from there to California.

"Corinne, you look tired," Auggie said when we walked toward Air Force One.

"Early mornings," I mumbled. "No Starbucks."

"There will be coffee on the plane." The President walked past us, flanked by Secret Service agents. "Breakfast, too."

Most people might have apologized to Madam President. Or thanked her.

I wasn't in the mood.

On any given day, who's to say who is more important than those who surround them? We both had jobs to do. Some people are just more cheerful than others early in the morning. I'm not in the cheerful camp.

"Cabbage," Rafe cautioned.

"Yeah."

When the President was far enough ahead, Auggie snickered.

"Auggie," I warned.

"Yeah."

~

"Where did that come from?" August read what I typed over my shoulder while we flew over Chicago.

I worked on my book while Rafe sat beside me and Auggie held a cup of coffee in his hands and read what I typed.

"This is my fancy tablet," I said. "James ordered it for me. It's not as heavy or as big as a laptop, and the cover is a keyboard. It fits in my purse," I added.

"James has an ulterior motive," Auggie said. "He wants the ending on that book."

"I'm working on it," I said. "It keeps me from worrying about other stuff."

"Anything I should be concerned about?" Auggie asked.

"I sure hope not," I said.

~

The first thing on our agenda when we arrived in Sacramento was to go to the bombed capitol building with the Governor. It was time to pull on my wig so I could appear in public with Madam President.

Rafe and I had gone blond for this event, and not by choice. I figured James' fantasies probably played a role in the choice of hair color, but I didn't say that.

News crews packed a nearby parking lot as we drove into the designated area at the ruined capitol building. We had half an hour scheduled there before we loaded into the vehicle again and drove to the memorial service.

"Cori, are we being watched?" Auggie said beside me as we walked a few discreet steps behind the President and the Governor.

"By millions," I gave the obvious answer. "If you mean are we being watched by somebody who wants us dead, well, I think that's a given. I just don't feel them close," I added.

"Good. Let me know if that changes."

"Will do."

I'd already checked the Secret Service agents and the guards with the Governor. So far, so good. They were doing their jobs and weren't bent on destruction.

The capitol building was a mess; Ted Ryan and his cohorts had orchestrated the bombing so the dome would fall, leaving a gaping hole in the building. The whole structure was considered unstable, and I wondered if they'd be able to save much of it.

The Sacramento Police and Fire Chiefs joined the President and the Governor as we approached the front steps—those were still intact, leading the way to a gaping ruin.

"I don't care what she looks like, that's her," Cutter pointed at the woman following the President.

"The witch?"

"Yes. That's her."

"As far as I'm concerned, there are two witches there. You know where a woman's place is, and it isn't the White House."

"I can't get close to her; she'll recognize me," Cutter sighed. "I'd love to take her out, though. There's no way she and the others should have survived in London."

"The death of the Secretary of State should have sealed the deal," Cutter's companion agreed. "You should be on your way to the presidency. Instead, you managed to lose the source and you're on every watch list the FBI, CIA and NSA have."

"The house was burning and Becker was dead. What did you expect me to do?" Cutter whined.

"Take the fucking body with you."

"Hey, there's no need for that," Cutter held up his hands as he stared at the gun his companion pulled from a jacket pocket.

"You're of no use to us."

Cutter didn't have time to protest before he was shot three times in the heart. "Don't worry, we'll take care of the witches. That's our job," his companion stepped over Cutter's body and headed for the door.

Corinne

Madam President discussed the rebuilding of the capitol while Cutter died in a motel room in Canada.

Auggie, Cutter just died, I said. That was a blow. He had information I needed, and now it was impossible to get it.

"Who?" Auggie was beside me quickly while Rafe carefully watched everybody around us.

"I don't know," I whispered. "All I know is that he was shot. Probably because he was a liability and didn't haul Becker's body with him when he ran out of the house in Utah."

"Can you tell me where to send the authorities to collect him?"

"Verbena Motel on the outskirts of Chilliwack, British Columbia," I said. Auggie stepped away and pulled out his cell. The President cut her eyes in our direction for a moment before going back to the Governor's conversation.

"Auggie, he hadn't been there longer than five minutes," I attempted to defend myself during the drive to the memorial service. He wanted to know why I hadn't told him immediately where Cutter was. The truth was complicated. I needed connections, and dead people generally don't reveal needed information.

Everything Cutter owned in the U.S. had already been searched, with no results. What he had that I wanted was in his head. I needed names and images, and I didn't have those. I didn't expect Colonel August Hunter to understand that.

Cutter's death left me with Mary Evans and General Baikov. I no longer had a link to those in the U.S. who were involved. No matter who they were, though, they had money. Enough to kill a Vice President in an attempt to take over the White House.

The President sat across from Auggie, Rafe and me, a solid frown on her face. As pissed as Auggie was, she may have been more so. I had to work to fight down a panic attack.

"We will discuss this later," Madam President said as the vehicle swung into the parking garage of a hotel. Police and guards swarmed the building as we climbed from the car and walked toward waiting elevators.

Rafe hadn't said a word the whole time, so I waited for his ass-chewing, too.

~

The service lasted three hours. I was grateful nobody shot at us during that time. Nobody spoke as we loaded into the vehicle to drive to the Governor's Mansion for the private meeting. I had a feeling Auggie and I were destined for a private meeting, too.

I wasn't wrong.

"What the fucking hell, Corinne," August exploded the moment the door shut behind us.

"Sometimes I do know stuff," I said, attempting to control my trembling. "But I have my reasons, Auggie."

"You will not call me Auggie during this meeting. You lost that privilege the minute I learned you withheld information." His anger beat against my bruised emotions, making me want to cower away from him, and I certainly didn't want to point out that I'd withheld information from the beginning. He was pissed about many things and I was receiving the brunt of his fury. Anything else I said would only make it worse.

"You knew where Cutter was in Utah, didn't you?" he snapped. "We wondered how Nick was able to track him so easily. You gave him money and sent him straight to the location. If you'd told me, we could have brought all of them in—Becker included, and yet you take matters into your own hands."

I had no excuses he would listen to, and I'd already said I had my reasons. I remained silent and worked to keep my breathing even. *Don't panic, don't panic, don't panic,* I repeated to myself.

"I'll have a talk with the President and we'll discuss your punishment on the flight home." August stormed out of the room, leaving me breathing raggedly and slumping in my chair.

～

Rafe didn't sit with me during the flight to D.C. I figured he was pissed, too—I could tell him where General Baikov was, no problem. What I needed was Baikov's information, and a dead Russian General did me no good whatsoever. Rafe intended to kill him the moment he found him, and that would cause another source of information to evaporate.

I worried that all my resources would end up dead and my leads would die with them. Fear and exhaustion plagued me during what felt like the longest plane ride of my life.

～

Confined to quarters, my computer was taken away and Rafe moved himself out of my suite. The worst of those punishments was Rafe's defection—he hadn't even given me a chance to explain. No, I wouldn't have told him everything, but he hadn't told me everything, either.

I had two weeks of solitary confinement in my rooms to consider my actions, as August and Madam President put it. Well, she wasn't getting my vote ever again.

～

Notes—Colonel Hunter

"Let's look at this from a logical standpoint," Shaw said. "You'd just gotten the notification from your wife's lawyer, you were secretly pissed that Corinne gave money to Nick to track down Becker, you learn she could have told you more about Cutter, including where he was, and you exploded."

"The President supported me the whole way," I blustered. Was I beginning to feel guilty?

You bet.

I felt responsible for the breakup between Rafe and Cori, too. I couldn't fix that; I'd lost it and told him she could see where Baikov was. His face went dark immediately and I knew I'd done the wrong thing.

Shaw was telling me what I already knew.

"We need her help," Shaw went on. "Face it, she's saved your life, the President's life, the sitting Vice President's life and the Prime Minister's life. Do you think for a moment that she wouldn't have told you if the President or anyone else was in danger? She didn't see the Sacramento bombing because she'd never seen Ted Ryan before he posted his video on the Internet. She has to see them, or haven't you figured that out, yet?"

"Stop," I held up a hand. "Look, I already feel like a bastard. You don't have to rub it in."

"She refuses to talk to me, now. I can't get to her. Right now, nobody can. She isn't talking and if what James tells me is true, she isn't eating, either."

"Fuck. Look, what's the word from Maye? Do we have anything?"

"There's a huge crowd of school kids scheduled for a tour at the museum tomorrow. It would be just like our quarry to hide in those numbers," Shaw observed. "I've already asked Maye to be extra careful and look for adults."

"Good. Keep me posted." I left Shaw's office as quickly as I could.

∼

Ilya

Colonel Hunter called a halt to Krav Maga lessons while Corinne was confined to her quarters.

Just as well, I might have done inadvertent harm. Angry couldn't begin to describe how I felt. She could have given me Baikov's location after seeing his photograph. I could have taken the fucker down immediately.

She'd withheld that information, just as she'd withheld information on Cutter from Colonel Hunter. If Corinne didn't know before that she was playing with fire where Baikov and I were concerned, then she knew it now.

James refused to spot me while I lifted weights.

I didn't care. I could take care of myself.

Corinne

There was so much that so many people didn't know. I hunched my shoulders as I walked down a sidewalk in Silver Spring. Getting out had never been a problem, no matter how well Colonel Hunter imagined his villa was guarded.

Nick would get back the following day. Maybe he could tell them when they were in danger; I was currently out of the business. Auggie and Ilya had played their hands; I'd played mine. I still held cards, too, while their hands were empty. There was one last thing I had to do before I dropped out of sight.

Maye, I sent to her, *Mary Evans will be disguised and in a wheelchair tomorrow.*

Notes—Colonel Hunter

We had to break down the door—she'd moved a heavy dresser in front of it. I had no idea how she could get past the cameras outside her windows after that. It wasn't difficult to determine actually—the soldier watching those feeds had fallen asleep.

I played the images back twice—she'd crawled through the

window as if it were something she did every day and walked—*yes, walked*—off the property.

Nobody stopped her.

I thought Rafe would go crazy when I told him. I'd never heard him curse in his native language, but I'm glad I didn't understand anything he said. At least he didn't have to tell the President that Corinne had gone AWOL.

That was my job.

"I was angry. So angry with her," Rafe slammed his fist onto the kitchen counter. That's where I'd found him, brewing coffee. "Now she is outside without help." He cursed again.

"And she has vital information."

"You know they will kill her if they learn of this."

I was just as sure as Rafe was that Cutter had pointed her out to whomever he was serving. He knew the Program was still alive—he'd shot at Nick, after all. He'd called Corinne a witch. His cronies had that information, just as they had information on everyone else in the Program.

Cutter had gotten killed for his trouble—his body had already been transported back to the U.S. by Canadian authorities. He'd served a purpose, but after Becker and Gene died, that purpose died with him. Somebody, somewhere, had Becker's blood and enough information to do whatever they wanted.

"We have to get Cori back," I fumed.

"Where would she go?"

"I don't have a clue."

"Perhaps the beach? She said she wanted a beach house."

"Which one?" I shook my head at Rafe. "Never mind, I'll get everybody I know to start looking for clues. She has no money—that I know of. Wait, where the hell did she get the money she gave Nick? Everything she had was destroyed in the Mansion."

"I am beginning to believe that Corinne is smarter than all of us."

"And three steps ahead," I snapped. "James," I shouted while I headed for the stairs and the second floor.

Corinne

One of my lawyers has offices in Silver Spring. All my e-mail correspondence with him is read by James or someone else in the Program.

I wasn't at his office because of that.

I was at his office for something else.

He'd never laid eyes on Sarah Fox or Corinne Watson.

"Ms. Dane?" the receptionist stood. "Bryan is waiting for you in his office."

I didn't just write as Sarah Fox. I also wrote other books—as Carol Dane. All those books I'd written as Carol Dane had been done at the library, on a laptop I kept at a storage facility. I no longer had a key to the storage facility—it had been destroyed in the Mansion bombing.

Bryan Kellogg, one of my lawyers, had a key, along with an envelope full of other things in case I needed them.

Things like credit cards, cash, keys and banking information.

All registered to Carol Dane.

"Here are the things you requested," Bryan smiled and handed a large manila envelope to me. He'd tried to ask me out before. I always said no. I didn't intend to change my answer.

"Thank you for this," I held up the envelope and smiled back.

"How was your trip to France?"

"Enlightening," I said.

"Let us know if you need anything else."

"I will. Thanks again."

A cab dropped me off at the storage facility. I waited until he drove away to walk to the unit I rented.

Opening the garage-like door after pulling off the lock, I set the lock inside the unit and nodded.

The car was registered to Carol Dane and draped with a car cover.

Flipping the cover back, I revealed the front bumper of my silver Mercedes. In the trunk was a laptop and enough cash to do me for a while.

I laid my envelope on the car's hood and pulled the rest of the cover off before piling it in a corner. Then I found the car keys inside the envelope, tossed the envelope on the passenger seat and climbed in.

The car started right up.

So many things needed doing, before I allowed myself the time and a corner somewhere to weep my heart out.

"Miss Dane, we hardly expected you to arrive unannounced," the desk clerk breathed. He was a fan; that was easy to see.

Carol Dane owned a condo on Myrtle Beach. The transaction had taken place in written and e-mail correspondence two years earlier. A third, local attorney had taken care of everything else, and he had no idea that Carol Dane was fiction, just as Sarah Fox was.

"Everything you sent is in boxes, and the furniture is still wrapped in plastic," he admitted. "Since we didn't know what you wanted done with it."

"Are the washer and dryer hooked up and ready to go?"

"All the appliances should be ready for use."

"Then you've done a spectacular job," I smiled at him. "Thank you. Oh, one more thing—this is a writing retreat for me. I'd appreciate it if nobody knew I was here."

"You got it," he said, grinning back. "I'm just so excited that you're finally here."

"Me, too," I said.

I thought he might follow me into the elevator to the top floor where my condo was, but he didn't. I rode up the elevator, clutching my purse, the laptop bag and the manila envelope. I had to hold it together until I got inside my condo. Then I could cry as much as I wanted.

When I opened the door, boxes were everywhere. Yes, Carol Dane had ordered everything online I thought I might need, and left instructions for the deliveries to be left inside the condo. I just hadn't realized how much room those boxes would take. Some were stacked atop one another.

I shut the door behind me and locked it. I couldn't even sit on the sofa against the wall without pulling heavy, dusty plastic off it first. Somewhere in the boxes was a vacuum and cleaning supplies.

Those would have to wait. I headed straight for the bathroom, sat on the edge of a huge whirlpool tub and let the tears fall.

Maye

A sea of school-age children shuffled past me, few of them appreciating their surroundings as they were led through the Smithsonian's Natural History Museum. Weary teachers and a few parents listened as well as they could to the docents explaining what this article or that artifact actually was, all while carefully watching third and fourth-grade students poke, tease and giggle as they made their way past priceless treasures.

So far, none of them had been in a wheelchair. More were coming, however; the next group had been dropped off and were being herded into the building. Holding back a sigh, I watched as a sparring match occurred between two boys before a teacher broke it up. Deliberately I shut out their mental accusations that the other boy had started the fight.

The target wasn't in this group.

Stepping into an alcove and adjusting the camera strap around my neck, I waited for the next batch of children to arrive.

Ilya

"James, did she have any friends on the outside?" I asked. He and I sat in the kitchen, morosely consuming coffee. I watched as James picked at a bag of microwave popcorn, chewing kernels absently while he considered my question.

"Her old neighbors in Arlington," James shrugged. "She made cookies for them and watched their cats when they went out of town."

"Do you have access to a vehicle?"

"Yes," James offered a hesitant answer.

"Good. You drive. We will question these neighbors."

"But Colonel Hunter," he protested.

"Is busy," I said. "We will go. Immediately."

"I guess it's better than sitting here," he agreed.

Ten minutes later, we were driving through the gate at the villa in a small, black car that had an excuse for an engine in it. Someday, I intended to have my own transportation again. I had no idea at present when that day might come.

"Hello?" The word was a question, and failed to encompass a much larger statement—one that said *I don't know you*. While Eric Borden didn't appear frightened by James, he was terrified of me. We stood on Eric's porch, which was as narrow as the three-story house it fronted. It was nearly identical to the empty one next door—the one Corinne had called home for five years. I wished she'd chosen to go there; it would have made things easy.

She was much too smart for that.

"We were just wondering if you've seen Cori—Corinne, lately," James said. "We're old friends and having a hard time catching up with her."

"She's in France," Eric said, stepping back and attempting to shut the door. I laid a palm against the door, stopping its momentum.

"You have heard from her," I narrowed my eyes at Eric, watching as the fear in his eyes increased.

"I just, I, I," he swallowed with difficulty.

"Tell me," I demanded. "She is in danger, and anything you say may prove important."

~

"A storage unit?" James' voice was close to cracking as we studied the unit. It was large enough to hold a car and other belongings. Most of those things were now missing. Eric had a key to the lock, and his voice and his hands shook as he'd handed it over. We'd left him behind, trembling and gaping as we drove to Corinne's storage facility.

Only a few boxes and bags lined the back wall; things Corinne didn't want to take with her. I went through them as quickly and efficiently as possible. One box held old manuscripts. I barely paid attention to them as I rummaged for something that might be used to find Corinne.

"She didn't want us to know," James whispered. "So her neighbor did a lot of this for her, or she took a cab so we wouldn't trace her car. Damn."

"Here," I handed a business card to James. It was an attorney's card, with the words "Call me," handwritten on the back. I'd found it at the bottom of one of the boxes.

"This is one of the lawyers Sarah Fox uses," James mumbled, staring at the card as if it might catch fire at any moment.

His cell phone rang. Colonel Hunter was calling, demanding to know where we were and what we were doing.

Maye

The third group looked very much like the first and second. Sounded very much like the first and second. Except there were three in wheelchairs. Two of them were teachers, with students crowding about them. The other was a tiny, male student—much too small for Mary Evans to emulate in disguise.

With students asking both teachers questions, I began to doubt Corinne's information. Still, I watched this final group as the docents began the tour.

Until one of the docents approached the wheelchair-bound female teacher. "Miss Vernon," she gushed, "Do you remember me?"

I caught the mental gear-switching as the woman attempted to invent a viable answer. That answer wouldn't be driven by mere forgetfulness. Instead, it was calculating and cold as she replied, "Of course I remember you; I just can't recall the name."

She was my target. Tapping the radio strapped to my belt, I sent a message to agents waiting nearby before lifting the camera I'd hung around my neck. "Excuse me," I called out, "Would you mind if I took a photograph for the new brochure?"

The docent couldn't be more pleased as I walked toward her. "This is my third-grade teacher, Miss Vernon," the docent giggled. "She's the reason I'm working here, now. She made me so curious about everything."

"Miss Vernon" wasn't happy. I realized she wore a mask and wondered for a moment where the real Miss Vernon was. That would have to wait. I knew my backup was closing in as the docent posed beside Mary Evans' stolen wheelchair. The children were pulled away by two teachers as I made ready to snap the pictures.

I only had time to take one before two FBI agents approached Mary Evans. "Ma'am," one of them said, "Please come with us."

She was out of the wheelchair fast—I'll give her that, but her attempt at taking the poor docent hostage was thwarted—I'd already punched Mary in the face before she could pull the poor girl against her.

Children snapped cell phone photographs as the prosthetic mask was pulled away from an unconscious Mary Evans, and she was handcuffed before she regained consciousness. I watched in satisfaction as she was led away, her steps unsteady. I'd hit her quite hard, as it turned out.

Colonel Hunter wouldn't even bother to ask if I'd used too much force on this one.

~

Notes—Colonel Hunter

Madam President wasn't pleased when she received news of

Corinne's disappearance—until she learned that Corinne was instrumental in capturing Mary Evans.

Corinne's last mental communication was with Maye, and Maye had looked at everyone who arrived at the Smithsonian in a wheelchair the day after Corinne's disappearance.

We had Mary Evans in custody now, although she'd attempted to take a hostage. She learned she was no match for Maye. We needed Corinne, now, to take a look at our prisoner, but Corinne was gone.

I'd been forced to order Rafe and James back to the villa—they'd gone hunting for Corinne on their own. Word was they had information that could prove useful, but that remained to be seen. We'd tabled it for a bit while Mary Evans was settled into a makeshift cell at the villa.

Rafe wanted to choke information out of Mary Evans about Baikov, but Shaw held both of us back. Mary Evans, or whatever her true name was, wasn't talking. We left her alone for a while, determined to vet anyone who came near her during her confinement.

I sat in my office while James worked on assignments, and he wasn't talking much, either. It wasn't difficult to tell he wanted to go out again to search for Cori.

That's when Richard knocked on my door.

"Dr. Farrell?" I said as he walked in and took a seat.

"I found this," he slid an envelope across my desk. I recognized Corinne's handwriting immediately.

"What the hell?" I said, lifting the flap and pulling a single sheet of paper out.

Richard, the letter began, *if you want any information from the male prisoner, have Rafe say the following words in Russian to him, in the exact order given.*

Green.

Yellow.

Seven.

Red.

Nine.

Eight.

White.

Sincerely,

Corinne.

"What is this supposed to do?" I shook my head at Dr. Farrell.

"No idea, but I'm willing to give it a try. Nothing else has worked."

"James, get Rafe in here," I called.

In ten minutes, the four of us stood outside the prisoner's cell. Rafe held the letter in his hand. I nodded to him.

"*Zee-lyo-niy,*" Rafe said in a heavy accent.

"*Zhol-ty.*"

"*Syem.*"

Dr. Farrell and I stared as the prisoner's eyes went from cloudy to clear and he began to sit up straighter on his bunk. By the time Rafe said the last word—*bye-liy,* the prisoner was completely focused —on Rafe.

He spoke for the first time, too, in Russian. I didn't understand it.

"He asks what I wish to know," Rafe turned to me.

Holy, fucking hell.

CHAPTER 15

otes—Colonel Hunter

    The prisoner didn't know much. He only had the name of a handler, and that turned out to be an alias. *Kill the dark-haired man and take the woman* were his instructions. He didn't recall exactly how he'd gotten into the U.S. He only said *plane*.

Rafe had to translate for us; I didn't understand Russian and Dr. Farrell only knew a smattering.

"Ask if he has any brothers or sisters," Farrell suggested.

Rafe asked the question and received a reply. He went still for a moment. "He says he is Five. He has four brothers. One and Two are dead. They are all the same. Look the same, same fingers," Rafe held up a hand.

"So they're clones?" I asked. This would explain the conundrum we'd run into before, with identical faces and fingerprints.

"I believe that's true," Rafe responded. "Whatever it is, you can bet Baikov is in it up to his nose."

"This takes Russian nesting dolls to another level," James muttered. "A copy of a copy of a copy."

"Ask why the dark-haired man was targeted," Dr. Farrell suggested. "And why the woman was targeted, too."

Rafe asked and waited for the answer.

"He does not question," Rafe translated. "He also asks why I resemble the dark-haired man."

"We'll skirt that issue. Ask him about General Baikov, instead," I suggested.

Rafe asked. The prisoner cringed and offered no answer. Rafe cursed.

"He's merely a tool—a weapon," Dr. Farrell shook his head. "I'll draw blood and see what we come up with. Tell him to cooperate with me," he instructed Rafe.

Rafe relayed the instructions.

Corinne

Brushing away the occasional tear, I opened boxes, washed new dishes (after I found the box with dishwasher tabs in it), washed new clothing, put things away and hung artwork on the walls.

Furniture was unwrapped and the bed was made up. I had a spectacular view of the water, but that didn't matter at the moment. How foolish and needy was I, that I longed for Ilya's embrace? For him to murmur soft words so I'd feel wanted and safe?

For years, I'd done without those things, I reminded myself. A few weeks of having those things made me shake and weep like a schoolgirl. I broke down boxes and piled them in a corner before searching out the instructions for disposing of oversized garbage at the condo.

I had to arrange for the delivery of groceries, too.

Corinne, Maye's voice entered my mind. *Tell us where you are.*

No deal, I replied. *Tell Colonel Hunter to fuck off.*

The President says to come back. All is forgiven.

On her side, maybe, I said. *I haven't forgiven. Sorry.*

We can protect you.

I can take care of myself.

Dr. Shaw says you only have three weeks of medication left.

You think I don't know that? I wiped fresh tears away.

Rafe wants to talk to you.

Tell him he had his chance. He fucked it up.

We know you're upset. They only want to talk to you, Corinne.

It's too late for that. I have things to do. Bye.

Ilya

"She's stopped talking," Maye reported.

As disagreements went, this was going horribly wrong. After talking with the clone in the basement, our fears for Corinne's safety had increased. "James," I turned to him. He frowned at me. "Show me the card we found—the one from Cori's lawyer. Do you think he might know something?"

"He knows her as Sarah Fox. All her correspondence with him is through e-mail," he answered reluctantly.

"I want the name," Colonel Hunter snapped. "I'll contact him."

"You'll just mess everything up between him and her," James grumbled. "Or between him and Sarah Fox, anyway."

"I don't give a fuck. We need her back. If this one doesn't know anything, we'll go to the second and then to her editor. I'll find military attorneys and editors and hire them into the Program. She won't have to go outside for anything."

"You'll just be locking her up again," Shaw pointed out. "You locked her up to begin with, then stuck her in a smaller cell and took away her writing. What did you expect?"

"Stop beating me over the head with this," Colonel Hunter complained. "I have enough worries with the divorce right now."

"Then perhaps we should go downstairs and talk about that," Dr. Shaw said.

"I'll be down in half an hour."

"Good." Shaw left Colonel Hunter's office.

"Maye, you can go, too," he waved her away. "Thank you for trying."

"She's important," Maye replied. "I wish I'd known that at the beginning. We were so full of ourselves." She walked out without saying anything else.

After Maye was gone, Colonel Hunter turned to me. "It's hard to send flowers and a card if you don't know where to send them," he muttered.

"Tell me about the bodies collected—the ones who shot at us and at Maye and Nick," I said.

"Farrell can explain this better than I can. We only got superficial information—all the organs, tissue and everything had turned to ugly goo by the time the forensics specialists got to work on them. They couldn't get anything from any of it; all they had was skin, hair and fingerprints. We didn't want to tell the rest of you—didn't want you to worry."

"What the hell can cause that?" I asked. Hunter was right not to tell the rest of us; that was frightening.

"Farrell worries that it may be an overdose of the drug—like a suicide pill for anyone else. It might explain how easy it was to kill them—they were already dying."

"How the hell did Baikov get his hands on the drug?" I exploded. "I was told the Program was airtight."

"That's obviously not true," Colonel Hunter replied dryly. "Cutter saw to that, and who knows who may have leaked information before that. Farrell says the clones are at least in their mid-twenties."

"How long has the Program existed?" I hissed.

"Longer than I've been alive," Colonel Hunter sighed. "Perhaps not longer than you've been alive, but who actually knows?"

"Farrell," I said. "He knows; I'll bet money on it."

"It's likely classified. Without the President's permission, I can't allow you to ask."

"We need Corinne. Fucking hell. *I* need Corinne," I growled.

"If I were in the President's good graces at the moment, I'd talk to her about this. As it is," Colonel Hunter shrugged uncomfortably.

"She's responsible for this mess, too, don't forget that," I said.

"But you know how that works. It's never the boss's fault."

"I know that better than anyone."

∼

Corinne

How convenient was it that he'd traveled outside the country? I stared at a photograph of the previous President. Gary Bridges had given the photographer a slight smile for the image used on his library website.

"You know something, don't you?" I muttered. I'd spent time attempting to track those who'd funded his campaign. Somehow, they and Cutter were mixed up in all of this. It wouldn't surprise me at all if former President Bridges didn't hold vital cards.

How do you accuse a former President?

He still had Secret Service agents surrounding him, wherever he was. With the current laws, too, it wasn't necessary to reveal or even claim knowledge of those who'd ran ads and alternate campaigns on his behalf. As long as the money didn't go directly into anybody's war chest, then government was for sale to the highest bidders.

Sure, the IRS was attempting to crack down on those nonprofits who pushed their chosen candidates toward election. They had varying degrees of success. I figured with enough money, you could hide anything from anybody.

Whoever backed Mary Evans, General Baikov and a certain Asian dictator would know how to accomplish all those things. If he, she or they could steal crowns and priceless works of art, then kill anybody they wanted no matter whom, where or when, they could hide whatever they wanted.

Forcing my mind away from that puzzle, I went in search of possibilities. The Russians had the drug. Somehow, they'd gotten their hands on it. They'd gone after a different result than we had, however. They'd found people who survived the drug, then set about cloning them. Who knows how long that had taken?

I'd seen something in Richard Farrell's face, though. Saw his suspicions, although he hadn't been present at the time. The ones who had been present during the drug's discovery were all dead.

That sucked. It made me wonder if any of the others (now dead) had tried the drug and didn't survive. Dr. Farrell didn't know of it, but it could have happened.

I wanted to discuss these things with Auggie and Rafe, then remembered I was pissed at both and far away from them on top of that. Taking a seat at the kitchen island, I opened my laptop and focused on two reported incidents occurring in Russia; one in 1969 and the other in 1986.

"What's the population?" Death asked.

"Around twenty-five hundred," War replied.

"This one will be easy, but anything after that will pose problems," Famine pointed out.

"Are we sure this will work?" Conquest wondered.

"I'm sure," Death answered. "Very sure. The experiments prove it."

"That was only five people," War pointed out. He sneezed, then took time to adjust his mask and red robes.

"Are we sure," Conquest began again.

"We have been appointed. Stop whining," Death hissed. He was dressed in silvery-gray and a hood covered his face.

"We will not question he who appointed us," War said. "We have agreed. It is done. I merely question the efficacy of the derivative—to make sure it is ready."

"I still say we should have someone else deliver it," Conquest suggested.

"No. We only need someone to get us into the closed system first. This task is appointed to us. We will make the first kill. All will know that we are bringing the apocalypse with us."

"Except we get to ride in style, instead of on horses," Famine, dressed in black robes and hood, laughed.

"Remember when the book was written," Death chided. "Vehicles were unheard of. Instead, we have horsepower to take us where we wish to go."

"Then let's go. People are waiting to die in Montana. After that, we will bring war."

∾

Corinne

Richard, I thought at Dr. Farrell, *I hope you've found the locating chip on Mary Evans by now. If you haven't, you may get surprise visitors.*

∾

Notes—Colonel Hunter

"It was embedded in the back of her neck and almost too tiny to find," Dr. Farrell said. "I sent it away from here to be destroyed."

"Corinne told you to look for it?"

"With that mental ability she seems to have, yes."

"What was Ms. Evans' reaction to the unplanned surgery?" I asked.

"She threatened to kill me before I had her sedated," Dr. Farrell smiled.

"Do you have anything planned this afternoon?" I asked.

"Nothing at the moment."

"Would you like to visit Silver Spring with me?"

"Of course."

"James," I called out. "Get Rafe. You can go if you want. Get Nick, too, he can drive."

∾

Armed with a photograph of Corinne, we left the vehicle parked in front of Bryan Kellogg's office, leaving Nick behind to guard it. Once inside the building, the receptionist informed us that we didn't have an appointment.

"We do, now," I flashed an official ID I carried for emergency purposes. I hadn't been named Secretary of Defense, yet, but I had all the perks of the office already.

Following her down a long hallway, we walked into the lawyer's office. "We need information on Sarah Fox," I said.

"I haven't heard from her in months," the lawyer sputtered. "I've never actually seen her; all our transactions are carried out through mail or e-mail."

~

Ilya

I wasn't satisfied with his answer. Pulling the photograph away from James, I shoved it under the lawyer's nose.

"That's not Sarah Fox," he insisted. "That's Carol Dane."

~

"That little hellion," Colonel Hunter complained the moment we were inside the vehicle. "All this time she's been publishing under two pen names."

"I like Carol Dane's books," James muttered. "Almost as much as I like, well, fuck. Corinne writes both."

"James, I want information on any property transactions, rentals, you name it, that you can find for Carol Dane," Colonel Hunter demanded. James began the search on a small tablet immediately.

Ten minutes later, we were on our way to the nearest air base. We were flying to Myrtle Beach, and I hoped Corinne would be there when we arrived.

"Last book she published as Carol Dane was six months ago," James reported as we swung onto a highway. Nick knew his way around; that was easy to see.

Colonel Hunter was on his phone quickly, ordering a military jet for our flight. It would take roughly an hour to get there. Once again, I hoped Corinne would still be there. She'd bought herself the beach house she wanted under a second pen name. It was exactly what I would have done.

Corinne

I hadn't slept the night before, so I decided to attempt a nap. I woke minutes after I'd fallen asleep. I knew two things. One had to come first, though.

Maye, get everybody out of the villa, I shouted mentally. *Do it now. Don't wait!*

Notes—Colonel Hunter

Halfway between the air base and Myrtle Beach, I received word from Shaw. The villa was now a pile of smoking rubble. Everybody had gotten out after Corinne warned Maye.

Everybody except the two prisoners, that is. There hadn't been time to get them out. Mary Evans and the clone were dead.

Twice now, Corinne had saved lives, although I felt she'd be upset that Mary Evans was dead. That source of information was gone. The clone had given us everything he could, but that wasn't much.

"The villa has been destroyed," I announced while the plane descended toward the airport. "Corinne warned Maye, so the prisoners were our only casualties."

"Mary Evans' backer had enough information from that fucking chip," Rafe muttered. "Next time, I want to be more difficult to find."

"I'm with him," Richard nodded in Rafe's direction.

"Right now, an underground bunker sounds really good," James hunched his shoulders.

"I hope you backed everything up," I told him.

"I always do," James said. "We just lost paper copies, that's all."

Corinne

I had a car—I could have driven away.

They would have found me eventually—the car was registered to Carol Dane and they had that identity, now.

I'd played my hand. I'd lost this round.

I waited for their arrival, feeling exhausted, hungry and defeated. Auggie was in a hurry—it took him twenty minutes to get from the airport to my condo, and that included getting a rental car.

At least they knocked first before kicking the door in.

"What the hell is that?" I yelled as they stood outside my condo. "I was on my way to open it for you." I pointed at the door, which now lay flat on the entryway tiles. Ten seconds earlier, it had been happily connected to the door hinges, guarding (ineffectively) the entrance to my condo. "You're gonna pay for that," I shouted at Colonel August Hunter.

He didn't have time to reply. Rafe stalked in, but Ilya pulled me into his arms. I cried while he whispered soothing words.

"The others are at the building in Arlington," Auggie sighed as he studied my empty refrigerator. "Corinne, when did you eat, last?"

"I don't remember." I wiped my face as Rafe let me go.

"Fuck," Rafe said.

"I was going to order something," I defended myself.

"Load up, we'll find a diner somewhere and then decide what to do while we eat," Auggie said. He'd been on the phone with Leo Shaw and the President almost from the moment he walked in. He was looking for something to drink after his conversation. He found an empty fridge instead.

"Cori, you look exhausted," Auggie said as we walked out the door.

Nick had fixed it as well as he could, but the door would still have to be replaced.

"Yeah."

"Your car still here?"

"Yes."

"Good. Rafe and I will ride with you. Nick will drive Richard and James."

"I'll drive," Rafe pulled the keys from my hand.

"Don't trust me?" I asked, frowning at him.

"Cabbage, you look as if you could collapse at any moment. Generally, it is wise to stay alert while driving."

"Yeah."

Auggie ate while studying a list of potential locations for the Program. James sat beside Auggie and read the same list. Richard and Nick discussed replacing what had been replaced after the Mansion bombing.

Rafe and I watched and listened to the others while having turkey sandwiches and soup. "Want dessert?" he asked softly.

"No. I'm already stuffed," I said.

"Then we'll have ice cream later."

"That sounds good."

"While we talk."

"Yeah."

"We only need half the building for this division of the Agriculture Department," the Vice President pointed out. "The rest is forty thousand square feet of updated and unused space."

"That could provide a front for the Program," the President studied the diagram on her computer. "It's on the outskirts of DC, so it's an ideal location. Plenty of parking area around it, so it will be easy to protect."

"It's your call, Madam President."

"Then let's do it. Get someone working on furniture and supplies. Is there room for a cafeteria and a dining hall?"

"Here," the Vice President pointed. "There's a smaller, executive kitchen and dining room here." He pointed to a second location. "We can combine spaces to make suites, and most of those spaces already have a bathroom and shower installed."

"Not much of a view," the President frowned.

"It will do until we find something better."

"True. Send a message to Colonel Hunter."

Corinne

By nightfall, we had newly assigned quarters—in the ugliest brick building imaginable.

The front portion was taken up by a division of the Agriculture Department, and all of it was surrounded by a large parking lot. The others were spending the night at the building in Arlington—the one that looked as if the Mystery Machine should be parked out front. At least they had beds, even if they did have ugly, outdated bedspreads.

Auggie wanted to check out the new digs, so we'd be sleeping on the floor. "Cori, I don't want you to take this the wrong way, but I'm placing you in an interior suite. I caught your window-climbing act, you know," he said.

"Then stop being an ass," I bristled. "You think I can't get away from you again?"

"I knew this was coming," Auggie muttered. "Look, can we table the shouting match until we get this mess sorted out? I have to make a report to the President, and I don't want to get her hackles up, too."

"Madam President can kiss my ass," I said.

"Cori, don't go there."

"Yeah? Tell me again about my free speech."

Leo Shaw arrived around midnight with Maye and a trunk full of sleeping bags. If he hadn't, we'd be forced to sleep on tiled floors.

"You should flee while you still can," I told Leo when he hefted his sleeping bag over a shoulder and began searching for a sleeping space.

"Corinne, it isn't the end of the world," he said. "Thank you for saving our asses again, by the way."

"Well, as asses go, yours is at the top of my *to save* list," I said. "Auggie dropped several notches."

"I heard that," Auggie shouted from down a narrow hall.

"I don't care if you did," I shouted back.

"Corinne, perhaps you should refrain from aggravating everyone and help me find a suitable suite of rooms," Rafe said.

"Oh, are we rooming together again?" I asked. He frowned at me. "We will talk," he said, taking my elbow. "Now."

"I was angry," he admitted. "Very angry. Until I realized I have done similar things in the past—allowed one to live when I needed information. I warn you, however, that if I find him, he will die."

"I understand that," I said. "I wouldn't ask you to do otherwise."

We sat in separate corners to have our discussion. He wanted to hold onto me. I wanted to see where we stood with one another, first.

"What will you do if I kill him?" Ilya asked.

"Try to find the next source of information," I shrugged. "There will be others; I just don't know how many people will die in the interim."

"This troubles you."

"Yes. I can't say who, but I'm uncomfortable now," I said. "The morning may bring terrible news and I don't have information or images to stop it."

"Cutter was not aware of whatever it was?"

"No. See, when someone withholds information from a source, I can't see it at all. Especially if I've never seen the source. If I've seen both, it becomes so much easier."

"A disturbing flaw."

"More than disturbing. Extremely dangerous. When I warned Maye to get everyone out of the villa, it's because I saw their deaths coming, not who was facilitating those deaths."

"Corinne, you will remind me not to interfere with your abilities from now on."

"Ilya, I don't want to interfere with how you feel. That's up to you. If you're mad, then you're mad. Just like anybody else."

"Including you."

"Yes. I was pissed at you and Auggie. Still am, actually. You have no idea how much that hurt."

"He and I may be more willing to listen to you from now on."

"Hmmph."

"I have ground to make up."

"You both do."

"Will this be our suite?" he asked, looking around.

"I hate the whole building," I grumped. "And no window? That's a requirement for my writing. I had an ocean view—for a whole day."

"It still belongs to you," he pointed out.

"And it may as well be on the moon."

"I believe your door will be repaired soon."

"Right."

"My love, I know you are not happy. I would make that otherwise, if I could."

"Corinne?" Leo Shaw knocked on the door and called out.

"Just a minute." I rose stiffly from my corner and went to let Dr. Shaw in.

"I wanted to set up an appointment with you for tomorrow," he said.

"I don't know whether that will help," I observed. "My insecurity inbox is getting crowded."

"What would make it better?"

"A trip to the office supply store."

"They're all closed at the moment. I'll see what I can do for later."

"Cool."

"Corinne suspects that bad news may come with the morning," Rafe said. "So we may have to plan carefully."

"Do you have any idea?" Leo began, offering a concerned frown.

"None, and that's extremely upsetting. I feel uncomfortable, though, and that's never a good thing."

"She hasn't seen the ones responsible, so she can't say what they are planning," Rafe offered.

"I guessed as much. Look, I can give you something to help you sleep."

"I'd prefer not to do that," I said. "I can't warn anybody if I'm knocked out."

"Point taken. I'll go have a word with Colonel Hunter," Leo said. "Corinne, don't escape again. I'm not sure my heart can take it."

After he closed the door, Ilya stepped up behind me. "My heart cannot stand such a blow again, either."

"You started it."

"Are we pointing fingers, now?"

"Yes. I'm tired, grumpy and somebody moved out without letting me explain."

"I regret that."

"Fine. I regret not telling you that I wanted to keep Baikov alive for personal reasons."

"I understand that, just as you understand me."

"Understood."

"Good. Very good. Might I remove your clothing, now?"

"As soon as James is done with us."

"What?"

The knock on the door came immediately. "Come in," Rafe called out.

"Colonel Hunter wants to see both of you," James said.

"What time is it?" I asked, surprising James.

"After midnight. Why?"

"So it's early morning?"

"Technically speaking."

"Yeah."

We followed James down the hall until we reached the rooms August claimed for his office. A cell phone was in his hand and a stunned expression was on his face as Leo Shaw stood nearby, unsure as to what to do.

"Colfer, Montana was the target," Auggie said. "Only twenty people survived, and some of them aren't human anymore."

otes—Colonel Hunter

"Somehow, they introduced a variation of the drug into the water supply," Madam President informed us. Shaw and I sat in her office while she explained what she knew. The media was going nuts with the information that nearly two thousand people had died the night before. A few residents hadn't drank water or bathed in it, and those had already been moved away from Colfer.

Initial reports leaked intentionally by the White House said the cause of the deaths was mass poisoning. In a way, that was true. "I suspect they chose that particular town because it was close to the Canadian border and they had sufficient amounts of the derivative drug to test on Colfer's water supply. Face it—Cutter died in Canada, so it makes sense they had a base there."

"Where do you suppose these perpetrators are, now?"

"They could be anywhere—they'll know we can make that connection, so it's likely they've abandoned the site. Once inside the U.S., they could go anywhere. They've had time to drive or fly away from Colfer after delivery of the drug. Corinne mentioned a small plane before, when Cutter was on his way to Canada. If they had something like that waiting, they really could be anywhere."

"I've ordered all departments to begin a search, but we don't have any specific targets. This is impossible," Madam President rose to pace. The rest of us rose with her—it wasn't proper etiquette to sit while the President stood.

I'd had my meeting with Rafe and Corinne much earlier—their guesses coincided with mine, so I felt comfortable presenting them to the President. Richard Farrell was on his way to Montana with three of his former collaborators—they'd be in charge of testing the Colfer water supply and sterilizing it afterward.

"What are we going to do with the ones who survived the drug?" the President asked.

"Are you sure all of them will live?" I asked.

"Roughly half of them are experiencing breathing problems. Those are the ones who don't look human anymore. Three of those can't speak. At least not in English."

"What do you think we should do?"

"Make them comfortable and let nature take its course."

"I think we ought to let Corinne decide."

"I want her kept away from this. It's upsetting enough for me. What do you think it will do to her? I sure as hell don't want her taking an unplanned vacation, again. We have to keep a tight leash on her and her abilities."

At that moment, I wanted to shout at the President. She considered Corinne an object—a tool to keep her alive and in office. If Corinne escaped, she couldn't control that asset. It made me angry. I reined that in and nodded my acceptance.

From then on, I planned to give Corinne as much free rein as I could. So far, she was the one keeping all of us alive. I knew enough to be grateful. Those around Cori cared about her. Madam President needed to get her thinking straight on this one.

I knew what Richard said the moment he learned there were survivors. "They wanted to kill everybody," he'd said. "But they rushed the use of the drug without testing it thoroughly. It's probable that they only used a limited sampling of victims. When all of them died, they determined the experiment a success."

If we didn't report what actually happened, then the ones behind the massacre would attempt to do it again. I had no idea how long it could take to produce enough of the drug to test it on a larger population, or whether it had to be placed in the water supply or could be delivered another way. I needed to speak with Richard again.

Soon.

❧

Corinne

Auggie was exhausted when he returned from his meeting with the President. I knew there had to be some survivors who'd ingested the drug—the odds were in their favor. Madam President didn't want anyone to know. It wouldn't be difficult—hide the information and stick them somewhere so they couldn't get to anyone else.

That would present problems and Auggie knew that. The perpetrators would think their massacre a total success, when that wasn't the case. People had survived. Whether they could now comfortably live on the planet was anybody's guess.

"Cori," Auggie said. He'd found me sitting on the floor next to Rafe in the smaller kitchen, clutching a cup of coffee as if it were salvation in a world gone mad.

"Auggie?" I said, turning my eyes up to him.

"Let James know what you need in the computer department. Whatever you want, he'll provide. You'll have access to departmental files from anywhere my codes will work. Look at people. Anybody and everybody that you want. Tell me if there's anything I ought to know. While James is getting your equipment, try to get some sleep."

He turned and walked out of the kitchen without another word. "Thanks, Auggie," I called out softly.

❧

Furniture and beds were moved in not long after, and Ilya and I made

235

ours up. He pulled me onto it and settled my head against his shoulder.

Both of us were troubled by the events in Colfer. I worried about what could happen next—the possibilities were terrifying. "Cabbage, try to sleep," he murmured before kissing my forehead. "We cannot save the world if we do not have the strength."

Notes—Colonel Hunter

"I can't say for certain that they won't find another way to distribute the drug to a larger population," Richard said. He'd phoned back after I placed the initial call. "The victims here are similar to those we examined before—few are intact inside."

"You've seen this before—I mean before those we asked you to examine recently."

"Early on, when an incorrect dosage was given to a volunteer. It has to be carefully calculated."

"You have the calculations for those in the Program?"

"I do."

"Will you forward them to me?"

"Of course. Those who didn't ingest the drug are sequestered and are being given excuses as to why the bodies of their loved ones must be cremated—I believe the story is that others might be poisoned if the body remains intact."

I cursed at Richard's explanation. "What have they done with the drug survivors?" I asked. I wanted to blame the lies on the FBI, Homeland Security and the CIA, but ultimately, the President had to give permission. She'd left me out of those decisions.

"Three died before transport arrived," Richard answered my question. "I wasn't told where they were taken after that."

"You asked, didn't you?"

"Yes."

"Fuck."

"I agree wholeheartedly."

~

Corinne

When I woke, Ilya was up and gone already. He'd slipped away after I'd fallen asleep.

Shuffling toward the kitchen, I found Auggie, Rafe, James and Leo having dinner. I'd slept all day, almost. We now had a table, chairs, a portable island and Chinese takeout.

"Beef and broccoli?" I asked.

"Here." Auggie shoved a carton toward me. "Rice," Rafe offered another carton. I took both and loaded a paper plate. Rafe poured a plastic cup of wine for me.

"I hope we get wineglasses soon," I said, spearing a chunk of broccoli with a plastic fork.

"I'd like cutlery that doesn't break," Leo said.

"I agree," I said. "Plastic belongs at picnics. With the ants."

"Every city and town in the country is now prepared to guard their water supply," Auggie offered while I ate. "I'm worried they'll find another way to introduce the drug."

"Nick and Maye?" I asked.

"On their way," Auggie said. "They were having a sparring match when the food arrived, so they went to clean up, first."

"Somebody say food?" Nick walked in.

"There's plenty, help yourself," Leo said.

"Corinne, are you eating my broccoli-beef?" Nick pretended offense.

"I didn't eat all of it," I complained. He shocked the hell out of me by giving me a hug. "Thanks for the early warning," he said before pulling out a chair and filling a plate. "Since I didn't say that before."

"No problem," I shrugged.

"Hey, Corinne," Maye walked in and went straight for the kung pao chicken.

"How are you doing?" I asked.

"I'm good. I've lost two katanas in two bombings, but those can be replaced. What do we have to do to catch the creeps responsible for Montana?"

"I need to see their faces," I sighed. "Or have somebody tell me who they are."

"Baikov?" Auggie asked.

"Baikov doesn't know. What Baikov has is possible information on the ultimate jerk behind all the other jerks. The ultimate jerk can tell me who else is paying him to get what they want, or who works for him to make all the evil happen. Mary Evans could have given us something. She probably knew the ultimate jerk's minions were gunning for her the minute she got caught. She decided not to talk anyway."

"You think he'll find somebody else to do what she did for him?"

"Yeah, and that worries me. He and or she likes the ones who don't have an ounce of humanity in them. That's what I've seen in Mary Evans' eyes every time—cold, calculating cruelty."

"If he's so hard to find, how do these people contact him to begin with?" Nick asked.

"I think he contacts them," I said. "With the Internet and the media, it isn't hard to see who might want something. How tough would it be to send someone—say, Mary Evans or somebody like her—to make suggestions?"

"That's frightening," Leo shook his head.

"There's something else you should know," I said.

"What's that?" Auggie asked.

"James, look up Claire Fabre and Jean Caillot," I said. "Their obituaries should show up from six years ago in Paris."

"Yeah," James nodded. He tapped on his tablet for a moment. "Here it is—says they were killed by burglars in their apartment. Says they worked for the Louvre until a few months before their deaths, but they'd quit shortly after the terrorist attack there."

"They were in on it, and got killed for their cooperation," I said. "Probably had a Swiss bank account or something set up, which evaporated the moment they were killed. It doesn't say they were working anywhere since they left the Louvre."

"Corinne, you've been a busy girl, haven't you?" Auggie blinked at me.

"It's amazing what you can do with an alias and free Wi-Fi at the library or at a coffee shop. I've been particularly motivated lately, but my Internet access has been limited."

"Why are you telling us this now?" Maye asked.

"Because I trust everybody here," I said. "Do you remember Ted Ryan?"

"I can't get him and the Sacramento bombing out of my head," Leo replied. "Why?"

"Because he couldn't wait to brag about what he'd done. He wanted the world to know. I think the ones responsible for Montana won't be able to stop themselves from bragging either," I said. "I just worry about what else they might do before they start bragging."

"Honey, there's something you ought to know," I told Ilya the moment we were alone in our suite.

"What's that?" his arms curled about me and he pulled me close.

"It's about the drug. You know they call the Program *Cloud Dust*."

"I do. I wondered why."

"Me, too. I think I may have an answer, but it's scary."

"Tell me, then." He led me toward our bed and we settled upon it. "I'm sure you're familiar with reported incidents in 1969 and 1986 in Russia," I began.

The deaths in Montana may as well have happened on another planet. So many bodies were either unrecognizable or missing. Family members were shown in news reports, holding signs with photographs of loved ones who would never come back to them.

Faked autopsy reports abounded, all orchestrated by the U.S. government. All the victims would be cremated, too—the excuse was that the poison in their bodies could cause problems. Family members would receive an urn with their loved ones' ashes, after the government was done with the investigation.

I felt sick—the television was turned on in our brand-new cafeteria and it was inevitable that I'd see all of it. So much of it was speculation and lies, and at that moment, I wanted to strangle the President plus the heads of the CIA, FBI and Homeland Security.

"Cori?" August asked as I made my way out of the cafeteria without eating.

"Going to the other one. The one without a television in it," I said.

"Rafe?" he asked.

"Sitting in our suite mulling over the price of good Scotch," I lied. "He should be out in a few." Actually, Ilya was in our suite, thinking about the information I'd given him and drawing his own conclusions as to who was involved and what they'd accomplished afterward.

"I'll come with you," Auggie offered. "I don't want to see that shit, either. It's disturbing."

"Yeah."

Rafe leaned in to kiss me when he found Auggie and me morosely silent as we drank coffee in the smaller kitchen.

"I know it's a mess, cabbage," he murmured. "It isn't your fault."

"None of it is," Auggie leaned back and stretched. "You'd have done something about it if you'd had proper information. I understand your reasons now for letting Cutter go as long as you did—he had information we desperately need. We have to find the ones responsible for this and do it soon."

Auggie had no idea he and Rafe were discussing different topics. I didn't enlighten him. "Have you eaten?" Rafe interrupted the conversation while walking the few steps to the fridge and opening the door to study its contents. He shuffled things around, looking for something suitable to eat.

"Didn't feel hungry," I admitted.

"I'll make eggs and toast. Colonel Hunter, do you want anything?"

"I'll have the same," Auggie grunted. "I'm not too hungry, either."

~

Madam President's personal cell phone rang, with the First Gentleman's caller ID in the window. "Graye?" she answered the call.

"Oh, I'm not Graye," the electronically enhanced voice said. "But I can deliver the next election to you if you want it."

"Who is this?" President Sanders demanded.

"I can give you the election by handing you those responsible for Montana," the voice went on. "I want something in return."

"What the hell would that be?" Amelia Sanders asked.

"I'll send a photograph. I want both. Alive. I'll call back in two days. I can't guarantee what may happen between now and then. Think about my offer and give an answer in two days, Madam President."

The President stared as a photo arrived on her cell. It was of Corinne and Rafe, taken during the meeting at Camp David.

~

Notes—Colonel Hunter

"What do you suppose will happen in the next two days?" I'd never seen the President so distraught. It was understandable—the one Corinne sought was also seeking her. He'd learned of her importance, likely through General Cutter. Rafe, too, was on the agenda, and I figured it was the Russians—Baikov in particular—who wanted him.

"If there's another Montana, the entire country will go crazy," I acknowledged. "What concerns me is that he'll be betraying those responsible for Montana, therefore, there's no guarantee he won't betray you, too."

"There is no good way out of this," the President shook her head. "I'm trading lives for lives if I concede, and potentially more lives if I refuse."

At least she didn't mention her presidency, or the continuation of it in this conversation. Corinne could determine the President's sincerity, but I didn't want to frighten her with this. Not yet, anyway. "Have you attempted to track the call?" I asked.

"Of course. It's untraceable, according to at least three agencies."

"Did anyone record it?"

"Of course not."

"Not good."

"He didn't even say not to try, or not to talk to anyone about the call. What is that supposed to mean?" she flung out a hand and stood to stare out a window at the White House lawn.

"It probably means he's so confident now that he's taunting us with it. He's destroyed two secure locations. Killed the Vice President. Stolen who knows what from some of the most secure places on the planet. Made attempts on many important lives, and would have succeeded, if not for Corinne."

"This means that Cutter received information from Dalton, then passed it along to his backers, who handed it to this murdering thief."

"That is the most likely scenario, yes. Information is often more valuable than gold, and information on Corinne—who wouldn't pay any asking price for that kind of talent?"

"We had it in our backyard for six years and didn't even know it," Madam President's shoulders sagged. "Corinne was wise to hide it, I think."

"The ultimate question, in my opinion, is what Cutter's backers want, other than a desk in the Oval Office. Why go to the trouble of killing an entire town, when there are other ways to get what they want?"

"Perhaps it's a way of exposing the Program."

"By using it against the people? They just killed twenty times what we have, and none of those volunteered. Besides, it was your predecessor who created the Program, and then insisted that it continue, even when so many," I stopped. "He's in this, too. I'll bet money on it."

"He appointed you to the Program," the President pointed out.

"I'm not naïve," I said. "He appointed me because he was pissed at the Joint Chiefs, since the Joint Chiefs never liked me. Not even for a minute. You see he assigned me to what he considered the most worthless of the survivors."

"Does he know that's changed?" She turned and lifted an eyebrow.

"I don't know," I answered honestly. "If he and Cutter had regular conversations, then it's likely. If that didn't happen, he may be out of the loop unless he's connected to Cutter's backers. If he's connected to Cutter's backers, then he's in this just as much as they are."

"If he's one of Cutter's backers, that's a problem," Madam President sighed. "You know how they all feel about a woman in the White House."

"I remember the attack ads," I said. "Clearly. He didn't come out and endorse Cutter, because he didn't want to alienate the women voters. His cronies endorsed Cutter, however, even after you'd been selected as the nominee at the convention."

"They pressured me to drop out of the race. Kept telling me I didn't have a chance against the opposition, when a man would," she shook her head. "Colonel Hunter, what the hell is going on? I realize that every president faces the prospect of wars, assassinations and every other difficulty you might imagine, but this time, the situation is jacked up—as if another level has been added to the game and we're scrambling for instructions on how to play it."

"Things began to change when the Program was introduced," I said. "I know what all the sci-fi novels and comic books are about, but this is reality and we don't have anybody who can swoop in and save the day. Without names or images, Corinne can't point to anyone. Without that information, the others can't do anything to protect us. Hell, we're scrambling just to stay alive on most days."

"I'm making the announcement tomorrow—that you're the new Secretary of Defense," Madam President sighed. "I realize that may paint a target on your back, but I'm getting pressured by both sides to make the call."

"I understand. I'll let Cori know. Do you want me to talk to her about this newest threat? It's likely she'll know about it anyway."

"Go ahead and tell her. Rafe, too. They need to know that somebody is after them."

"Thank you, Madam President."

Corinne

I knew the minute we walked in Auggie's new office. Madam President had been approached. She'd been offered the next election, in exchange for Rafe and me.

Fuck.

For now, she was saying no. I worried that her decision might waver in the next few days.

"You know he'll do his worst, just to convince her," I said before Auggie had a chance to talk.

"Perhaps someone will include me?" Rafe asked quietly.

"Corinne was right," Auggie said. "The one behind all this does approach people. He offered the President the next election and the ones behind the Montana massacre—in exchange for both of you."

"The ones responsible for Montana didn't make a very good deal with their benefactor, then," Rafe observed. "Obviously they forgot to include provisions—such as avoiding capture or prosecution for their crimes."

"Or, maybe they're just so megalomaniacally rich they think they're above all that," I said. "The ultra-wealthy sometimes fall into that trap. Generally they're correct; their money does cover a multitude of sins."

"Cori, I don't think that's a word," Auggie pointed out.

"Megalomaniacally?"

"That's the one. James," Auggie shouted. James appeared within seconds.

"Get photographs of all the wealthy people in the U.S.," Auggie said. "Give them to Cori. We have killers to catch."

"We have new orders and a new batch of the drug," Death reported.

"I wasn't aware that our people could move that fast," Famine said.

"It came from higher up," Death said. "We have enough to kill ten thousand or more."

"We won't get into the next water supply so easy," Conquest pointed out.

"This batch isn't designed to go in the water supply. It's in mist form and can't be seen by the naked eye. The drug can be inhaled and still work. It's genius, actually—ours were toying with the idea, but they said it was a long way off. We have it now, courtesy of our benefactor."

"We pay for that," War said.

"We donate. He told us at the beginning that money clears the way with the uncooperative. We have a mission, and we can afford the donations."

"Ten thousand people? Do we have likely targets?"

"I have several—marked on this map," Death said, tapping a key on his computer. A map of the United States popped up, with several locations circled. He then pulled up another window on the screen, listing events.

"I like this better," Conquest grinned as he pointed out a specific event. "We can offer our congratulations with an air event they can't refuse. Not only will we achieve our objective, it will be recorded."

Corinne

Rafe thought a Krav Maga session, followed by weight lifting and a run would help. While I normally suck at Krav Maga, I was so distracted I got mangled. Rafe didn't intend to hurt me and truthfully, I wasn't really hurt but he did amazing acrobatics to keep that from happening.

"Maybe we should just run," I said as he lay on top of me. "If I trip, it'll be my own fault."

"You're too distracted," he rolled to the side and rose with an easy, graceful movement. I felt like a slug attempting to stand on its tail when I got up.

"I have no idea why," I replied with a hint of sarcasm. "You know something else will happen before he calls back."

"I'll be happy to hand myself over—and deliver my version of justice."

"Which brain are you thinking with?" I asked sweetly.

"I can protect both of us," he said.

"I'm getting a headache," I responded.

"Then let's go to the kitchen and get something to drink with your aspirin."

James was already there when we arrived, taking a coffee break. "What are we going to do, Cori?" he pleaded, as if I had answers for everything.

"Honey, I don't know," I sat beside him and rubbed his back. "I have a feeling the enemy is about to flex his muscles big time, just to see how we'll react."

"How many do you think he'll kill this time?" Auggie walked in. "Madam President will make the announcement tonight that I'm the new Secretary of Defense," he added. "I want you and Rafe with me at the press conference."

"I'd prefer not to wear the wig," I complained.

"I believe that disguise is compromised already," Auggie muttered as he popped a coffee pod into the brewer. "I honestly don't care if you dress in jeans, although the President will likely complain."

"Congratulations, Auggie," I said. "You deserve it. I just wish it were a better time to take that position. She should have put you there to start with, instead of attempting to appease Cutter's camp. That could have saved us time and trouble."

"You think Cutter already knew about the Program?" Auggie asked.

"I think he knew something—what crumbs the previous administration saw fit to give him. Madam President handed all of it to him on a plate."

"I remember what you said when he was given the job," James said. "You told us the virus had been introduced. Man, we should have shot him then and taken the jail time."

"Oh, his cronies were doing their happy dance," I said. "I don't want to visit you in jail, honey. Let somebody else take out the bad guys. Somebody who can get away with it," I added.

"That means Maye, Nick, Rafe or somebody from another agency," Auggie sighed. We just need to know who the targets are and where they are. We can send the cavalry after that. Cori, have you had any luck with the photographs of wealthy people?"

"Not yet," I grumped. "Don't get me wrong; a bunch of them are steeped in felonious behavior, but it doesn't include murdering a town in Montana."

"Let's table that for now and focus on the other thing. I'd love to hand the information to Madam President before she gets that call tomorrow."

"That would be a coup—new Secretary of Defense solves Montana mystery," James framed a journalistic headline with finger quotes.

"I'd have to say my team was responsible," Auggie pointed out. "Cori, why don't you and Rafe look at photographs until we have to leave for the White House?"

"We can look while we're on a treadmill," Rafe said.

"Joy."

"You have your orders," Death said into his cell phone. "Tonight, we begin."

"You are sure, Commander?"

"Yes. Once we attack, the retaliation will be swift. You must not be deterred, even when it seems our allies have turned against us. It is his will."

"We are strong. None shall stand against us. We go tonight."

"I'll expect a report afterward—be at the rendezvous point for extraction afterward."

"It will be done. Thank you, sir. The end times are upon us."

"The end times are upon us," Death agreed and ended the call.

Corinne

"I'm not finding anything," I said. "I've gone back through some of these twice. Nobody sticks out." A computer monitor was hooked to my treadmill, and I'd walked while I studied photographs.

"Nobody?" James walked on a treadmill beside mine, while Rafe ran on a treadmill on my other side.

"Nobody," I shook my head. "This sucks."

"We have to get cleaned up soon, for Colonel Hunter's appearance at the White House press conference."

"I know. How should I dress?"

"Nice, but dark clothing," James grinned. He'd been invited, too, since his pay grade would rise with Auggie's. Auggie was considered a civilian since he was no longer active in the regular military—that had transpired after his assignment to the Program more than eight years earlier. Almost two years after his selection as a special consultant, he'd been assigned to me.

Being classified as a civilian, with no regular active connection to the military for more than seven years was a requirement to be Secretary of Defense. Auggie fit the bill perfectly. His rank should have been higher when he officially retired eight years earlier, but as he'd said often enough, there were some in the military who didn't like him.

At least the Senate approved of him—the President couldn't appoint him without their consent.

"Cabbage," Rafe extended an elbow after stopping his treadmill.

I took his arm. I waved at James as Rafe steered me out of the gym.

"I really don't feel good about this," I said as I put diamond studs in my ears. Rafe stood behind me, combing his hair. We were nearly ready to go.

"I am not comfortable, either. We will get through this, my love, as we are only watching from the side."

"I'm worried for Auggie. And the President, although she's still on my shit list."

"That is the way with leaders—they cannot be all things to all people, though we expect it of them always."

"Ilya, something will go wrong—we both know it. We just don't know what form it will take."

"I know. People will die to prove a maniac's point. It remains to be seen whether we will be counted among the dead."

"That's scary," I hugged myself and mumbled.

Cameras clicked in the White House press room as Auggie stepped toward the podium. Rafe and I stood in a corner away from the cameras to keep an eye on Auggie and the President.

One journalist caught my eye and forced me to draw in a painful breath. He'd gotten information from an undisclosed source. That information included video and photographs. *Oh, God, Auggie*, I sent to him. *Civilian Security Services has gone nuts in Afghanistan and wiped out three villages.*

CHAPTER 17

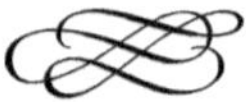

orinne

"I only have preliminary information," Auggie said when he responded to that journalist first. "I have been made aware of the situation, but we are scrambling for more intel."

I fed information to Auggie mentally, while the journalist stood and stared—he imagined he had an exclusive, straight from the source. He did, but he didn't know about me.

His information says at least six hundred are dead, including children, I sent to Auggie. Gunned down and left where they fell. These guys are cutting a swath through the Afghan hills, with nothing to stop them.

Leo Shaw nodded as Auggie looked in his direction, then left the room. The military was about to get involved with this.

Leo was probably more than surprised when I included him in the mental conversation. James, too.

James, I need photographs of all those assholes in Afghanistan—the Civilian Security guys, I said. Somebody has to have those records. Get me the same on whoever has a stake in that company, too.

I watched as he gave a slight nod and followed in Leo's wake. No matter how you looked at this, it would reflect badly on the President—those people were on the government payroll. I suspected they wanted a war, and probably had a good head start on creating one.

The fortunate thing, I suppose, was with the dropping of that bombshell, it was the best excuse ever for ending the press conference and going straight to work. The Press Secretary took over and handed out standard platitudes while Auggie, Rafe and I walked out of the room with Madam President.

"What the hell is happening?" the President demanded as Auggie walked so fast I had to trot to keep up.

"Corinne has more information than I do, but that's about to change," Auggie snapped. "Somebody get the Secretary of the Air Force on the phone. We have to plan an air strike."

"Some—if not all—the Civilian Security Services personnel we have in Afghanistan just went batshit crazy and attacked villages, killing everybody," I said. "That's the gist of it, and until James can get me photographs, that's really all I can give you."

"Then you have anything you want, Corporal," Madam President nodded at James while Auggie and Rafe broke into a run.

That's how I ended up in a room full of computers while James ran record after record of the Civilian Security Services employees in Afghanistan. I ticked them off as on or off the list as we went through photograph after photograph.

James made two lists while we went through the records—one titled *yes* and one titled *no*. Three-quarters of the way through more than thirty-five hundred records, I developed a nosebleed and a headache. I kept going. Madam President paced behind us while I updated information as I studied photographs and held bloody tissues to my nose.

"They're driving to this village," I pointed out the fourth target on a map someone else had pulled up on a second computer.

"Get that information to Colonel Hunter," the President shouted at her Deputy Chief of Staff. He was on a phone nearby, relaying information to wherever Auggie had gone with Rafe.

The Deputy Chief delivered the message. "He asks if you want to send drones," he held a hand over the receiver and asked.

"I want whatever it will take to stop these bastards," the President said. "I want an air strike on that convoy as quickly as possible. Send both, since we have no idea what kind of weapons they have."

"Yes, Madam President. Colonel Hunter, use whatever force is necessary to kill the rogues before they reach the next target. Send in manned and unmanned aircraft."

"Do not fire on any villages," the President added.

"Did you get that?" the Deputy Chief asked. "Good. Yes. Immediately. Madam President, he says he'll have bodies airlifted out when they're done," the Deputy Chief hung up the phone.

"Good. Thank you. Corinne, if you and James will come with me to the Oval Office? Andrew, ask Colonel Hunter and his guard to meet us there when everything is in motion."

"Yes, Madam President."

~

"Corinne, what can you tell me?" the President sat heavily on her desk chair and leaned her elbows on the desk.

"I couldn't get a clear count on fatalities," I said, slumping onto a guest chair. "I gave the village names to James, so he can tell you approximate populations. I believe the number of deaths they handed to the journalist are very conservative."

"Do we still have him in custody?" the President turned to one of her Secret Service agents. I recognized him as someone who'd ridden to the Vice President's funeral with us.

"We do, but he's protecting his source."

"Of course he is," the President muttered. She had a headache, just as I did, but her nose wasn't bleeding; mine was.

"Can I get a cold, wet cloth?" I asked, pulling the red-soaked tissue away from my nose.

The agent opened the door and shouted for someone to bring tissues and a cold, wet cloth. Leo, Rafe and Auggie walked in before the cloth arrived.

"Corinne?" Leo scooted James over on the sofa we occupied, then pulled my hand and the bloody tissue away from my nose.

"I have a headache," I mumbled.

"I don't doubt it," Leo muttered.

"Here's the cold cloth," the agent handed it to Leo.

"Lean forward a little," Leo said before placing the cold cloth on the bridge of my nose and pinching gently. "Breathe through your mouth if you have to," he said. "The pinching and the cold should help the blood clot," he explained.

In less than five minutes, the bleeding had stopped. "Thank you," I mumbled. "Can I have some water, now?"

Leo Shaw grinned and nodded. "Want something for your headache, too?"

"Ibuprofen?"

"We'll see."

An hour later, we received information that the convoy had been bombed and the cleanup crew dispatched to retrieve bodies, vehicles and weapons. Auggie had to stay with the President to field incoming questions and deal with the press. Rafe stayed with them. Leo, James and I were driven back to our ugly, temporary building.

"No more for you tonight," Leo said as I asked James for information on the ones who owned the Civilian Security Services; I knew they had to be responsible for the killings in Afghanistan. "James and I can handle that through regular channels," Leo continued. "You're going to bed."

After a dose of ibuprofen, I climbed into bed and attempted to sleep. That didn't take long—Leo told the nurse who brought the ibuprofen that it was only that. As it turns out, it held a sleep aid, too. I intended to have a talk with Dr. Leo Shaw—once I was fully conscious and not so sleepy I couldn't move.

Ilya

The only images televised were taken from far away with Telephoto lenses or from the air, also with Telephoto lenses. The air, too, about a football stadium in Georgia was being tested for remains of the drug.

Journalists were abuzz with the poison's second use—the same poison that reportedly killed two thousand or more in Montana. The government in that southeastern U.S. state had convened and officials from Homeland Security and other agencies were arriving quickly to discuss necessary actions and investigations.

Authorities were forced to examine the scene in hazmat suits—the drug had been loosed as mist by an innocent-looking small plane, dragging a congratulatory sign behind it. The concoction had been invisibly sprayed as families and graduates sat in a rapidly warming stadium with very little breeze to provide relief from the heat.

What I could see from televised images showed bodies slumped in their seats or scattered across the turf of the field. It looked as if a multicolored wheat field had been harvested by a giant sweep of a scythe.

Deaths occurred outside the stadium, too—it couldn't be avoided since the mist had been released in the air. That meant the college campus was on lockdown, and bodies lay on grassy lawns where they'd fallen, once the mist was inhaled.

The drug was being used as a form of chemical warfare, and that was unacceptable.

Notes—Colonel Hunter

I wanted to tell Shaw that anyone might have made the same mistake, especially a physician, when one of his patients needed rest. The truth was, if Corinne had been awake and allowed to study photographs of Dante Dolsen and three others connected to Civilian Security Services, she might have told us what else they'd planned.

Instead, we had no idea and were in the process of getting four wealthy businessmen extradited from Canada when we learned what else was on their agenda.

An outdoor college graduation ceremony was gassed with a mist version of the drug and more than ten thousand died, in and outside the stadium. A handful of others had been affected and changed, the same as in Colfer, Montana. Just as before, other departments took the lead on that, and I'd only received perfunctory calls from the President so far, although I had a meeting scheduled with her later.

The country was going nuts, Afghanistan was ready to declare war after the killings there and several other Middle Eastern countries were siding with them. Ugly demonstrations were occurring across the Middle East, while effigies of the President alongside American flags were being burned in the streets. My meeting with Madam President would cover initial responses to the debacle in the Middle East.

I drank a cup of coffee in the cafeteria while watching the news with Rafe and James. None of the media coverage was good and the population, understandably, was panicked. We needed more information, and we needed it soon. Just like the attack at the Louvre —it looked as if Americans were involved in these acts of terrorism.

"We need to be able to point a finger at these assholes," I muttered, slapping my cup onto the table.

"I'll see if I can get Corinne up," Rafe nodded to me.

Neither he, James nor I had gotten any sleep; we'd been up all night, following the events in Afghanistan. Madam President had spoken with authorities in the country, who were understandably incensed that nearly fifteen hundred of their citizens had been killed by Americans under contract with the U.S. government.

"Get coffee in her, then see what we can do about this mess," I nodded. It didn't matter that the Americans who'd done the killing were rogues operating outside the law and at someone else's command. The mere fact that we'd sent them into Afghanistan to begin with bloodied our hands as well.

We also needed information as to why the ones behind Civilian Security Services chose to kill in Montana and Georgia. That information had to be provided to the media, who were making wild speculation on how and why the government failed to protect them.

Dante Dolsen was the primary owner, with more than half ownership of Civilian Security Services. He was also an American, just as the other three were, but all four lived in Canada.

All four protested our emergency request to the Canadian government to extradite them and sought a judicial review of the Minister's surrender order. They had enough money to convince anyone that they were uninvolved with the events in Afghanistan. They hadn't been linked yet to the U.S. attacks.

An official call to the IRS indicated that a large portion of Civilian Security Services' investments were likely held in Canadian or other foreign banks, and they'd been avoiding proper taxation for years. Recent legislation had been passed in an attempt to close that loophole, but the problem lay in forcing financial institutions from other countries to obey U.S. tax laws.

"James," I said. "Have those photographs ready for Corinne, since Rafe is going to get her up. We only need five minutes of her time if she's still groggy. Make sure every television in this fucking facility is turned off, too, while you're at it."

"Yes, sir."

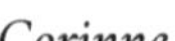

Corinne

"My love, wake now. We need you." Ilya's voice woke me. Groggy didn't begin to describe how I felt—Leo had given more than enough of a sleep aid to an exhausted person to keep them sleeping round the clock.

"Honey, no," I mumbled. "Sleep."

"I know," he rubbed my back gently. "You have to get up. Colonel Hunter needs your help. Everyone needs your help." His lips were warm against my temple as he kissed me.

"Feel awful," I said.

"I know. Headache gone?" Fingers brushed hair away from my face.

"No."

"We'll find something for it. Come with me, my darling. Ten minutes of your time is all we require."

That's how I ended up shuffling beside Rafe down a long hallway, wearing a bathrobe and shambling along like a drunken gazelle. Rafe kept a hand on my arm so I wouldn't wander into walls as we walked.

"Coffee?" Rafe said as he and I walked into Auggie's office.

"Here." James' voice—I couldn't see him since my eyes attempted to close once I stopped moving.

"Drink this," a paper cup was shoved into my hands. If I'd been awake, I'd have savored the warmth of it. Instead, I drank, the hot brew almost scalding my tongue as I swallowed.

"Here, Cori," I heard a wheeled office chair as it rolled backward. Hands pushed me onto it and I sat. "We really need you to look at these pictures," Auggie said. I swallowed another mouthful of coffee and forced my eyes open.

Four photographs were displayed on a computer screen, so I fought to bring them into focus.

"Dante Dolsen," I whispered as I stared at his image. "Dead."

"Francis Pike," I went to the next photograph. "Dead."

"Karl Graham," I named the third man. "Dead."

"Langston Coffman," I nodded at the fourth photograph. "Dead."

"What the hell?" Auggie exploded behind me. His cell phone rang. I listened and drank more coffee as he spoke to someone in the CIA. All four owners of Civilian Security Services had died moments earlier while visiting their attorney's office.

The pilot of the plane was found six hours later—he'd been driving westward as fast as his truck would take him. Rafe was asleep, as was Auggie when the call came. Les Banks was in an Arkansas jail, waiting for the FBI to arrive and question him. Local authorities had already gotten some information about the mist he'd sprayed on an unsuspecting college stadium crowd in Georgia.

Sure, he'd pulled a banner behind his plane that said *congratulations, graduates*, but that wasn't the only thing he'd been asked to do.

"Leo, stop fretting. I don't think we could have stopped much of this, even if we'd known in advance," I said. He'd taken the call, then relayed information to James, Nick, Maye and me.

"I just feel responsible," he muttered.

"Then stop. You didn't do any of that crap," I said. My head still hurt, but I hadn't taken anything else for the pain since Rafe ousted me from our bed. He slept there, now. I could only imagine the scenarios played out across the nation as people speculated on the massacres in Georgia and Afghanistan.

The White House deliberately leaked information that the owners of Civilian Security Services were responsible for all of it, including Montana, but nobody had a good reason for any of it. That didn't stop them from making wild suppositions, however.

As wild as those suppositions were, they were far from the truth. Auggie and I would have a discussion about that—when he woke.

"They're saying that CSS was testing chemical weapons," Maye said.

"That's plausible," Leo sighed. We'd moved to the small kitchen to have a cup of coffee and discuss the pilot's arrest in Arkansas. "Do you think we'll get anything useful out of the pilot?" Leo turned to me.

"I doubt it. The money was good, as long as he didn't ask questions. He had no idea he was about to murder ten thousand people."

"Where are the survivors? With the ones in Montana?" Nick growled.

"Nick, we don't have any authority in the matter," Leo sighed. "I wish we did. I think Richard might work with them, and I wouldn't mind helping, but we've been cut out of it."

"We knew what we were walking into, up to a point," Nick said. "And it was still a shock. What will it do to those people?"

"It's complicated, and I don't feel comfortable discussing it," Leo shook his head.

I knew what he was saying—what the drug had done to me. How I'd wakened in unfamiliar surroundings in a body unfamiliar to me. After the trauma in Paris, there'd been a second trauma waiting. Poor Leo; he'd done his best to get me through all that, but some things would never fully heal, I think.

"I need more coffee." I stood and lifted my cup. To illustrate my point, I yawned on the way to the coffee maker.

That's when the call came from the President. Mr. Evil had called her back, just as he said he would. She wanted to see all of us in her office.

～

Notes—Colonel Hunter

At least I'd had four hours' sleep before I had to rise and go to the White House. Rafe looked better than I did when we loaded into vans for the trip. Mentally, he was older than I. Physically, after the drug, he was much younger.

I'd never felt my age as much as I did right then.

Corinne still didn't look good, though. She was worn out; that was easy to see. Leo was still troubled, although he was better now than when I'd seen him before going to bed.

Corinne convinced him somehow that the massacre in Georgia wasn't his fault—that others deserved the blame. She was right, but we worried that she could have kept it from happening if she hadn't been asleep.

The trip to the White House seemed to take forever. Armed guards and Secret Service surrounded our group the moment our vans were parked, and we were ushered quickly into the White House.

Madam President waited in a private study.

"He called back, just as he said he would. Pointed out that all four involved in Montana, Georgia and Afghanistan are now dead. How the hell did he accomplish that?" the President asked after we'd been seated. "Preliminary medical reports say they died of natural causes. Can we believe that? How did he manage to kill them that way?"

"What did you say to him?" I asked quietly.

"I told him no. I pointed out that he'd arranged for four deaths, after promising them something. I had no desire to work with him in the beginning, and this reinforces my decision."

"What did he say?"

"He turned to blackmail." Madam President covered her face with her hands. "He says he'll kill again if he doesn't get what he wants, only it will be more people next time. Colonel Hunter, we already have a panicked country. What will happen if he delivers on his threat on a much grander scale? How are we to extricate ourselves from all this?"

"I don't know," I shook my head. "I think we should call everyone together and discuss it."

"They're on the way, now. Dr. Shaw, we have a comfortable space arranged for you and these," she swept out a hand, encompassing Maye, Corinne and the others. "We'll keep you informed. Be advised that this could take a while."

Corinne

"Did you get enough sleep?" I asked Rafe as we settled on a love seat. The room we'd been led to was tastefully decorated and comfortably furnished, but I wanted to be anywhere except where I was.

The blackmailer, whoever he was, wanted Rafe and me. Madam President was considering it, just to avoid another massacre. She already had enough trouble at her doorstep, and if giving up two people made that go away, then why wouldn't she consider it?

I liked to think that she really didn't know what she was giving away, but squashed that thought immediately. Rafe grimly accepted our fate, and was already plotting ways to handle it.

As was I. The thing that terrified me most?

That someone would insist I be blindfolded.

"I've had enough sleep," Rafe responded distractedly. I held back from asking further questions. He was busy thinking, just as I was.

~

Notes—Colonel Hunter

"They're asking for Corinne and Rafe." The Vice President's words were flat as he shook his head. He didn't want that to happen—they'd saved his life.

"I hope you'll excuse the question, Madam President," the Secretary of Commerce said, "but I don't understand who these people are."

"I know. These two are very talented special agents. He either wants to use them or kill them; he hasn't said which."

"So he has us by the balls, if you'll pardon the sexism attached to that comment," the Secretary of Agriculture said.

"Yes," the President replied. "We turn them over, or we get another Georgia."

"Why would he want them?" the Secretary of Homeland Security asked. I could tell he was pissed because he hadn't heard of either one. I wanted to strangle him—it was easy enough to see that he was interested in any talent that might help his department.

"I've worked with them," the Vice President said. "They saved my life in London."

"Is that how you got out of Downing Street alive?" someone else asked.

"Yes. I can't reveal more than that, it's still classified as need-to-know."

"There are things you should know," the President sighed. "This same person was behind the terrorist attack at the Louvre. He manipulated those events in order to steal valuable paintings and works of art. He is also behind the thefts and deaths in London and Edinburgh. You see what we're dealing with, here? With Corinne and Rafe, he can be assured of getting in anywhere and getting out again with very little trouble. That's how talented they are."

"We have to weigh two lives against tens of thousands?" the Attorney General asked.

"We do." Madam President's shoulders slumped. She knew, just as I did, what they'd already decided.

"Did he provide a time and place to turn them over?"

"Yes. We have an hour, and it'll be in one of the tunnels leading away from White House."

"How the hell?" the Attorney General exploded.

"I didn't stay on the phone to discuss how he knew. The clock was already ticking," the President snapped. "Now, if you don't have a suggestion as to how we're going to inform two of our agents that we're trading them for civilian lives, then shut up."

"Madam President, we don't make deals with terrorists," I reminded her as we made our way to the room where Shaw and the others were.

"We don't have a choice," she hissed. We'd left the cabinet in the meeting room and walked away with only the Vice President and two Secret Service agents at our heels. "If we could have questioned those pricks in Canada before they dropped dead of who knows what, then we might have learned something. We have nothing on this man—if it is a man. The voice is disguised every time."

"What did he tell you to do, then?" I asked, attempting to keep my voice civil. This was the worst kind of betrayal, in my book. Yes, it might save lives in the interim, until the bastard wanted something else. He only had to threaten us again. We were setting a dangerous precedent, and choosing a path we couldn't change or abandon, once we were on it.

"We have to meet outside the tunnel entrance. He said no weapons and only two others—no Secret Service and no cameras. He said to turn everything off; he'll know if we don't."

"Three people to escort Corinne and Rafe?"

"That's what he said."

"Fuck."

Corinne

Ilya, they're going to trade us, I thought at him.

"I know," he murmured as he pulled me against him and kissed my temple, his breath warm and soft against my skin. Too many scenarios ran through my mind as he held me close—scenarios from more than six years earlier, when I'd witnessed torture and death at the hands of the deranged.

I didn't imagine this would be any better—after all, the one behind all this didn't seem to worry about killing—had been behind the killings I'd witnessed in France, actually, just to steal paintings and a crown.

Whomever or whatever he or she was, they'd become bolder. More convinced that they were untouchable. In their sociopathic mind, they were invincible.

They wanted us—Rafe and me—to do their dirty work. Rafe could provide shielding for us, and I could lead him through any maze and past any keypad to get us in anywhere. Cutter had provided that information, through Dalton.

"How will he blackmail us to cooperate?" I pulled away from Rafe. "We know somebody wants you dead. I think this guy wants us alive."

"I do not know," he replied, his eyes betraying worry. "I have no one left. Baikov saw to that."

"This is so fucked up," I mumbled.

"It is certainly that. Cabbage, we will go. And we will destroy him."

"He'll expect us to try."

"I know that. He does not know all we are capable of."

"True."

Madam President, Auggie, the Vice President and two Secret Service agents walked through the door, interrupting our conversation.

"Cori, this is the last thing I would have agreed to," Auggie said. He'd asked for a few minutes alone with Rafe and me. The others had left the room to give us privacy.

"I know that," I said. "I don't think anybody here really wants that. I just worry that this won't be enough."

"That is also my concern," Rafe said.

"And mine. This is a slippery slope, and nobody can see the bottom of the pit we've dropped into," Auggie agreed. "That's why I've brought this." He handed each of us a small capsule. I'd never seen one before; nevertheless, I knew what it was—a means to commit suicide.

"Absolute last resort," I turned to Rafe.

"Agreed."

"We have to leave in a few minutes," Auggie said, and his voice broke. "Cori, I love you. Not the way Rafe loves you—you're the daughter I never had. Be safe. Please. Stay in contact with me as long as you can."

"I will." I wanted to weep. One shouldn't meet the enemy while one is crying; I worked to keep my vision clear. We walked out of the room together, my hand held firmly in Ilya's, my eyes on Auggie's broad shoulders as he led the way.

"Those four in Canada," I spoke as Auggie dropped back beside Rafe and me, "They wanted to facilitate the apocalypse," I explained. "They called themselves the four horsemen. Took on those names to describe themselves. Thought they'd been given divine instruction to do that."

"What the hell would make them think that?" Auggie exploded.

"You'd be surprised what some people will believe," I said. "If it fits well in the beliefs they already hold. Provide some smoke and mirrors and presto—you have a man-made apocalypse. Of course, it never hurts to have so much money you can make just about anything happen, including a war in the Middle East."

"And someone to rely on who can make those things happen without leaving even a trail of smoke behind," Auggie muttered.

"Remember that same someone ended up betraying them," I said.

"I remember."

～

Madam President and her Chief of Staff, Hal Prentice, walked ahead of us. I only saw the backs of their heads as we made our way through underground passageways beneath the White House.

I'm sure the President kept her Chief of Staff informed—as much as she could—that was his job. I'd just never seen him in person. Well, there was no time for proper introductions now. Our time was winding down and we were nearing our destination.

Rafe walked beside me, his face set and so silent I barely heard his footsteps. Yes, I was seeing the spy who'd worked for the Soviet Union for so many years, and even beyond the days after the cold war ended.

They'd coerced him. I knew it; I'd merely waited for him to volunteer that information. After the next few minutes, that opportunity might never come. Reaching out, I gripped his fingers with mine and squeezed. *I love you*, I sent to him. He lowered his chin in acknowledgment.

～

Notes—Colonel Hunter

A war raged within me. I wanted to grip the throats of the ones forcing us to give up Corinne and Rafe, so I could squeeze the life from them. I would enjoy watching the light leave their eyes as they died. This is how anyone might feel when they are faced with such helpless feelings—when someone they care for is in danger.

Rafe would go down fighting—I had no doubt of that.

Poor Corinne didn't stand a chance. She'd see exactly what they were, and if they didn't kill her outright, would attempt to force her to do unspeakable things.

A heavy door loomed ahead of us, with a keypad glowing softly at its center. On the other side of that door lay disaster. I glanced at Corinne. She was pale. Shaking already. I offered a silent prayer to anyone listening as the President reached for the keypad and entered her private code.

$\sim$

Corinne

When the door swung open, we saw nothing except a narrow, concrete entrance sloping upward, and beyond that, ornamental shrubs and trees, hiding the entrance. In the distance I could hear sounds of traffic—people going here and there on their daily journeys, unsuspecting that the fate of the world might hang upon the next few minutes.

"What time is it?" Madam President asked.

"We have two minutes," Chief of Staff Hal Prentice replied. "We're not late." He stood next to the President, blocking her from any attack that might come from the greenery above as he spoke.

"Where are they?" Madam President betrayed her nervousness by rubbing her arms.

Rafe reached out and pulled me against him. I knew his shield was up, but Madam President was too far away to include in his protection. I wondered in a distracted fashion if she realized that. Auggie, on the other hand, was close enough to be included in Rafe's protective bubble.

My breath caught when the Chief of Staff called time and the ones who'd come for us revealed themselves.

CHAPTER 18

*C*orinne

They detached themselves from concrete walls, their clothing blending so well with the surface they'd seemed a part of it. That wasn't the most frightening thing, however.

All eight of them looked exactly like Becker.

Not only had Cutter's cronies developed a way to kill thousands with Becker's blood, they'd learned to create clones, just as the ones who'd sent assassins after the rest of us had. How they'd managed to replicate so many so quickly was a mystery. Each clone held a weapon as they took steps in our direction.

"Becker, that's close enough," Auggie commanded.

"That name has no meaning to us," one of the clones replied. "We are here to collect those two." He nodded in Rafe's and my direction. I worked to keep my breathing even—they had orders to keep me alive and kill Rafe, once they got us away from there.

"How many of you are there?" Madam President's voice quavered. Hal Prentice, still standing between her and the approaching clones, gripped her elbow to steady her.

"That is not our information to provide. Command them to come with us quietly, or we will kill all present."

"That wasn't part of the deal," she snapped.

"It will become part of the deal if they are not given to us willingly."

"Come, cabbage," Rafe urged softly, pulling me with him toward the waiting clones. I had no idea how they intended to get us out of there. It didn't really matter; Rafe would be dead and I'd be a prisoner if they had their way.

Ask them if he's watching—the one who sent them, I mentally instructed Madam President. I worried about the consequences if I refused to cooperate.

Rafe's life mattered most to me at that moment.

"Is he watching? I want to know," Madam President's voice wobbled again.

"You are so shortsighted," the spokesman replied.

And you are so dead, I sent directly to him. He dropped immediately, as did the seven others who flanked him.

Madam President screamed. Yes, I knew someone else was there—someone who hadn't yet revealed himself.

Or, in this case, *herself.*

Ilya

I went cold. Eight clones died before my eyes, in less than three seconds. All eight. I glanced at Corinne. Her nose was bleeding.

Words ran through my mind. Corinne's words, as she sat behind a computer, studying photographs.

Dante Dolsen, dead.

Francis Pike, dead.

Karl Graham, dead.

Langston Coffman, dead.

She'd killed them while she stared at their photographs. While she was in the nation's capital and they were in Canada.

My blood went from cold to frozen. Eight clones lay dead in front of us when the hidden one revealed herself.

Was she human?

Not now.

I blinked, too, at the one she held hostage, a gun pointed at the woman's temple.

Colonel Hunter's wife, Laci.

~

Notes—Colonel Hunter

She had arms and legs, like a human. Very little past that resembled any human I'd ever seen. Covered in greenish-brown scales, she appeared more lizard-like than human. She was also dressed in camouflage, to keep us from seeing her until she chose to reveal herself.

She pointed a fucking gun at Laci's head.

I had no idea how Becker's clones had suddenly dropped dead, but suspicions were forming in my mind. Those would have to wait until later. Yes, Laci had filed for divorce. I still loved her, and it broke my heart to see her threatened like this. Obviously, the enemy had covered all his bases.

Corinne and Rafe had stopped walking the moment Laci and her captor appeared. I could tell that the deaths of Becker's clones disturbed the lizard woman. *Greatly.*

I didn't have time to dissect that fact. I had to figure out how to get Laci away from her.

"Let her go," Corinne said. "Or you'll end up like the Beckers."

"I will kill her if you do not come with me," lizard woman replied. I could see sharp teeth as she spoke—teeth made for killing, not chewing.

Did she swallow her prey whole or in chunks? I fought down nausea.

~

Corinne

This was my last hand. The ace I'd held until the end, so the others wouldn't be so afraid of me they'd attempt to kill me or run away.

There hadn't been any choice. Lizard lady probably knew her minutes were numbered, but she'd been given strict orders to haul Rafe and me away. The thing that terrified me the most? There were others just like her. And I mean *just* like her. In every way, down to the smallest scales on her little pinky.

Her boss, though, whoever he was, wasn't going to get what he wanted. Not today. With a narrowing of my eyes, I watched her fall. All of it seemed to happen in slow motion. Lizard woman crumpled. Laci dropped to her knees, sobbing. Auggie ran toward her. I looked past him at Madam President, who was forcefully tossed to the ground by her Chief of Staff, Hal Prentice. Hal then pulled a gun and aimed it at Auggie.

Seeing his face—focusing on it for the first time, told me so many things. He'd been contacted months ago. *He* was behind the helicopter bombing and the passing of Rafe's information to the Russians. *He* was kept in the loop as much as possible by the President herself.

He was a clone.

Like Mary Evans, this version worked for the enemy. He'd never wanted Auggie in charge of the Program, because Auggie was a straight shooter. He'd advised the President to name Cutter after General Edwards' death. He'd been instructed to kill Colonel August Hunter now, after Rafe and I had been safely squirreled away. Even with the failure of the first part of the plan, he was still following orders.

Could I kill him with my talent?

I tried. Something prevented it.

I screamed and ran toward Auggie and his wife. Rafe called my name dimly behind me. I shoved Auggie aside.

The gun went off.

I was outside Rafe's protection.

The bullet hit me in the chest.

～

Ilya

I wanted to kill him a second time. He'd emptied his weapon at me while I stalked toward him. He should have known better than to attempt to run. Hal Prentice lay at my feet, his neck broken, glassy eyes staring at me in surprise.

"Get back," Leo Shaw shouted behind me. I turned swiftly.

What was he doing?

Colonel Hunter was shoved away from Corinne's body. Dr. Shaw pulled a syringe from a pocket and plunged it into Corinne's neck. I screamed Corinne's name; I know I did.

Colonel Hunter and the President of the United States did their best to hold me back as I struggled to get to Corinne.

Notes—Colonel Hunter

"August, I'm so sorry."

Laci's apology salved part of my guilt.

Just not all of it.

Shaw and Richard Farrell were with Corinne's body. Six hours had passed since the incident, and there was no news.

Either Cori was dead, or the drug was taking hold.

We'd had to sedate Rafe. He wanted to kill all of us, I think.

"She's like a daughter," I mumbled, working to keep the tears from my eyes.

"I was jealous. Of her. Of your job," Laci wept. "I was so stupid."

"Laci, don't cry. You make me want to," I said, sitting beside her and wrapping my arms around her shoulders.

Madam President's phone had remained curiously silent. That concerned me. I pondered that while I held my wife and wiped away her tears.

Did Corinne's talent frighten the enemy so much he'd backed off?

Now I knew why she wanted to see him so badly. To kill him. To make him pay for all those he'd killed just to get this painting or that bauble for somebody else.

I knew a certain Asian dictator who'd better watch his back if Corinne happened to survive. Actually, I knew a lot of people who ought to watch their backs.

∼

"I have information, connecting Hal with Hugh Lawrence." The FBI Director handed a flash drive and a file to the President. "The information is sketchy—what we could put together in the last few hours since you requested it."

"But why?" Madam President had worked hard to keep tearstains from showing. It wouldn't do to show that weakness to anyone.

"Did Hal push Cutter for the Secretary of Defense position?"

"Yes." The President lowered her eyes. "Right after General Edwards was murdered."

"We have information on plenty of calls between Lawrence and your Chief of Staff, two months before Lawrence died. There are odd transfers of funds, too, that have been coming to Prentice's bank accounts since then."

"He was connected to this whole mess?" The President's voice trembled.

"It looks that way. We'll know more in the next few days."

"No wonder he was never in a meeting with Corinne," the President muttered.

"What's that?" the Director asked.

"Nothing. Thank you for this—I'll take a look immediately. Bring the other information when you have it."

"I will."

"One more thing, Director."

"Yes?"

"I want the body turned over to a special team for an autopsy."

"I'll make arrangements."

∼

Ilya

Days have passed. The President, Colonel Hunter and many others have turned their attention to the growing unrest in the Middle East. The U.S. government is taking the blame for the deaths in Afghanistan, when they had little to do with it.

I knew now that the Civilian Security Services rogues who did the killing were already dead when their convoy was bombed—satellite images and air strike pilots confirm that the vehicles weren't moving when the missiles were launched. Many of them looked to have been wrecked where they were—Corinne had killed them while they were en route to their next target.

Yes, it was frightening, and I understood why she held that information back until there was no other choice. I sat beside her bed —as often as Dr. Shaw would allow it.

She had no idea that we trusted her—with our lives. I reached out to push a tendril of hair behind an ear. A moan, as soft as a whisper, escaped her lips.

Corinne

You float in a bubble.

At least I did, poised between death and another life. If I chose the latter, would they run from me, knowing I could kill them with a thought?

All I had to do was see them—or their photograph—once, and I could do it.

You have no concept of time.

Whether it had been days or weeks while I struggled to make up my mind, I had no idea.

Should I stay?

Faced with the prospect of no friends and few allies, what incentive did I have?

That's when I felt the mental brush against my soul, the words gentle. Careful.

Shhh. Ilya's here, my darling. Ilya's here.
It was all I needed to know.

The End

www.ingramcontent.com/pod-product-compliance
Lightning Source LLC
Chambersburg PA
CBHW070428120726
47910CB00003B/697